"Are you taking this anywhere?" Matt asked.

Not a morning person, it took Amy a moment to process what he meant. And then she realized that by "this," he was referring to the fact that her hand had drifted disturbingly low on his abs. If she moved her fingers a fraction of an inch down, she'd have quite the palmful.

Their legs were entwined. At some point in the night, the sleeping bag had fallen away and there was no barrier between them. Matt was warm and hard.

Everywhere.

Amy inhaled as the long forgotten heat of arousal continued to build within her. Worse, her fingers itched with the need to move south.

"Amy." Matt's voice was pure sin, not a warning so much as a statement, and her fingers reacted without permission, gliding downward.

Matt groaned, then slid a hand into her hair, tilting her head up to his. He searched her gaze. "Just checking to make sure you're awake," he said, then rolled her beneath him...

"Jill Shalvis is a total original! It doesn't get any better."
—**Suzanne Forster,** *New York Times*
bestselling author

Praise for
Jill Shalvis
and Her Novels

Head Over Heels

"[A] winning roller-coaster ride . . . [a] touching, character-rich, laughter-laced, knockout sizzler."
—*Library Journal* (starred review)

"Healthy doses of humor, lust, and love work their magic as Shalvis tells Chloe's story . . . Wit, smoking-hot passion, and endearing tenderness . . . a big winner."
—*Publishers Weekly*

"The Lucky Harbor series has become one of my favorite contemporary series, and *Head Over Heels* didn't disappoint . . . such a fun, sexy book . . . I think this one can be read as a stand-alone book, but I encourage you to try the first two in the series, where you meet all the characters of this really fun town."
—*USAToday.com*

"The writing is, as always, very good. Shalvis makes her characters seem like reflections of ourselves, or at least our relatives. She also makes the scenarios real, not too sweet or too violent. Definitely a good choice for a rainy afternoon."
—*RT Book Reviews*

"Witty, fun, and the characters are fabulous."
—FreshFiction.com

"It is fabulous revisiting Lucky Harbor! I have been on tenterhooks waiting for Tara and Ford's story and yet again, Jill Shalvis does not disappoint...A rollicking good time...If you have not read the first book yet, this one will certainly compel you to do so...*The Sweetest Thing* is shiny and wonderful book goodness."
—RomanceJunkiesReviews.com

"This is a fun and flirty story of past loves, secrets, and three sisters whose lives draw the reader in. For a good-time romance, check this one out."
—*Parkersburg News and Sentinel* (WV)

"A fun-filled, sexy, entertaining story...[satisfies] one's romantic sweet tooth."
—TheRomanceReader.com

Simply Irresistible

"Hot, sweet, fun, and romantic! Pure pleasure!"
—Robyn Carr, *New York Times* bestselling author

"4 stars! [I]ntroduces some wonderful characters with humor, heartwarming interaction, and an abundance of hot sex. Readers will be eager for the next story."
—*RT Book Reviews*

"This often hilarious novel has a few serious surprises, resulting in a delightfully satisfying story."
—LibraryJournal.com

"Heartwarming and sexy... an abundance of chemistry, smoldering romance, and hilarious sisterly antics."
— *Publishers Weekly*

"Shalvis's writing is a perfect trifecta of win: hilarious dialogue, evocative and real characters, and settings that are as much a part of the story as the hero and heroine. I've never been disappointed by a Shalvis book."
— **SmartBitchesTrashyBooks.com**

"One of those books that totally and absolutely encapsulates its title... utterly irresistible. The romance instantly jumps off the page... Jill Shalvis seems to have a golden touch with her books. Each one is better than the previous story."
— **RomanceJunkiesReviews.com**

"A beautiful start to this new series. The characters are as charming as the town itself. A pleasure to read."
— **FreshFiction.com**

"A Jill Shalvis hero is the stuff naughty dreams are made of."
— **Vicki Lewis Thompson,** *New York Times* **bestselling author of** *Chick with a Charm*

"Jill Shalvis has the incredible talent for creating characters who are intelligent, quick-witted, and gorgeously sexy, all the while giving them just the right amount of weakness to keep them from being unrealistically perfect."
— **RomanceJunkies.com**

Also by Jill Shalvis

At Last

♥

Jill Shalvis

FOREVER

NEW YORK   BOSTON

Copyright © 2012 by Jill Shalvis
Excerpt from *Forever and a Day* copyright © 2012 by Jill Shalvis

Forever
Hachette Book Group
237 Park Avenue
New York, NY 10017
www.HachetteBookGroup.com

Printed in the United States of America

First Edition: June 2012
10 9 8 7 6 5 4

Forever is an imprint of Grand Central Publishing.
The Forever name and logo are trademarks of Hachette Book Group, Inc.

The Hachette Speakers Bureau provides a wide range of authors for speaking events. To find out more, go to www.hachettespeakersbureau.com or call (866) 376-6591.

The publisher is not responsible for websites (or their content) that are not owned by the publisher.

ATTENTION CORPORATIONS AND ORGANIZATIONS:
Most HACHETTE BOOK GROUP books are available at quantity discounts with bulk purchase for educational, business, or sales promotional use. For information, please call or write:

Special Markets Department, Hachette Book Group
237 Park Avenue, New York, NY 10017
Telephone: 1-800-222-6747 Fax: 1-800-477-5925

To those who've ever been on a journey of their own.
May you find your own hope, peace, and heart.

At Last

Chapter 1

♥

Everything's better with chocolate.

I'm not lost," Amy Michaels said to the squirrel watching her from his perch on a tree branch. "Really, I'm not."

But she so was. And actually, it was a way of life. Not that Mr. Squirrel seemed to care. "I don't suppose you know which way?" she asked him. "I happen to be looking for hope."

His nose twitched, then he turned tail and vanished in the thick woods.

Well, that's what she got for asking a guy for directions. Or asking a guy for anything for that matter... She stood there another moment, with the high-altitude sun beating down on her head, a map in one hand and her Grandma Rose's journal in the other. The forest around her was a profusion of every hue of green and thick with tree moss and climbing plants. Even the ground was alive with growth and running creeks that she constantly had to leap over while birds and squirrels chattered at her. A city girl at heart, Amy was used to concrete, lights, and people flipping other people off. This noisy silence and lack of civilization was like being on another planet, but she kept going.

The old Amy wouldn't have. She'd have gone home by now. But the old Amy had made a lifelong habit out of running instead of taking a stand. She was done with that. It was the reason she was here in the wilds instead of on her couch. There was another reason, too, one she had a hard time putting into words. Nearly five decades ago now, her grandma had spent a summer in Lucky Harbor, the small Washington coastal town Amy could catch glimpses of from some of the switchbacks on the trail. Rose's summer adventure had been Amy's bedtime stories growing up, the only bright spot in an otherwise shitty childhood.

Now Amy was grown up—relatively speaking—and looking for what her grandma had claimed to find all those years ago—hope, peace, heart. It seemed silly and elusive, but the truth was sitting in her gut—Amy wanted those things, needed them so desperately it hurt.

It was harder than she expected. She'd been up since before dawn, had put in a ten-hour shift on her feet at the diner, and was now on a mountain trail. Still on her feet.

Unsure she was even going in the right direction, she flipped open her grandma's journal, which was really more of a spiral notepad, small enough that it fit in the palm of her hand. Amy had it practically memorized, but it was always a comfort to see the messy scrawl.

It's been a rough week. The roughest of the summer so far. A woman in town gave us directions for a day hike, promising it'd be fun. We started at the North District Ranger Station, turned right at Eagle Rock, left at Squaw Flats. And with the constant roar of the ocean as our northward guide, headed straight to the most gorgeous meadow I've ever seen, lined on the east side by thirty-foot-high prehistoric rocks pointing to the sky. The farthest one was the tallest, proudly planted into the ground, probably sitting there since the Ice Age.

We sat, our backs to the rock, taking it all in. I spent some time drawing the meadow, and when I was done, the late afternoon sun hit the rock perfectly, lighting it up like a diamond from heaven, both blinding and inspiring. We carved our initials into the bottom of our diamond and stayed the night beneath a black velvety sky...

And by morning, I realized I had something I'd been sorely missing—hope for the future.

Amy could hear the words in her grandma's soft, trembling voice, though of course she would have been much younger when she'd actually written the journal. Grandpa Scott had died when Amy was five, so she couldn't remember much about him other than a stern face, and that he'd waggled his finger a lot. It was hard to picture the stoic man of her memories taking a whimsical journey to a diamond rock and finding hope, but what did she know?

She hiked for what felt like forever on the steep mountain trail, which sure had looked a whole lot flatter and straighter on the map. Neither the map nor Rose's journal had given any indication that Amy had been going straight up until her nose bled. Or that the single-track trail was pitted with obstacles like rocks, fast-running creeks, low-hanging growth, and in two cases, downed trees that were bigger than her entire apartment. But Amy had determination on her side. Hell, she'd been born determined. Sure, she'd taken a few detours through Down-On-Her-Luck and then past Bad-Decisionsville, but she was on the right path now.

She just needed that hope. And peace would be good, too. She didn't give much of a shit about heart. Heart had never really worked out for her. Heart could suck it, but she wanted that hope. So she kept moving, amongst skyscraper-high rock formations and trees that she couldn't even see the tops of, feeling small and insignificant.

And awed.

She'd roughed it before; but in the past, this had meant something entirely different, such as giving up meals on her extra lean weeks, not trudging through the damp, overgrown forest laden with bugs, spiders, and possibly killer birds. At least they sounded killer to Amy, what with all the manic hooting and carrying on.

When she needed a break, she opened her backpack and went directly to the emergency brownie she'd pilfered from work earlier. She sat on a large rock and sighed in pleasure at getting off her feet. At the first bite of chocolately goodness, she moaned again, instantly relaxing.

See, she told herself, looking around at the overabundant nature, this wasn't so bad. She could totally do this. Hell, maybe she'd even sleep out here, like her grandparents had, beneath the velvet sky—

Then a bee dive-bombed her with the precision of a

kamikaze pilot, and Amy screeched, flinging herself off the rock. "Dammit." Dusting herself off, she stood and eyed the fallen brownie, lying forlorn in the dirt. She gave herself a moment to mourn the loss before taking in her surroundings with wariness.

There were no more bees, but now she had a bigger problem. It suddenly occurred to her that it'd been a while since she'd caught sight of the rugged coastline, with its stone arches and rocky sea stacks. Nor could she hear the roar of the crashing waves from below as her north-ward guide.

That couldn't be good.

She consulted her map and her penciled route. Not that *that* helped. There'd been quite a few forks on the trail, not all of them clearly marked. She turned to her grandma's journal again. As directed, she'd started at the North District Ranger Station, gone right at Eagle Rock, left at Squaw Flats...but no ocean sounds. No meadow. No diamond rock.

And no hope.

Amy looked at her watch—six thirty. Was it getting darker already? Hard to tell. She figured she had another hour and a half before nightfall, but deep down, she knew that wasn't enough time. The meadow wasn't going to magically appear, at least not today. Turning in a slow cir-cle to get her bearings, she heard an odd rustling. A human sort of rustling. Amy went utterly still except for the hair on the back of her neck, which stood straight up. "Hello?"

The rustling had stopped, but *there*, she caught a quick flash of something in the bush.

A face? She'd have sworn so. "Hello?" she called out. "Who's there?"

No one answered. Amy slid her backpack around to her front and reached in for her pocket knife.

Once a city rat, always a city rat.

Another slight rustle, and a glimpse of something blue—a sweatshirt maybe. "Hey," she yelled, louder than she meant to but she *hated* being startled.

Again, no one answered her, and the sudden stillness told her that she was once again alone.

She was good at alone. Alone worked. Heart still racing, she turned back around. And then around again. Because she had a problem—everything looked the same, so much so that she wasn't sure which way she'd come.

Or which way she was going. She walked along the trail for a minute but it didn't seem familiar so she did a one-eighty and tried again.

Still not familiar.

Great. Feeling like she'd gone down the rabbit hole, she whipped out her cell phone and stared down at the screen.

One bar...

Okay, don't panic. Amy never panicked until her back was up against the wall. Eyeing the closest rock outcropping, she headed toward it. Her guidebook had said that the Olympics' rock formations were made up of shales, sandstone, soft basalts, and pillow lava. *She* would have said they were sharp and craggy, a fact attested to by the cuts on her hands and legs. But they were also a good place to get reception.

Hopefully.

Climbing out onto the rocks was fine. Looking down, not so much. She was oh-holy-shit high up.

Gulp.

But she had *two* bars now for her efforts. She took a moment to debate between calling her two closest friends, Grace or Mallory. Either of the Chocoholics were good in a tough situation, but Mallory was Lucky Harbor native, so Amy called her first.

"How's it going?" Mallory asked.

"Taking a brownie break," Amy said casually, like she wasn't sitting on a rock outcropping a million feet above earth. "Thought you could join me."

"For chocolate?" Mallory asked. "Oh, yeah. Where are you?"

Well, wasn't that the question of the day. "I'm on the Sierra Meadows Trail...somewhere."

There was a beat of accusatory silence. "You lied about meeting you for a brownie?" Mallory asked, tone full of rebuke.

"Yeah, that's not exactly the part of my story I expected you to fixate on," Amy said. The rock was damp beneath her. Rain-soaked mosses adorned every tree trunk in sight, and she could hear a waterfall cascading into a natural pool somewhere nearby. Another bush rustled. Wind? Or...?

"I can't believe you lied about chocolate," Mallory said. "Lying about chocolate is...*sanctimonious*. Do you remember all those bad girl lessons you gave me?"

Amy rubbed the spot between her eyes where a headache was starting. "You mean the lessons that landed you the sexy hunk you're currently sleeping with?"

"Well, yes. But my point is that maybe you need *good* girl lessons. And good girl lesson number one is *never* tease when it comes to chocolate."

"Forget the chocolate." Amy drew a deep breath.

"Okay, so you know I'm not all that big on needing help when I screw up, but..." She grimaced. "*Help*."

"You're really lost?"

Amy sighed. "Yeah, I'm really lost. Alert the media. Text Lucille." Actually, in Lucky Harbor, Lucille *was* the media. Though she was seventy-something, her mind was sharp as a tack, and she used it to run Lucky Harbor's Facebook page like New York's *Page Six*.

Mallory had turned all business, using her bossy ER voice. "What trail did you start on and how long have you been moving?"

Amy did her best to recount her trek up to the point where she'd turned left at Squaw Flats. "I should have hit the meadow by now, right?"

"If you stayed on the correct trail," Mallory agreed. "Okay, listen to me very carefully. I want you to stay right where you are. Don't move."

Amy looked around her, wondering what sort of animals were nearby and how much of a meal she might look like to them. "Maybe I should—"

"No," Mallory said firmly. "I mean it, Amy. I want you to stay. People get lost up there and are never heard from again. *Don't move from that spot.* I've got a plan."

Amy nodded, but Mallory was already gone. Amy slipped her phone into her pocket, and though she wasn't much for following directions, she did as Mallory had commanded and didn't move from her spot. But she did resettle the comforting weight of her knife in her palm.

And wished for another brownie.

The forest noises started up again. Birds. Insects. Something with a howl that brought goose bumps to her entire body. She got whiplash from checking out each and every noise. But as she'd learned long ago, maintaining a high level of tension for an extended period of time was just exhausting. A good scream queen she would not make, so she pulled out her sketch pad and did her best to lose herself in drawing.

Thirty minutes later, she heard someone coming from the opposite direction she *thought* she'd come from. He wasn't making much noise, but Amy was a master at hearing someone approach. She could do it in her sleep—and had. Her heart kicked hard, but these were easy, steady footsteps on the trail. Not heavy, drunken footsteps heading down the hall to her bedroom...

In either case, it certainly wasn't Mallory. No, this was a man, light on his feet but not making any attempt to hide his approach. Amy squeezed her fingers around the comforting weight of her knife.

From around the blind curve of the trail, the man appeared. He was tall, built, and armed and dangerous, though not to her physical well-being. Nope, nothing about the tough, sinewy, gorgeous forest ranger was a threat to her body.

But Matt Bowers was *lethal* to her peace of mind.

She knew who he was from all the nights he'd come into the diner after a long shift, seeking food. Lucky Harbor residents fawned over him, especially the women. Amy attributed this to an electrifying mix of testosterone and the uniform. He was sipping a Big Gulp, which she'd bet her last dollar had Dr. Pepper in it. The man was a serious soda addict.

She understood his appeal, even felt the tug of it herself, but that was her body's response to him. Her brain was smarter than the rest of her and resisted.

He wore dark, wraparound Oakley sunglasses, but she happened to know that his eyes were light brown, sharp, and missed nothing. Those eyes were in complete contrast with his smile, which was all laid-back and easygoing, and said he was a pussy cat.

That smile lied.

Nothing about Matt Bowers was sweet and tame. Not one little hair on his sun-kissed head, not a single spectacular muscle, nothing. He was trouble with a capital *T*, and Amy had given up trouble a long time ago.

She was still sitting on the rock outcropping, nearly out of sight of the trail, but Matt's attention tracked straight to her with no effort at all. She sensed his wry amusement as he stopped and eyed her. "Someone send out an S.O.S.?"

She barely bit back her sigh. *Dammit, Mallory. Out of all the men in all the land, you had to send this one...*

When she didn't answer, he smiled. He knew damn well she'd called Mallory, and he wanted to hear her admit that she was lost.

But she didn't feel like it—childish and immature, she knew. The truth was, her reaction to him was just about the furthest thing from childish, and that scared her. She wasn't ready for the likes of him, for the likes of any man. The very last thing she needed was an entanglement, even if Matt did make her mouth water, even if he did look like he knew exactly how to get her off this mountain.

Or off in general...

And if *that* wasn't the most disconcerting thought she'd had in weeks...

Months.

"Mallory called the cavalry," he said. "Figured I was the best shot you had of getting found before dark."

Amy squared her shoulders, hoping she looked more capable than she felt. "Mallory shouldn't have bothered you."

He smiled. "So you *did* send out the S.O.S."

Damn him and his smug smile. "Forget about it," she said. "I'm fine. Go back to your job doing..." She waved her hand. "Whatever it is that forest rangers do, getting Yogi out of the trash, keeping the squirrels in line, et cetera."

"Yogi and the squirrels do take up a lot of my time," he agreed mildly. "But no worries. I can still fit you in."

His voice always seemed to do something funny to her stomach. And lower. "Lucky me."

"Yeah." He took another leisurely sip of his soda. "You might not know this, but on top of keeping Yogi in line and all the squirrel wrangling I do, rescuing fair maidens is also part of my job description."

"I'm no fair maiden—" She broke off when something screeched directly above her. Reacting instinctively, she flattened herself to the rock, completely ruining her tough-girl image.

"Just the cry of a loon," her very own forest ranger said. "Echoing across Four Lakes."

She straightened up just as another animal howled, and barely managed not to flinch. "That," she said shakily, "was more than a loon."

"A coyote," he agreed. "And the bugling of an elk. It's dusk. Everyone's on the prowl for dinner. The sound carries over the lakes, making everyone seem like they're closer than they are."

"There's elk around here?"

"Roosevelt Elk," he said. "And deer, bobcats, and cougars, too."

Amy shoved her sketch book into her backpack, ready to get the hell off the mountain.

"Whatcha got there?" he asked.

"Nothing." She didn't know him well enough to share her drawings, and then there was the fact that he was everything she didn't trust: easy smile, easy nature, easy ways—no matter how sexy the packaging.

Chapter 2

*If God had meant for us to be thin, he wouldn't
have created chocolate.*

Matt loved his job. Having come from first the military, then Chicago SWAT, the current shortage of blood and guts and gangbangers in his workweek was a big bonus. But his day as supervisory forest ranger for the North District had started at the ass crack of dawn, when two of his rangers had called in sick, forcing him to give the sunrise rainforest tour—a chore he ranked right up there with having a root canal.

Without drugs.

Talking wasn't the problem. Matt liked talking just fine, and he loved the mountain. What he didn't love were the parents who didn't keep track of their own children, or the divorcees who were looking for a little vacay nookie with a forest ranger, or the hard-core outdoor enthusiasts who knew ... everything.

After the morning's tour, he'd measured the snowmelt and then gone to the Eagle Rock campsites to relocate one royally pissed-off raccoon mama and her four babies from the bathroom showers. From there, he'd climbed up to Sawtooth Lake to check the east and west shore-lines for reported erosion, taken steps to get that erosion under control, patrolled all the northern quadrant's trails for a supposed Bigfoot sighting, handled some dreaded paperwork, and then come back out to rescue a fair, sweet maiden.

Only maybe not so sweet…

She was still sitting on the rock outcropping, her mile-long legs bent, her arms wrapped around them, her dark eyes giving nothing away except her mistrust, and he felt the usual punch of awareness hit him in the solar plexus.

So fucking beautiful. And so full of 100 percent, hands-off-or-die bad attitude.

She wasn't his usual type. He preferred his women soft, warm, giving, with a nice dash of playful sexiness, so he had no idea what it was about Amy Michaels. But for the past six months, ever since she'd moved to Lucky Harbor, they'd been circling each other.

Or maybe it was just him doing the circling. Amy was doing a whole lot of ignoring, a real feat given that she'd been serving him at the diner just about every night. He could have asked her out, but he knew she wouldn't go. She turned down everyone who asked her.

So instead Matt had regularly parked himself at Eat Me, fueling himself up on diner food and her company when he could get it. Then he'd go home and fantasize about all the other ways she might keep him company, getting off on more than a few of them.

Today she wore low-riding jeans and a black tank top that hugged her curves, revealing slightly sunburned shoulders and toned arms. Her boots had both laces and zippers. City girl boots, meant to look hot.

They did.

"You going to tell me what's going on?" he asked.

"Nothing's going on."

"Uh huh." She was revealing a whole lot of nothing. Basically, she would admit to being lost over her own dead body.

Usually people were happy to see him, but not this woman. Never this woman, and it was a little baffling. He knew from watching her at the diner, serving everyone from the mayor to raunchy truckers with the same impassive efficiency, that she had a high bullshit meter and a low tolerance for anything that wasn't delivered straight up. "So Mallory's what, on crack?" he asked.

"She thinks she's funny."

"So...you're good?"

"Pretty much," she said.

He nodded agreeably. Fine by him if she didn't want to break down and admit to being lost. He enjoyed her fierceness, and the inner strength that came with it. But he still couldn't just walk away.

Or take his eyes off her. Her hair was a deep, rich, shiny brown, sometimes up, sometimes falling softly about her face, as it was today. She wore aviator sunglasses and lip gloss, and that tough-girl expression. She was a walking contradiction.

And a walking wet dream. "You know this trail closes at dusk, right?"

She tipped her head up and eyed the sky. Nearly dusk. Then she met his gaze. "Sure," she said with a tight smile.

Hmm. Not for the first time, he wondered how it'd be

to see her smile with both her eyes and her mouth at the
same time.

She retied her boots, those silly boots that didn't have
a lick of common sense to them. He was picturing her in
those boots and nothing else when she climbed off the
rock and pulled on her cute little leather backpack, which
was as impractical as her boots. "What are you doing all
the way up here?"

"Just hiking," she said carefully. She was always careful with her words, careful to keep her thoughts hidden,
and she was especially careful to keep herself distanced
from *him*.

But Matt had his own bullshit meter, and it was deadly
accurate. She was lying, which stirred his natural curiosity and suspicion—good for the cop in him, dangerous
for the man who was no longer interested in romantic
relationships. "Hiking out here is big," he said. "But it
can be dangerous."

She shrugged at this, as if the dangers of the forest
were no match for her. It was either cocky, or simply the
fact that she'd spent a hell of a lot of time in far more
dangerous situations. He suspected the latter, which he
didn't like to think about.

She moved back to the trail, clearly anxious to be rid
of him. Not a surprise.

But along with Matt's BS meter came a honed ability to
read people, and he was reading her loud and clear. She was
exhausted, on edge, and his least favorite: scared, though
she was doing her best to hide that part. Still, her nerves
were shining through, and he knew it was because of him.

He wasn't sure what to do about that. Or her. He
wasn't at all used to explaining himself, but he needed to

explain a few things to her. Such as exactly how lost she was. "Amy—"

"Look, I appreciate you coming out. I did lose track of time, but I'll be going now, so..."

Knowing the value of a good, meaningful silence, Matt waited for her to finish her sentence.

She didn't.

Instead, she was clearly waiting for him to leave, and he suddenly got it—she wanted to follow him out. Pride sucked, as he knew all too well. "Okay, then," he said. "I'll see you at the diner real soon."

"Right." She nodded agreeably, the woman who was the singularly most disagreeable woman he'd ever met.

Having much more time than she, he leaned back against a tree, enjoying the flash of annoyance that crossed her face. "Right," he mirrored. It'd been a hell of a long day, and it was shaping up to be a longer night. He didn't have enough Dr. Pepper left to get him through it, but he was perfectly willing to try.

Amy sighed with barely concealed annoyance and stalked off down the path.

In the wrong direction.

Funny, Amy thought, how righteous indignation could renew one's energy level, not to mention make them stupid. And oh, how she hated being stupid. Even worse was being stupid in mixed company. She'd done it before, of course. Too many times to count. She'd thought she'd gotten past it but apparently not.

"Need help?"

With a grimace, she slowly turned to face Matt. Yeah, she needed help, and they both knew it.

He was still leaning against the tree, arms crossed over his chest, the gun on his hip catching the sun. He looked big and tough as hell, his shoulders broad enough to carry all her problems. His hair brushed his collar, a little shaggy, a lot tousled. Sexy. Damn him. He stood there as if he had all the time in the world and not a concern in his head.

And of course he didn't. *He* wasn't lost.

But there was something else, too. There was a sort of...crackling in the air between them, and it wasn't a bird or insect or frigging elk call either.

It was sexual tension. It'd been a long time, a real long time, since she'd allowed herself to acknowledge such a thing, and it surprised the hell out of her. She knew men, all of them. She'd been there, done that, bought *and* returned the T-shirt. She knew that beneath a guy's chosen veneer, whatever that may be—nice guy, funny guy, sexy guy, whatever—lay their true colors, just lying in wait.

But she'd been watching Matt for months now, and he was always...Matt. Amused, tense, tired, it didn't seem to matter, he remained his cool, calm, even-keeled self. Nothing got to him. She had to admit, that confused her. *He* confused her. "I'm actually okay," she said.

He expressed polite doubt with the arch of a single brow. Her pride was a huge regulation-sized football in her throat, and admitting defeat sucked. But there was ego, and there was being an idiot. "Fine," she said. "Just tell me which way is south."

He pointed south.

Nodding, she headed that way, only to be caught up short when he snagged her by the backpack and pulled her back against him.

She startled, jerking in his hands before forcing herself to relax. It was Matt, she reminded herself, and the thought was followed by a hot flash that she'd like to blame on the weather, but she knew better.

He turned her ninety degrees. "To get back to the ranger station and your car, you want to go southwest," he said.

Right. She knew that, and she stalked off in the correct direction.

"Watch out for bears," Matt called after her.

"Yeah, okay," she muttered, "and I'll also keep an eye out for the Tooth Fairy."

"Three o'clock."

Amy craned her neck and froze. Oh sweet baby Jesus, there really was a bear at three o'clock. Enjoying the last of the sun, he was big, brown, and shaggy, and *big*. He lay flat on his back, his huge paws in the air as he stretched, confident that he sat at the top of the food chain. "Holy shit," she whispered, every Discovery Channel bear mauling she'd ever seen flashing in her mind. She backed up a step, and then another, until she bumped into a brick wall and nearly screamed.

"Just a brown bear," said the brick wall that was Matt.

"Would you stop sneaking up on me?" she hissed over her shoulder. "I hate to be sneaked up on!"

Matt was kind enough not to point out that *she'd* bumped into him. Or that she was quaking in her boots. Instead, he set his drink down and very softly "shh'd" her, gently rubbing his big hands up and down her arms. "You're okay," he said.

She was okay? How was that possible? The bear was the size of a VW, and he was wriggling on the ground, letting out audible groans of ecstasy as he scratched his back on the fallen pine needles, latent power in his every move. Sort of like the man behind her. "Does he even see us?" she whispered.

As she spoke, the bear slowly tipped his big, furry head back, lazily studying Amy and Matt from his upside down perch.

Yeah, he saw them. Reacting instinctively, she turned and burrowed right into Matt. "If you laugh at me," she warned as his warm, strong arms closed around her, "I'll kill you."

He didn't laugh or mock her. For once, he was unsmiling, his jaw dark with stubble, eyes hidden behind his reflective Oakleys. "No worries, Tough Girl," he said, his warm, strong arms closing around her. "And anyway, I'm hard to kill."

Chapter 3

There's more to life than chocolate,
but not right now.

As Matt drew Amy in close, he thought that laughing at her was just about the last thing on the list of what he felt like doing at the moment. Kissing her was on the list. Sliding his hands down her back to cup her sweet ass and rub up against her was also on the list.

But laughing? No. She'd nearly leapt out of her own skin a second ago, and it hadn't been all fear of the bear. Nope, a good portion of that had been when Matt had touched her unexpectedly. That bothered him, a whole hell of a lot. "I've got you."

"I've usually got myself," she murmured into his chest. "I'm just not much of a bear person." Her voice was soft and full of the reluctant gratitude he knew she'd never actually express. He liked this better than the wariness she usually showed him, but not even close to what he'd rather she be feeling.

He ran his hand up and down her back, trying to soothe

the quivers he felt wracking her, trying *not* to notice how good she felt against him. Or how...fragile.

He'd never thought of her as fragile before, ever. He'd spent a lot of time watching her carry loaded trays at the diner and knew she was actually strong as hell. "You're not going to be bear bait," he promised, turning her so that she was behind him. "Not today anyway."

She grabbed a fistful of the back of his uniform shirt and pressed up against his back. "How do you know?"

"Well, you're behind me, for one thing. So if anyone's going to be bear bait, it'll be me. And brown bears are extremely passive. If we take a step toward him, he'll take off."

She let go of him, presumably so he could do just that, even giving him a little nudge that was actually more like a push. With a laugh, Matt obliged and stepped toward the bear, waving his arms. With a look of reproof, the bear lumbered to his feet and vanished into the bush.

Amy collected herself with admirable speed, which was just the slightest bit of a bummer because he'd been enjoying the contact. "A lot can happen this far out here on the mountain," he said. "You need to be ready for anything."

"Yeah, I'm getting that, thanks." In those ridiculous but sexy-as-hell boots, she moved unenthusiastically to the trail.

"Sure you don't want an escort out?" he asked. *Or some more comforting...*

"I've got it."

Just as well since he was out of the practice of comforting a woman. Several years out of practice, actually, since his ex had so thoroughly shredded him back in

Chicago. He was still watching Amy hike off into the sunset when his radio squawked, and then Mary, his dispatcher, came on. "You find her?"

Mallory had called his office an hour ago, and Mary had reached him on the radio. Now Mallory was probably calling to check on Amy. "Yeah, she's on her way out now. I'm still up here near 06-04," he said, giving his coordinates.

"You might want to think about sticking overnight."

"Why?"

"One of the standing dead fell about twenty minutes ago, across the fire road at 06-02."

His route out.

"Can't get a saw up there until daybreak," she said.

This left him two choices—leave his truck and hike out like Amy or sleep up here. He wasn't going to leave his truck. Overnighting wasn't a hardship in the slightest since he had all his gear with him and had stayed out here many a night. "I'll stick. Take me off the board."

"Ten-four."

Matt turned and went in the opposite direction Amy had gone, stepping off the trail to take a considerable shortcut back to where he'd left his truck. He didn't hurry through the stands of spruce, hemlock, pine, and cedar. There was no need; he'd still beat her. And sure enough, when he'd gotten to his truck and four-wheeled farther down the narrow fire road to where it intersected with the Sawtooth trail, he came out just ahead of her. She came around a blind corner and kept moving, not seeing him.

"Amy."

She whipped around, feet planted wide, eyes alert, ready for a fight.

"Just me," he said easily.

"What the hell are you doing, besides trying to scare me to death?"

She'd been really moving. And, if he wasn't mistaken, she was also limping a little bit in her boots. "Just making sure you're still going in the right direction."

Breathing a little heavily, she tore off her sunglasses and narrowed her dark eyes at him, hands on hips. "You had your truck all along?"

"I offered you help. Think you're going to be okay for the three-mile hike back?"

"Three miles? What the hell happened to the '*moderate, two-mile round-trip hike that everyone can enjoy*' that the guidebook promised?"

"If you'd have stayed on the Sierra Meadows Trail, that'd have been true," he said. "But you cut over to the Sawtooth Trail."

She blew a strand of hair out of her face. "You need better trail signs."

"Budget cuts," he said. "Next time stay on the easy-access trails down by the station. Those are clearly marked."

"Easy is for pansies."

"Maybe, but at least all the pansies are safe for the night. Because once it gets dark out here, it's best to stay still. And that's in about…" He tipped his head back and studied the sky. "Ten minutes. Ever been out here at night?"

She glanced upward uneasily. "No."

"It's a whole new kind of dark. No street lights, no city lights, nothing."

"Why aren't you in a hurry then?"

"I'm not going anywhere tonight," he said. "The fire road's blocked until morning by a fallen tree, and I don't want to leave my truck."

"So you're going to stay out here all night?" she asked. "Beneath the velvet sky?"

"Nice description."

"It's not mine." She pulled a small penlight flashlight from her backpack and flicked it on in the dusk, looking relieved that it actually worked. "You don't think I can get back before dark, do you?"

"No."

She sighed. "So if I stay out here, you going to ticket me for not having a overnight permit?"

"I think I can cut you some slack."

It wasn't often he didn't know what he wanted to do with a woman. In fact, this was a first. She was obviously unprepared. All she had was a flashlight. No water, no tent, no sleeping bag, no food that he could see.

Not that it was a problem, since he was prepared enough for the both of them. Plus, he'd be sticking to her like glue, and not because he'd been lusting after her for months, but because she was a statistic waiting to happen. "I have camping gear, if you want to share." Christ, listen to him. Such a sucker for melted-chocolate eyes.

"I'm fine."

Her mantra. And there was no doubt that she *was* extremely fine standing there, her long, lithe body throwing off attitude as she looked at him with that devastatingly powerful gaze, shadowed by things he didn't understand but wanted to. "Sleep near your fire," he advised, playing it her way. For now. "Keep the coyotes back."

"Coyotes," she repeated faintly.

"And douse yourself in mosquito spray. It's getting to be that season. Keep your jean legs tucked into your boots when you lie down. You don't want any extra creepy crawlies getting up there."

She stared down at her skinny jeans, then at the boots that were most definitely *not* hiking sanctioned. "Creepy crawlies?"

"It's a little early for snakes, but you should keep a watch out for them, too," he said. "Just in case."

She nodded and took a long, uneasy look around them.

He had *no* idea what she thought she was doing, or why, but he wasn't *that* big an asshole to let her do it alone, no matter how brave she thought she was. "You know," he said quietly. "Sometimes, being alone isn't all it's cracked up to be."

She thought about that a moment. "You really have gear in your truck?"

"Standard operating procedure," he said, and it was true. But what wasn't SOP was to offer that gear to stranded hikers, no matter how sexy they were.

No fool, she slid him a long, steely-eyed look, and he did his best to look innocent.

"Listen," she finally said. "I might've given you the wrong impression when I...bumped into you with the bear thing."

"Bumped into me?" He couldn't help it, he laughed. "You tried to crawl up my body."

"Which is my point," she said stiffly. "My sleep-out adventure *isn't* going to include crawling up anyone's body."

"Will it include sleeping?"

She continued to study him, thinking so hard that he could smell something burning. He left her to it and turned to the surrounding woods, gathering dry kindling from the ground as the sky went from dusk to jet-black night in the blink of an eye. Moving to the center of the clearing, he quickly and efficiently built a fire, then grabbed the tent and sleeping bag. He raided his lockbox, pulling out—thank Christ—a can of Dr. Pepper, some beef jerky, a bag of marshmallows, and two bottles of water. "Honey, dinner's ready."

This earned him another long look across the fire.

"Tough crowd." Typical of mountain altitude, one moment it was a decent temperature, and the next, it was butt-ass cold. He moved closer to the fire, next to his camping partner, who was standing huddled-up as close as she could get without singeing her eyebrows. There was no moon yet, though a few stars began to glitter like diamonds in the huge, fathomless sky. Didn't get skies like this in Chicago, he thought, and took a moment to soak it in.

Amy was hands-out over the flames. He doubted her tank top was offering much, if any, protection against the evening breeze. This fact was confirmed by the way her nipples pressed against the thin knit material. Nice view. But he went back to his truck, grabbed his extra sweatshirt, and tossed it to her.

"What's this?"

"A way to get warm."

She stared down at it as if it were a spitting cobra.

"Works better if you put it on," he said.

"Wearing a guy's sweatshirt implies…*things*," she said.

"Yeah? What things?"

She didn't answer, and he dropped another log on the flames. By now she was visibly shivering. "It's just a sweatshirt, Amy, not a ring. It doesn't come with a commitment. Now my Dr. Pepper, *that* I'm not sharing."

She snorted and pulled on the sweatshirt without comment. It dropped past her hips to her thighs, swallowing her whole. She tugged the hood up over her hair, shading her face from him. "Thanks."

He should have just kept his mouth shut and let it go, but he couldn't. "Just out of morbid curiosity, what exactly did you think I'd expect in exchange?"

She slid him a long look that said it all, and once again he wondered what kind of assholes she'd come across in her life. "Come on," he said. "For a sweatshirt? I mean, *maybe*, if I'd given you the Dr. Pepper, that I could see. Or if I'd had to wrestle you from the bear . . ."

She actually smiled. It was a lovely smile that made her eyes shine, and he smiled back. "So who told you a guy gets sex for sharing his sweatshirt?" he asked.

"Guys only think about one thing."

He chewed on that for a few minutes, keeping his hands busy setting up the tent, tossing in his sleeping bag. "Sometimes we think about food, too," he finally said.

Amy laughed outright at this, and Matt felt like he'd won the lottery. He kicked a fallen log close to the fire and gestured for her to have a seat. When she did, he tossed her the beef jerky and marshmallows. "Dinner of champions. Which course do you want first?"

She eyed both, then opened the marshmallows. "Life's short," she said. "Dessert first."

"I like the way you think." He stoked the flames,

then pushed aside the two burning logs to reveal the hot ashes—the sweet spot for roasting marshmallows. Moving to the edge of the clearing, he located two long sticks then handed one to Amy.

She in turn handed him a marshmallow for his stick. Look at them, all companionable and domestic. They roasted in silence for a few minutes, Amy staring speculatively into the fire. "Being out here makes me want to draw," she said quietly.

He looked at her. "Wait— Did you just offer a piece of personal information?"

She rolled her eyes. "I'm not a complete social moron. I can do the casual conversation thing."

"But your drawing isn't casual to you," he said.

She held his gaze. "No. It's not."

Forget her great laugh. *Now* he felt like he'd just won the lottery.

"Do you draw?" she asked him.

Was she looking for common ground? He'd like to give it to her, but this wasn't going to be it. "Stick figures," he said, blowing on his marshmallow before eating it. "I'm good at stick figures when I have to be for a report, but that's about it. Doesn't mean I can't get how inspiring it is out here though. What do you draw?"

"Landscapes, mostly." She glanced around at the dark night. "I'd love to do the trees silhouetted against the dark sky. Or the waterfalls that I saw on the way up here. I can still hear them."

"Yeah, there's more than sixty glaciers melting out here," he said. "Along with all the heavy rains we got this year. All that water's rushing 24-7 to the sea."

She handed him another marshmallow from the bag,

and their fingers brushed. Her breath caught, and the sound went straight through him. She busied herself with her toasted marshmallow, popping it into her mouth, sucking some of it off her finger. He tried not to stare and thereby prove that she was right with *guys only think about one thing*, but Christ. She was *sucking* on her finger. A completely involuntary sound escaped him, and she stopped.

He met her gaze, and though he couldn't quite read her expression, she didn't look disgusted or pissed off. She nibbled on her lower lip for a beat, and suddenly it seemed like all the cool air got sucked out of the night, leaving only heat.

Lots of heat. But hell if he'd do one damn thing about it. Beautiful as she was sitting there by the fire's glow, he knew making a move on her would be fatal to any friendship they might have.

But she kept looking at him like she'd never really seen him before, and then suddenly they were a lot closer, their thighs touching. His hands itched to reach for her but he forced himself to stay perfectly still. Perfectly. Still. Which was how he knew that *she* leaned in first. Oh, yeah, but just as her mouth got to his, a coyote howled— a bone-chilling, hair-raising cry that was immediately answered by another, longer, louder howl that echoed off the mountain caverns.

Amy jerked, straightening up with a startled gasp.

"They're not as close as they sound," he said.

She nodded and leaned over to fiddle with her boot, using the ruse to scoot close again. He'd have teased her about it but he didn't want to scare her further off.

Another coyote howled, and then more joined in. Amy went rigid and set her hand on his thigh.

Matt silently willed the coyotes to come closer, but they didn't. Instead, when Amy realized where her hand was, she snatched it away. "Sorry."

"Don't be. You can hold on to me anytime." He threaded a row of marshmallows onto her stick for her, and then did the same for himself, watching Amy keep an eye on the shadows of the woods around them as though maybe, if only she concentrated hard enough, she'd be able to see through the dark.

"Not a big camper, huh?" he asked sympathetically.

"I'm more of a city girl."

"Which city?"

"New York. Miami. Dallas..."

"All of them?"

"Chicago, too," she said. "I moved around a lot."

He pulled his stick from the fire and wished he had chocolate and graham crackers to go with the perfectly toasted marshmallows. "I'm from Chicago," he said. "Born and bred in the rat race." Which he didn't miss. Not the weather, not the job, not the ex...Although he did miss his family. "When were you there?"

"Ten years ago." She shrugged. "Just for a little while."

He knew she was twenty-eight, so that meant she'd been eighteen when she'd been there. "You went to high school in Chicago?"

"No. I took the GED and got out early. Before Chicago."

"Ten years ago, I was just out of the Navy," he said. "Working as a cop. Maybe our paths crossed when you were in town."

"Yeah, not likely," she told him. "You were SWAT, not a beat cop running homeless teens off the corners."

He wasn't surprised that she knew he'd been SWAT. Everyone in Lucky Harbor knew everyone's business. He just wished he knew hers, but she'd been good at keeping a low profile. "You were a homeless teen?"

She let out a single syllable hum that could have been agreement or just a vague "don't want to talk about it."

Too bad that he did want to talk about it. "What happened to your parents?"

"I'm the product of what happens when teenagers don't listen in sex ed class. Nothing you haven't seen before on *16 and Pregnant*."

"That bad huh?"

She shrugged and stuffed the marshmallow into her mouth.

Conversation over, apparently. Which was okay. He'd get another chance. He enjoyed watching her savor each marshmallow like it was a special prize. He especially enjoyed how she licked the remnants off her fingers with a suction sound…

"You give good marshmallow," she said.

He gave good other things, too, but he kept that to himself.

When they were high on sugar, they balanced it out with the beef jerky. Amy unzipped her backpack, and he unabashedly peered inside, catching her drawing pad, colored pencils, a hiking guide, lip gloss, and a pocket-knife before she pulled out an apple and zipped the pack closed.

She was a puzzle, he thought. All tough girl on the outside, girlie-girl on the inside, and a whole bunch of other things he couldn't quite put a finger on yet.

She handed him the apple. He took a bite, then handed

it back. They shared it down to the core, drank their waters, and then Amy yawned wide.

"I'm sorry," she said, and yawned again. "I had the morning shift at the diner. I'm exhausted."

"Bedtime then." He stoked the fire, then rose and pulled her up as well, turning her toward the tent.

She stared inside at the still rolled-up sleeping bag. "This is yours. I can sleep in your truck."

"The bucket seats suck, and the truck bed's ridged and cold as hell. You've had a long day and need some sleep. Take the tent."

She bit her lower lip, her eyes suspicious again. "And you?"

"I'll be by the fire. I have an emergency blanket, I'll be fine."

"No," she said, shaking her head. "I can't let you do that. You'll get cold."

"Are you offering to share the tent?"

Her gaze dropped down to his chest, and she chewed on her lower lip again—which was driving him insane. *He* wanted to chew on that lower lip and then soothe the ache with his tongue.

"Sharing is a bad idea," she finally said. "A really, *really* bad idea." But she gave him another slow sweep. His chest, his abs, lower... Her pupils dilated, giving her away.

Either she had a head injury he didn't know about or looking him over had aroused her. "Sometimes," he said, "bad ideas become good ideas."

"No, they don't."

He didn't like to disagree with a woman, especially a pretty, sexy woman whom he'd been dreaming about getting naked and licking every inch of her body. But he absolutely disagreed on this.

Vehemently.

Instead of voicing that, he gave her a nudge into the tent. "Zip up behind you."

When she did, he let out a long breath and stood there in the dark between the fire and the tent for a long beat. *You're an idiot*, he told himself, and shaking his head, he moved closer to the flames. Leaning back, getting comfortable, or as comfortable as he could without a sweatshirt or his sleeping bag, he stared at the sky. Normally, this never failed to relax him, but tonight it took a long time.

A very long time.

It was his body's fault, he decided. He definitely had a few parts at odds with each other, but in the end, it was his brain that reminded him of the bottom line. He'd come here to Lucky Harbor for some peace and quiet, to be alone.

To forget the hell his life in Chicago had turned into.

And it *had* been complete hell, having to turn in his own partner for being on the take, then facing the censure of his fellow cops.

And then there'd been his marriage.

Shelly had never liked his hours or the danger he'd faced every day. In return, he'd never liked that she hadn't taken her own safety seriously enough. And when it had all gone bad and she'd gotten hurt...well, that had been another sort of hell entirely.

And his fault. He 100 percent blamed himself.

That had made two of them. Shelly had told him in her parting shot that he was better off alone, and he honestly believed that to be true. All this time he'd thought it...

At some point during this annoying inner reflection, he must have finally fallen asleep because he woke up instantly at the sound of Amy's scream.

Chapter 4

A day without chocolate is like a day without sunshine.

Breathless, heart pounding, Amy lay flat on her back in the pitch dark. *Shit.* Okay, so that was the *last* time she ever tiptoed into the woods by herself to find a nice, big tree to pee behind. Her downfall had been the walk back to camp. It'd been so dark, and her flashlight had given enough light for exactly nothing.

And she'd slipped on something and slid.

Down.

And down.

She'd lost her flashlight on the descent, and now she couldn't see much except the vague black outline of the canopy of trees far above her. Or at least she hoped those were trees. Claustrophobic from the all-encompassing blackness, and more than a little worried about creepy crawlies, she sat up and winced. Her left wrist was on fire. So was her butt. Great, she'd broken her butt. She could see the headline on Facebook now—*Amy Michaels cracks her crack during a potty break on the mountain.*

The worst part was that this was all her own fault. She was street smart and had been cocky enough to believe she could handle herself. Her mistake, because she should have known better—bad things could happen anywhere. They'd always happened to her, from back as far as when her grandma had died. Back then, a twelve-year-old Amy had gone to live with her mother for the first time, and oh how she'd hated that. Her mother had hated it, too, and Amy had grossly misbehaved, acting out in grief and teenage hatred. She'd sought attention, bad attention, in the form of inappropriate sex, using it as a way to manipulate boys. Then the game had been turned on her, and she hadn't liked it much. It'd taken her far too long to realize she was destroying herself, but eventually she'd given up dangerous sex. Hell, she'd pretty much given up men, no matter how gorgeous and sexy they were.

It'd been so long she felt like a virgin. At least an emotional virgin.

And now she was going to die as one.

A beam of light shined down on her from above. Not God. Not a fairy godmother. Just Matt, calling her name, concern clear in his voice.

"Down here," she said. *Where all the stupid girls end up on their broken butts.* "I'm coming."

"Don't move."

"But—"

"I mean it, Amy. Not a muscle."

"Well jeez, if you mean it . . ."

No response to that. Seemed the laid-back forest ranger wasn't feeling so laid-back right now.

He got to her quickly and without falling, she noted

with more than a little bitterness. And unlike her, he could apparently see in the dark. Crouched before her, he was nothing but a big, built shadow holding her down when she'd have gotten to her feet. "Stay," he said, voice firm.

"Stay?" she repeated with a disbelieving laugh. "What am I, a dog?"

"Where are you hurt?"

"Nowhere."

He flicked the light over her, eyes narrowing in on the wrist she was hugging to herself. "Hold this," he said, and put the light in her good hand so he could probe at her other wrist.

She hissed in a breath, and he slid his gaze to hers. "Can you move your fingers?"

She showed him just how much her middle finger could move.

"Nice," he said. "So nature call, huh?"

She didn't answer, distracting herself by shining the light around them to make sure they weren't being circled by bears or mountain lions. What she *did* see stole her breath more than Matt's gentle maneuvering of her wrist.

They were at the base of a meadow. "Sierra Meadows?"

"Yeah, although this is the back way in." Matt glanced up at her face. "Why?"

"No reason."

"Why do you try to bullshit a bullshitter? You were looking for Sierra Meadows?"

"Yeah."

"It's not a very well-known place," Matt said. "Hard to get to—well, unless you fall into it."

"Ha ha." She wondered how hard it'd be to find this place again on her own.

"So why Sierra Meadows?"

"I read about the wall of diamond rocks. I wanted to see them."

"They're a couple of hundred yards across a very soggy meadow from here. But worth seeing—in the light of day." He took the flashlight back. "I don't think your wrist is broken but you've got a good sprain going. What else hurts?"

"Nothing."

He obviously didn't buy this since he gave her a rather impressive eye roll and began running a hand down her limbs with quick, impassive efficiency.

"Hey!" She pushed his hand away. "I already had my annual."

Finished with her arms, legs, and ribs, he merely tilted her head back and looked into her eyes. "How many fingers am I holding up?"

"One," she said. "But as I already showed you, it's much more effective when it's the middle finger."

He smiled. "You're fine."

"I keep telling you that."

"Come on." Rising to his feet, he pulled her to hers.

At the movement, pain shot up her tailbone, but she controlled her wince and let him help her back up the hill.

"I've seen just about everything there is to see out here," he said at the top. "But I've never seen anyone fall down that ravine before."

"So glad to give you a first."

"You should have woken me up."

For a pee escort? Hell no. They were at their campsite now, and he gave her a little nudge toward the tent. She crawled inside and back into the sleeping bag, pulling it over her head, hoping to pretend that she was at home, in a warm bed. But at home, she never had worries about bears and mountain lions, and for all she knew also the big bad wolf. She certainly never shivered like this at home either.

When had it gotten so cold?

Her butt suddenly vibrated, scaring her for a second until she realized it was the cell phone in her back pocket. With some maneuvering, she pulled it out and read the text from Mallory.

> *Good girl lesson #2: When your BFF sends you a gorgeous guy, you call her and thank her. That's good manners. Good girl lesson #3: Stop scowling. You'll scare away the aforementioned gorgeous guy.*

Amy was definitely scowling and didn't plan to stop anytime soon. She considered hitting reply and telling Mallory exactly what she thought of the good girl lessons so far, but just then the sleeping bag was yanked off her head, and it wasn't the big, bad wolf. Actually, if she squinted, there *were* some similarities.

"Your arm," Matt said, on his knees, head ducked low to accommodate the tent ceiling. He had a first-aid kit and had pulled out an ACE bandage, which he used to wrap her wrist. Then he slapped an ice pack against his thigh to activate it and set her wrapped wrist on it. He pulled out a second ice pack and eyed her.

She narrowed her eyes. "What?"

"You going to let me look at it?" he asked.

Her free hand slid to her own behind. "How did you know?"

"Wild guess," he said dryly. "Let me see it."

"Over my dead body."

He let out a breath and dropped his chin to his chest for a moment. Either he was praying for patience or trying not to laugh. When he had himself together, he moved with his usual calm efficiency and unzipped her sleeping bag, yanking it from her before she could so much as squeak.

Which she did.

He ignored that and held her down effortlessly with one hand on her waist and one on her thigh. "Be still," he said.

Be still? Was he kidding? "Listen, I'm going to *be still* with my foot up your ass—"

"You're bleeding."

"What?" She immediately stopped struggling and tried to see what he was seeing. "I am not. Where?"

"Your leg."

He was right, there was blood coming through her jeans on her thigh. She stared at it a little woozily. She hated blood, especially her own. "Um . . ."

Matt was rifling through the first aid kit again. "Lose your pants. We need to clean that up."

Well if that didn't make her un-woozy right-quick. She laughed at him, making him lift his gaze from the box. "Oh, hell, no," she said.

The only light in the tent came from his flashlight, so she couldn't see his exact expression, but she had no trouble sensing his surprise. Probably when he said "lose your pants" to women they generally tore themselves out of their clothes, in a hurry to get naked for him. "Over my dead body."

She sensed more than saw his smile. "I administer a lot of basic first aid," he said in that calm, reasonable tone that made her want to do something to rile him up.

Too bad she'd given up riling men a good long time ago. "Just give me a Band-Aid."

"We need to clean the cut." His voice was all reasonable friendliness, but laced with unmistakable steel. Authority. And yet...and this made no sense...it was also somehow the sexiest voice she'd ever heard. She didn't often let herself get curious about the people in her life, but this time she couldn't seem to help herself. "After all you've done," she said, "How the hell did you end up out here in the boonies saving the stupid chick?"

He laughed softly, the sound warming her a little bit. "Always did love the outdoors," he said. "I was twelve when I first spent a night outside."

"You ran away when you were twelve?"

"No." He slid her a look that said he found it interesting that her mind had taken her there. Interesting, and disturbing. "My older brother took me camping," he said. "He warned me not to go anywhere without him, not even to take a leak." He laughed a little at the memory. "I thought, well fuck that."

The smile in his voice was contagious, and she felt herself relax a little. "What happened?" she asked.

"Woke up in the middle of the night and had to take a leak. I was way too cool to need an escort..." He paused meaningfully, and she grimaced.

"Yeah, yeah."

"So I stumbled out of the tent and went looking for a tree. Walked straight into a wall of bushes and got all cut up. Nearly wet myself before I got free." He laughed again and shook his head. "My brother reamed me a new one when I got back. Man, he was pissed off that I was hurt. I told him to chill, that everything was fine. And the next morning, everything was still fine. But by that afternoon, I had a hundred-and-three temperature. My mom stripped me down to put me in a cool bath and found a nasty gash on my arm that had gotten infected."

His voice was magic, Amy thought, listening to him in the dark. Low and a little gruff. Listening to him was like listening to a really great book on tape. No regrets about his past, and then there was his obvious affection for both his brother and his mom... both things she had no experience with.

"I also had poison oak," he said. "*Everywhere.*"

She gasped. "Oh, God." Gentle interlude over, she sat up so fast she bashed her head on his chin. "Do you think I have—"

"No." He pressed her back down, rubbing his chin with his spare hand. "But you do have a cut that could get infected if we don't clean it out."

"By morning?"

"By midnight."

She stared up at him, looking for a single sign that he was being a perv about this. Because if he was, then he was also a dead perv. But there kneeling at her side, he looked at her evenly, steady as a rock.

This was also totally out of her realm of experience as well, a guy wanting in her pants for non-sexual reasons.

Maybe the scratch was already infected, and she'd lost her mind. This was the only explanation she could accept for the teeny tiny smidgeon of disappointment. In which case, dropping trou was the least of her problems. So she blew out a sigh and unzipped her jeans. For a moment she panicked, unable to remember which underwear she'd put on that morning. She didn't know whether she hoped for laundry day granny panties, or something sexy. Laundry day granny panties…No, wait. Something sexy. *No!* Good Lord, she was losing it.

Shimmying the skinny jeans down to her knees wasn't easy or attractive, and Amy was also incredibly aware of Matt's big, solid presence at her side. And yep, he was right—there was a big gash on her thigh, curving around to the back. It was burning now, but she hardly noticed over the relief to find that she wasn't wearing granny panties. She was in the thin baby-blue, cheeky-cut panties that she'd gotten in a sale pack of three. Which is where the bad news came in, because they were a lot like wearing nothing. Worse, they said "booty-licious" across the butt, but luckily he couldn't see that.

There was a beat of complete silence.

And then another.

And then yet another.

Finally, she looked up. Matt was still as stone, his hands on his own thighs, eyes dilated nearly black.

"Matt?"

"Yeah?"

"You okay?"

"Working on it." His voice sounded unusually tight.

"I thought you said you did this a lot."

"Yeah. I do. But apparently not with anyone I'm wildly attracted to."

This caused certain reactions in her body that were best not experienced in mixed company. "It's just panties," she finally whispered.

"And they're really great panties," Matt agreed. "But it's not the panties, Amy. It's you."

She wasn't sure what to say to that, or even how to feel. She should feel weird; she knew this. Instead she felt...

Attractive. Sexy.

It'd been so long since she'd thought of herself in this way that it took her by surprise. So did the yearning running through her.

They were silent for another long minute. Then she heard Matt blow out a very long breath. In the next beat, he was cleaning her wound with a clean pad and antiseptic, which hurt like hell. She distracted herself by watching his long and callused fingers work on her. They felt decadent on her skin, like a long-denied treat. And it *was* long denied, being touched, being cared for.

Too long.

"Turn over," Matt said.

She hesitated, everything in her balking at his quiet command—just as at the same time, she was completely turned on by it.

"Amy."

She turned over. There was another long beat of silence as Matt took in the rear view, and she risked a glance over her shoulder. His face was more angles than curves, his silky hair brushing the collar of his shirt. He was so broad in the shoulders he blocked out any light the moon might have given them. This left only the meager glow from the flashlight, but she wasn't afraid of the dark.

Or him.

She was safe with him. She knew that. But at the same time, she was about as unsafe as she could get.

She knew that, too.

By the time he finished bandaging her up and she pulled her pants back up, they were both breathing a little unsteadily. He handed her the ice pack for her tailbone. She put it in place, and there was a long silence.

"You're still shivering," he said, and lay down beside her. "Come here, Tough Girl." He pulled her in close. The sleeping bag, still unzipped, was between them. He didn't try to get into it with her, simply wrapped her up in his warm arms and held her until she stopped shivering.

"Better?" he whispered against her hair.

He was rock solid against her, the muscles in his arms banded tight. Yeah, she was better. "Much, thank you."

He started to pull away but she slid her arms out of the sleeping bag and around his neck, pressing her face into his throat. It was a move that startled them both. It was also a really dumb thing to do. Normally she had so much more sense than this, but he was turning her on with every little thing he did. She didn't understand it but she understood this—holding onto him had nothing to do with being cold.

"Amy." He stroked a hand down her back. "You're safe, you know that, right?"

Safe from bears and coyotes and creepy crawlies, maybe. But she wasn't safe. Not from the yearning flowing through her and not from feeling things she didn't want to feel. Feeling things like this left her open to being hurt. "We're not the only ones out here," she said. "Right before you found me on the trail, someone was in the bushes, watching me. I saw just a face."

"There are a few people out here on this mountain tonight," he said, and rubbed his jaw to hers.

"But that's not what I meant."

"I know."

Again he stroked a hand down her back. "When I first took this job, it'd been a while since I'd gone camping. And then as it turned out, on my first night out here, I was stalked."

She tipped her head back and tried to see his face. "By...?"

"Every horror flick I'd ever seen."

She found herself smiling. "Was the big, bad forest ranger scared?"

"I started a fire," he said instead of answering, and the typical guy avoidance of admitting fear made her smile in the dark. "But even after I had a roaring fire, I still felt watched."

"What did you do?"

His hand was still gliding up and down her back, absently soothing, not-so-absently arousing her further. "I got up and searched the perimeter," he said. "Often. I finally fell asleep holding my gun, and at first light was startled awake by a curious teenage bear."

"Oh my God," she said on a horrified laugh. "What happened?"

Amusement came into his voice. "I shot the shit out of a tree and scared the hell out of us both. I fell backward off the log I'd fallen asleep on, and the bear did the same. Then we both scrambled to our feet, and he went running off to his mama. If my mama had been anywhere within two thousand miles, I'd have gone running off to her just the same as the bear."

She burst out laughing.

"What," he said, smiling at her, "you don't think I have a mama?"

"I think you wouldn't go running off to *anyone* if you were scared. You'd stand firm and fight."

He shrugged. "I've had my moments."

"So your mom...?"

"Lives in Chicago with my dad, tending to the three grandkids my brother's given them. We talk every week, and they ask me when I'm going to give them a few as well."

"When are you?"

He shook his head. "Not anytime soon."

"Why?" she asked, fascinated in a way she couldn't explain even to herself. "Kids not for you?"

He shrugged. "My ex seemed to think I don't do love, at least not the kind of love a family requires. Said I wasn't good with people."

"You were married?" She was surprised, though she shouldn't have been. Matthew Bowers was a catch.

"For about twenty minutes," he said. "Just after I got out of the military."

"When you were a cop," she said.

"Yeah."

"Is that why she thought you weren't family material?" she asked. "Because of your job?"

"Partly. And partly because I failed her. But mostly because she was pissed off at me."

Amy wanted to ask how he'd failed, but that felt too intimate, especially given that she was lying in his arms with his ice pack on her ass. But his ex's words didn't make sense. He wasn't the sort of guy to fail a stranger, much less someone he cared about. What he'd done for her today proved that. His job might have brought him here to check on her, but it hadn't been his job or responsibility to stay the night with her and keep her safe.

And yet he'd stuck.

She'd had people in her life who *had* been responsible for her and hadn't stuck. "Matt?"

His wordless response vibrated through his chest to hers, and he turned his head so that his face was in her hair, inhaling as he rubbed her back.

"I think you're pretty good with people," she said softly.

She could feel him smile against her. "Thanks," he murmured. "Now tell me about you."

"Nothing as interesting as you."

"Try me," he said.

That was the *last* thing she intended to do. "Well, I don't have an ex-husband..."

"How about a mom? Dad? Siblings?"

"A mom. We're not close." An understatement, of course. Her mom had gotten pregnant as a teen and hadn't been mom material. "I was raised by my grandma, but she's gone now. She died when I was twelve."

"Any other family?"

No one she wanted to talk about. "No."

He tightened his arms around her, a small, protective, even slightly possessive gesture. It should have made her claustrophobic.

It didn't.

They fell quiet after that, and Amy wouldn't have imagined it possible since she was snuggled up against a very solid, very sexy man, but she actually fell asleep.

She woke up what must have been hours later, as dawn crept in, poking at the backs of her eyelids. For a moment, she stayed utterly still, struck by several things. One, she was no longer cold. In fact, she was quite warm, and the reason for that was because she'd wrapped herself like a pretzel around her heat source.

Matt.

She cracked open an eye and found him watching her from his own heavy-lidded gaze. He was looking pretty amused at the both of them. "Hey," he said, and to go along with that bedroom gaze he also had a raspy early morning voice. Both were extremely distracting. He wasn't looking like a forest ranger right now. He was looking sleepy, rumpled, and sexy as hell.

"Are you taking this anywhere?" he asked.

Not exactly a morning person, it took her brain a moment to process what he meant. And then she realized that by "this," he was referring to the fact that her hand had drifted disturbingly low on his abs. If she moved her fingers even a fraction of an inch south... "Sorry!" Face hot, she pulled back and closed her eyes. "This is all Mallory's fault."

"Actually," he said, looking down at his obvious erection. "It's not."

"No, I mean—" She broke off at his low, teasing laugh and felt her face flame again. "She sent you out here because she thinks something's going on with us."

"*Is* there something going on with us?"

She didn't want to touch that with a ten-foot pole. Or an eight-inch one. "It has nothing to do with us. It's payback for how I set her up with Ty at the auction a few weeks back."

"What if it's not?"

She met his warm gaze. "Not what?"

"Payback," he said.

Their legs were entwined. At some point in the night,

the sleeping bag had fallen away so that there was no barrier between them. He was warm and hard.

Everywhere.

She felt herself soften as the heat of arousal built within her. Worse, her fingers itched with the need to touch him.

"Amy." Matt's voice was pure sin, not a warning so much as a statement, and her hands reacted without permission, migrating to his chest.

"Mm," rumbled from his chest as he slid a hand into her hair, tilting her head up to his. He searched her gaze. "You're all the way awake, right?"

"Yeah. Why?"

"Just making sure," he said, then rolled her beneath him.

Chapter 5

Other things are just food. But chocolate is chocolate.

Matt had given distance his best shot but it hadn't worked out. As he pressed Amy into the sleeping bag, her teeth bit into that plump curve of her lower lip again. Her breathing went erratic, and her pulse raced at the base of her throat. Her gaze darkened with the same thing turning him inside out.

She wanted him.

That was only fair since he'd wanted her for months. Ever since he'd first caught sight of her in the diner working her ass off, the tough, wounded, beautiful woman with the heartbreaking smile that didn't quite meet her amazing eyes.

At the moment, she looked softer than usual. Her long, side-swept bangs were sticking up a little in one spot, falling across her forehead in another. Her mascara had smudged. She'd been driving him bat-shit crazy all night, her and those mile-long legs, which were tangled up in his. He'd always been a confirmed ass man, but Amy seemed to be expanding his horizons.

She was still wearing his sweatshirt and now it smelled like her. He wanted to shove it up to her chin and nuzzle every inch of her. And then kiss. And lick... All the erotic possibilities played in his mind, and he lowered his head until his mouth was only a breath from hers, giving her a moment to think about what was going to happen between them.

She stared up at him, her fingers in his hair. "Yes," she breathed, barely audible.

He kissed her then, and the soft, little sound that escaped her went straight through him like fire. Her hands tightened on him as if to hold him to her. Not that he was going anywhere. Hell, no. For months, he'd wondered how she'd taste, if the reality would be as good as the dreams. They were.

She tasted like heaven.

This was made all the sweeter by having her amazing body shrink-wrapped up against his, a situation that was blowing brain cells left and right. Hoping he had enough to spare, he deepened the kiss, opening his mouth wider on hers.

She made the sound again, a small murmur deep in her throat that held as much surprise as arousal. He could feel her heart pounding. No, wait, that was his, because for the first time in all these months, she'd let him in. Not only had she let him in but she'd melted against him, completely surrendering, pressing her warm body to his. Sliding her fingers in his hair, she murmured his name against his mouth, squirming closer, then closer still.

And just like that, he was in deep, deeper than he'd

been in some time. Warning bells clanged in his brain, but anticipation and erotic thrill overrode them. Slanting his mouth more fully over hers, he took everything she gave, wanting more still. So goddamn much more. He wanted all of her, panting his name, naked and writhing beneath him. Reaching for the hem of the sweatshirt, he went still when from outside the tent, he heard something—pine needles crunching. Someone was out there, walking around, and he lifted his head.

"What?" Amy whispered, hands still in his hair, her mouth wet from his. "A bear?"

He shook his head. Whatever was out there, it was definitely of the human variety. "Wait here." Rising off her in one fluid move, he adjusted himself as he left, not particularly wanting to meet an intruder with a boner in his pants the size of...well, the tent he'd just vacated.

The morning was so foggy he couldn't see much more than a few feet in front of himself but he carefully searched the clearing.

Empty of any mysterious intruders.

But someone had been here, he could see the footsteps in the morning dew. He checked out his truck, but everything seemed the same, with the exception of the flashlight he'd left on his rear fender. That was gone.

"Find anything?"

Matt turned to Amy. She stood with her back to the tent, a Swiss Army Knife in hand, ready for action. Her hair was wild, her wrist bandaged, her stance making it clear that she was ready to rumble. She was still in his sweatshirt, and he'd never seen anything so sexy. Probably she could wear a potato sack and he'd think she looked sexy. Probably he needed to also get a grip. "Nice job on the waiting thing," he said.

"I don't do the waiting thing."

Right. She could take care of herself. Message received loud and clear—except that it was his nature to do the taking care of, though really he should be over that by now. It'd been that exact characteristic that so completely detonated his life back in Chicago.

Which is why he was here. He needed to remember that. He was here for the quiet mountain life. It suited him. He liked being on his own, liked it a lot, and didn't plan to change that status anytime soon.

And yet here he was, wanting Amy. Unable to stop himself, he lifted a hand, cupping her face, running the pad of his thumb along her lower lip. She might look damn tough and on top of her world, but she sure was soft to the touch.

And he wanted to eat her up for breakfast. It'd be off the charts, he had no doubt.

But she took a step back. Okay, he'd expected that. Hell, he'd expected that last night, and he moved to his truck, grabbing his last Dr. Pepper—grateful their thief hadn't stolen that, too. He cracked it open and offered it to Amy first.

She went brows up. "Dr. Pepper for breakfast?"

"Breakfast of champions."

She took a sip, then studied him, looking amused. "What are you going to do if I drink it all?"

"Cry."

She laughed and lightened the tension considerably. Then he fell a little bit in love when she handed him back the rest of the soda.

"Not exactly what I'd have chosen for breakfast," she said.

Yeah. Him either.

They left shortly after that. Amy had to get to work, and she knew that Matt did, too. He would have taken her to the diamond rocks first but it was too foggy.

Plus then there was the real reason she'd passed on his offer. She wanted to be alone when she went and searched for her grandparents' initials.

And her hope...

An hour later, Matt had dropped her at her car, and she'd driven home. She took the longest shower known to man, not getting out until she ran out of hot water. When she'd dried off, she swiped the mist from the mirror and stared at herself. "You *kissed* him?"

Her reflection nodded, you 'ho.

Amy had no idea what she'd been thinking at all. Actually, she *hadn't* been thinking, that was the problem. She'd been *feeling*. Far too much.

At least there'd been no witnesses, she told herself. Well, except for their mysterious guest. With Amy's luck, that mysterious guest had been Lucille, and Amy and Matt would end up on Facebook as engaged, or something equally horrifying. Wouldn't that just make Mallory happy.

But would it make you happy?

The errant thought appalled her. She didn't need a man complicating her life, and she didn't need one to be happy either. Her life was complicated enough, thank you very much. She was very busy following her grandma's footsteps to find...well, she wasn't sure exactly, but hopefully she'd find herself.

Except, said a small voice, *if you really were interested in finding yourself, you'd have let Matt take you to the rocks.*

And really, what was she so afraid of? That she'd get to the end of Rose's journey and Amy's life would still be…meaningless? Because she didn't need a journey to feel that way. Her *life* made her feel that way, and had since her grandma had died.

Amy hadn't handled that scene too well. She was the first to admit it. By that time, her mom had pulled herself out of the gutter and had snagged a really great guy, the measurement of "great" being the size of his bank account, of course. Coming from the wrong side of the tracks to the only side that mattered, Amy had become the poster child for Poor Little Rich Girl, bumping up against a society she'd never been a part of and couldn't possibly understand. She'd chafed at the rules and had behaved textbook predictably, acting out with all sorts of mayhem. And she'd been good at it.

Until the day she'd run into real trouble. Bad trouble. Holy-shit trouble, and for once, it hadn't been her own doing. No, that honor had gone to her stepfather, who'd decided she needed to give him a little of what she was so freely giving to the boys her own age.

But he'd been no boy.

Amy had always been able to intimidate anyone who'd invaded her space without permission, but not him. Scared for the first time in her life, she'd tried to get help. But no one had believed her.

She'd been on her own.

She'd been on her own ever since, and it'd worked out just fine for her. She didn't need anyone.

But once in a while, like now, she felt a little flicker of need. Just to be held. Touched.

Wanted.

Matt had amplified those feelings, in a big way. And if they hadn't been interrupted this morning, she'd have acted on them. She had no idea where that would have left them.

Well satisfied, no doubt, as Matt had a magic mouth and magic hands. Her reflection sighed in remembered pleasure. She wanted more. That wasn't a surprise. What *was* a surprise was how badly she also wanted to run her hands over Matt's tough, sexy body. She'd felt him vibrating with that same need, every single muscle, and he had a lot of delicious muscles.

Mutual pleasure. They needed it. She wasn't looking for more, and after what he'd told her about his ex and how he didn't do love, neither was he.

Could it be that simple? *No.* Nothing was ever that simple. Which meant she needed to steer clear of one sexy Matthew Bowers. Very clear.

Matt wasn't much for cooking. He could do it—his mom had made sure of it—he just preferred not to. But there were limited dining options in Lucky Harbor: the Love Shack, the only bar and grill in town, or Eat Me, the diner. The Love Shack had great beer on tap.

Eat Me had Amy.

The day after their overnight adventure, following a long ten hours on the job, Matt entered the diner. He sat at a booth, and Amy brought him a soda. He could have kissed her for that alone. She was wearing a black tee with a silver zipper running amuck in a zigzag between her breasts, the kind that could open from the top or the bottom. Her jeans were low riding and faded, with a hole on one thigh, the denim there held together by a few threads across her taut skin. She was wearing the Ace bandage on her wrist. "The usual?" she asked. "Burger, fries?"

"Yeah. How are the injuries?"

"Fine. The thigh's a little sore but my wrist's a lot better."

"And the other injury?"

She raised a brow. "You are *not* asking me about my ass."

He smiled.

"You aren't smiling at the thought of my ass either," she said.

"Not funny yet?"

She just looked at him.

"Okay," he said, letting a smile break loose. "Not funny yet."

Lucille walked by the booth and stopped, touching Amy's wrist. "What happened, honey?"

"I fell hiking. It's nothing." Amy slid a long look at Matt, daring him to say a word.

Matt wasn't a complete idiot. He wanted this woman, naked. So he held his silence.

Lucille hitched a thumb at him. "You fell in Ranger Hot Buns's forest?"

This had Amy flashing a rare *real* smile. "What did you just call him?"

"Ranger Hot Buns," Lucille said. "Are you telling me you haven't seen the side poll on Facebook to rank the town's current hotties?"

Christ. Matt slouched down into his seat.

"It's doubled our traffic," Lucille said. "Matt's out in front of Dr. Josh Scott, but just by a nose. You need to come by and vote."

"I'll do that." Amy's tone said that she'd be voting for Josh.

Lucille walked away, and Amy slid him a speculative look. "I'll go put in your order. Ranger *Hot Buns*."

He snagged her by her good wrist before she walked away. At the contact, he felt a current of electricity go straight through him.

She looked down at his hand on her. Apparently he wasn't the only one experiencing the shock of connection between them. She tugged free, stepping back, looking a little off her axis.

He knew the feeling. Their chemistry was off the charts.

She turned and disappeared into the kitchen. He wasn't all that surprised when a few minutes later it was Jan, Eat Me's owner, who served him his food. Jan was fifty-ish, with a perpetual frown on her face and a black cap of hair that made her resemble Lucy from the Peanuts comic strip. "Where did Amy go?" he asked.

"Break," she said in her been-smoking-three-decades voice. "She took her break."

That night, Amy was trying to lose herself in a *Friends* marathon on TV, complete with a huge bowl of popcorn and two Snickers bars, when her phone rang.

"Chocoholics meeting tomorrow night," Grace said when Amy answered. "Mallory wanted me to call you and let you know. She'd have called herself but she was about to go jump Ty's bones."

Yeah, or she was avoiding Amy after the whole sending-Matt-to-the-woods stunt... "I don't know," Amy said. "Jan says we can't meet at the diner over chocolate cake anymore." A couple weeks back, the Chocoholics had accidentally destroyed the interior of Eat Me when their chocolate cake had gone up in flames thanks to some trick candles.

"Brownies," Grace said without pause. "We'll meet over brownies."

Brownies worked.

"Mallory says to prepare yourself," Grace warned her. "Apparently now that her life is in order, we're moving onto yours. She says we're going to be giving you good girl lessons." She laughed. "I'm sorry."

"And this is funny why?"

"Well not funny *exactly*," Grace said, still sounding amused. "A challenge, maybe."

"Hey, I would make a good good girl." *If she wanted...*

Grace snorted. "Okay. See you tomorrow night, good girl."

"Maybe I'm busy."

"Are you?"

Amy hesitated. She wanted to be busy getting back up the mountain to Sierra Meadows, but she wasn't crazy enough to do it at night. She'd wait for her next day off.

"Amy?"

"I'm free. I just really think our time would be better spent fixing *your* life first. I can totally wait."

Grace had worked as a financial wizard back East until several months ago. Looking for some happiness, she'd stuck around town, but the employment opportunities here were pretty limited. "Nice try but you're up," Grace said. "Oh, and bee-tee-dub, Facebook says you were getting cozy on the mountain with Ranger Hot Buns."

"Bee-tee-*what*?"

"*B T W. By the way.* Jeez, don't you ever surf the 'net?"

Amy sighed. "Brownies. Tomorrow night."

"We'll expect the Ranger Hot Buns story."

Amy hung up and then got a text from Mallory: *Good girl lesson #4: Omitting juicy details to your BFFs is a sin. You slept with him????????*

Amy rolled her eyes and typed a response: *Haven't you heard—good girls don't tell all. Especially to nosy friends who sneakily set their supposed BFFs up when they don't want to be set up.* Amy sent the text off, knowing Mallory would stew over that all night. It was a small consolation, because half an hour later, there came a knock at her door. Amy's entire body went on high alert, especially her nipples, so she knew exactly who it was.

Matt Bowers.

Aka Ranger Hot Buns.

She'd known he'd show up sooner than later. The question was, did she want him to?

He knocked again, a sturdy, confident sort of knock. She looked through the peephole. Yep, one sexy-as-hell, uniformed forest ranger stood at her door, armed, locked, and loaded.

And hot.

Looking her right in the eye, he raised a brow.

Still silent, she bit her lip in rare indecision. Obey the hormones? Or ignore the need humming through her...

"All night," Matt said. "I can do this all night."

Blowing out a breath, she opened the door.

He rocked back on his heels, hands in his pockets, perfectly at ease as he took in her appearance. "Pretty," he said.

She was in her oldest T-shirt and a pair of cutoffs. She looked like a garage sale special, and the worst part was...he most definitely did not. He was looking waaaaay too good. "I'm a mess."

"Maybe. But you're a pretty one."

She narrowed her eyes, and he laughed. "You know, most women like it when a man calls them pretty."

"I'm not most women."

"Yeah, I'm getting that."

"Why are you here, Matt?"

"Get to it?" he asked. "Is that what you're saying?"

"Yes. Get to it."

"All right. Direct. I like that. But you might not. It's about the kiss."

Her stomach suddenly had butterflies. "What about it?"

"You've been acting weird ever since."

"No, I haven't."

"Liar." He leaned against the doorjamb, settling in, making himself comfortable. "So it's been making me wonder. "Did I have bad breath?"

Was he kidding? He'd tasted like heaven. "No."

"Did I kiss like a jackass? A Saint Bernard?"

She actually felt a smile threaten. How did he always do that, make her want to smile? Make her...*want* him, desperately. It was a conundrum, a big one. She really hadn't had a single intention of getting tangled up in a man, but this man had come from nowhere and blind-sided her, and now she could think of little else. "No," she said. "You didn't kiss like a jackass or a Saint Bernard."

"Hmm." He stepped into her then, crowding her in the doorway.

"What are you doing?"

"Apparently I have something to prove." He pressed her up against the doorway. Fisting his hands in her hair, he kissed her. And just like that, with a single touch of his mouth to hers, her entire body disconnected from her brain. She kissed him back, too, hungrily pressing closer, as close as she could get.

The thing was, it'd been good the other night in the tent. Real good. But it was even better now—which made no sense. Neither was the way she could almost forget all her problems when he had his mouth on her. And what had begun as an irritating interruption quickly escalated into a heated frenzy, his body colliding with hers in all the right places. She was panting for air when he abruptly broke the kiss with a muttered oath and answered his radio.

She hadn't even heard the interruption.

"I have to go," he said, his breathing still a little ragged.

Nodding, she touched her wet mouth. "Yeah."

His gaze dropped to her lips, and his eyes heated again. He didn't want to go. He wanted her. Not that he'd ever made a secret of it, but the knowledge gave her a disturbingly warm glow.

"So we're good?" he asked.

Good covered way too much ground. "You've got to go, remember?"

"Amy—"

"Bye." Stepping backward into her apartment, she shut the door. Then stared at it. He was still standing there on the other side, she could *feel* him.

"I'm going to take that as a yes," he said through the wood.

She let out a startled laugh, then clapped a hand over her mouth. Hell no, they weren't good. Not when he'd just proven what she'd already known—they were so far beyond good it was scary. They were *combustible*.

But she knew the power of it now, she assured herself. And it was okay because all she had to do was stay clear.

Which was going to be a little bit like trying to keep a moth from the flame.

Chapter 6

Chocolate is not a matter of life and death—it's more important than that.

Matt spent a few mornings a week in the gym, usually in the ring with Ty Garrison. This morning they were doing their usual beat-the-shit-out-of-each-other routine. He ducked Ty's left hook, feeling pretty damn smug for one solid beat—until Ty snuck a right uppercut to his gut.

Matt hit the floor with a wheeze, and then it was Ty's turn to be smug. "Gotcha."

Hell, no. They'd been at it for thirty minutes, and Matt was exhausted to the bone, but the last one down had to buy breakfast. Kicking out, he knocked Ty's feet from beneath him. Then it was Ty's turn to land with a satisfying thud.

"Jesus," Josh muttered from the weight bench.

Josh was also a good friend, but he didn't know much about having fun. He was a doctor, which left his taste for occasional recreational violence greatly diminished.

"You keep going at each other like that," Josh said, "and you'll end up in my ER."

Breathless, Matt rolled to his back. "Sorry, I only play doctor with the ladies."

Josh snorted and kept lifting. In Josh's opinion, weights were much more civilized.

Matt swiped the sweat off his forehead with his arm, keeping a close eye on Ty, a formidable opponent, as Matt knew all too well. They'd been in the Navy together. Matt had left after four years of service and gone to Chicago.

Ty had gone on to the SEALs. He wasn't someone to mess with lightly so Matt stayed back and gave him a careful nudge with his foot. Actually, it might have been more of a kick, but he knew better than to turn his back.

Josh stopped lifting. "At least check him for a pulse."

Matt poked Ty again. "Not falling for the dead possum shit, man."

"I've got an adrenaline pin I can stick him with," Josh said mildly. "Hurts like hell going in, but it should wake him right up."

"Come near me with a needle," Ty grumbled, "and you'll be the one who needs medical attention." He groaned and rolled over, eyeing Matt. "And that was a total pussy move."

"Yeah? Who's flat on his back?"

Ty swore and laid an arm over his eyes, still breathing heavily.

Matt collapsed back to the ground himself. He felt like he'd been hit by a bus, but at least his brain was too busy concentrating on the pain rather than on what his next move should be with Amy. If he didn't come up with something good soon, those few kisses would be all he'd ever get, and they hadn't been enough.

Not even close.

Ty staggered to his feet. "Another round."

Ty liked to push himself. Matt didn't mind doing the same, but he'd prefer to move onto something else—say a big plate of food. "I'm starving."

"Yeah," Ty said. "Because you skipped dinner last night. Loved getting stood up, by the way. I could have been with Mallory, and dinner with Mallory includes things you've never offered to do for me."

Matt laughed. He'd have pegged Ty as the *last* guy on the planet to hook up with the same woman more than once, much less commit to her, but that's exactly what Ty had done. He'd gotten serious with Mallory Quinn, Lucky Harbor's sweetheart. "Told you," Matt said. "Something came up."

"Like . . . ?"

Like kissing Amy. "Had to see someone. About a work thing."

"A work thing? Since when do you work at night?"

"There was a lost hiker, and some follow-up." There. That was at least half the truth. Okay, maybe a quarter of the truth.

Ty flashed Matt a full-on smile. "You do remember I'm sleeping with the woman that Amy called first that day, right?"

Well, hell. "Fine, so I was visiting the lost hiker, who turned out to be Amy."

"Interesting," Ty said.

"What?"

"That you only go to the diner when Amy's working. And now you're finding excuses to 'visit' her."

Suddenly Matt was ready for round two after all. He pushed to his feet and gave Ty the "come here" gesture.

Ty, who'd never met a challenge he wasn't up for, grinned and came at him, but Josh whistled sharply through his fingers and stopped the action cold. He gestured to Matt's cell phone, which was buzzing on the floor.

"It's work," Josh said, tossing Matt the phone.

Ty sank back to the mat. "Handy, since I was going to hand you your own ass."

"Fuck if you were," Matt said, wisely stepping out of Ty's arm range before answering the phone.

Thirty minutes later, Matt was showered and on his way to Squaw Flats. A group of hikers had called in to report a theft from their day camp.

Matt parked at the trailhead and hiked up to the area. He took a report for the missing gear: a camera, an iPod touch, a smartphone, and a Swiss Army Knife. The campers hadn't bothered to lock up any of their stuff—a situation that Matt had seen a hundred times. He liked to call it the Mary Poppins Syndrome. People left the big, bad city for the mountains and figured they were safe because apparently the bad guys all stayed in the city.

The fact was that National Park Service Law Enforcement Rangers suffered the highest number of felonious assaults, as well as the highest number of homicides of *all* federal law enforcement officers. People never believed Matt when he spouted that fact, but it was true.

After taking the report, he spent a few hours in the area, a visible presence to deter any further felony mischief. He had four park rangers who worked beneath him, each assigned to a quadrant of the North District, and they patrolled daily, but the quadrants covered far too much area for them to be 100 percent effective.

Budget cuts sucked.

Since thieves rarely bothered to get a permit first, Matt detained everyone he came across to check them. At the south rim, he found two guys perched on a bluff, readying their ropes for a climb down into Martis Valley.

Lance and Tucker Larson were brothers, though you couldn't tell by looking at them. Tucker was tall and athletically built. Lance was much smaller and frail as hell thanks to the cystic fibrosis ravaging his twenty-something body. They ran the ice cream shop on the Lucky Harbor pier, and when the two of them weren't climbing, they were trouble seeking.

They both nodded at Matt, who gave them the once over, trying to decide if he needed to check their bags. The last time he'd found them up here, they'd been consuming Tucker's homemade brownies in celebration after a climb—brownies that had made their eyes red and put stupid-ass grins on their faces.

Not to mention, brownies that were also illegal as hell.

"Hey," Lance said with an easy smile.

Tucker, who was never friendly with anyone holding the authority to slow him down, didn't smile. Nor did he say anything.

"Any brownies today?" Matt asked.

"No, sir," Lance said. "No brownies on us today."

This made Tucker smile, so no doubt they'd already done their consuming. Great. "Careful on the rocks," Matt said. "You check our site for the latest conditions?"

"Mudslides," Lance said with a nod. "I'm hoping to see Tucker slide down the entire rim on his ass like he did last year in this very spot." He patted his pack. "Got my iPhone this time so I can get video for Lucille."

Matt shook his head and left them to it, intending to head back to the station, where a mountain of paperwork waited for him. But just outside the Squaw Flats campground, he found evidence of an off-site campfire. This was illegal, especially this time of year. The campfire was abandoned, but the ashes were warm, and as he stood there, he heard the footsteps of someone running away.

There was only one reason to do that: guilt. Someone had something to hide. Matt took off running, catching up to a figure dodging through the forest, off trail. A kid, maybe a teenager. "Stop," he said.

He didn't stop. They *never stopped*.

Matt sped up and caught the back of the kid's sweatshirt, yanking him to a halt. "Hold still," he said, when his arsonist fought to get free.

Of course he didn't, so Matt added a small shake to get his meaning across. The kid's hoodie fell back from his face, exposing dirty features, a snarling mouth, eyes spitting fury, and a surprise—he was a she. A scrawny she, who was lanky lean, as if three squares hadn't been a part of her recent program. "Let go of me!" she yelled, and kicked Matt in the shin. "Don't touch me!"

Christ. She was *maybe* sixteen. He let her loose, but before she could so much as lift another foot in his direction, he gave her a hard look. "Don't even think about it."

She lifted her chin in a show of bravado and crossed her arms tightly over herself. "I didn't do anything wrong."

Her voice was cultured and educated, but her clothes were dirty and torn and barely fit her. "Then why did you run?" he asked.

"Because you were chasing me." She didn't add the *duh*; she didn't have to—it was implied.

"Where're your parents?" Matt asked.

Her face was closed off and sullen. "I don't have to answer any of your stupid questions."

"You're a minor alone in the woods," he pointed out.

"I'm eighteen."

He gave her a long look, which she returned evenly. He held out his hand. "ID."

She produced an ID card from her ratty, old-looking backpack, careful to not let him see inside, which reminded him of yet another prickly female he'd come across, two nights ago now.

The girl's ID was issued by the Washington Department of Motor Vehicles for one Riley Taylor. The picture showed a cleaner version of the face in front of him, and the birth date did indeed proclaim her eighteen as of two weeks ago.

Handing the ID back, he nodded his chin toward the trail from which he'd come. "Was that your campfire back there?"

Her gaze darted away from his. "No."

Bullshit. "You need a permit or a paid campsite to overnight out here."

She just stared stonily at a spot somewhere over his shoulder. "I know that."

More bullshit. Matt eyed her backpack. "Some folks about a mile west of here were ripped off earlier today. You know anything about that?"

"Nope."

"What's in your backpack?"

She hugged it to her chest. "Stuff. *My* stuff."

His ass. The only thing that saved her was that when he'd grabbed her a minute ago, her backpack had seemed nearly empty. Far too empty to be carrying the stolen loot. She'd either fenced it already or she'd stashed it somewhere. "What are you doing out here?"

"Camping."

"With your family?"

A slight hesitation. "Yeah," she said.

More bullshit. "Where?"

"Brockway Springs." Again her gaze darted away.

She was racking up the lies now. Plus Brockway Springs was a campground about seven miles to the east. "That's a long way from here."

She shrugged.

"Look," he said. "You shouldn't be out here alone. You need to go back to your family. I'll give you a ride."

"No!" She took a breath and visibly calmed herself. "No," she said more quietly. "I don't take rides from strangers. I'm leaving now."

With no reason to detain her, there was little Matt could do to stop her. "Put your ID away so you don't lose it."

She once again opened her backpack, and he made no attempt to disguise the fact that he took a good look inside. A bottle of water, what looked like a spare shirt, and a flashlight. He put his hand on her arm. "Where did you get that flashlight?"

"I've had it forever."

It was the same model and make of flashlight that had gone missing off Matt's bumper the other night. It was also the most common flashlight sold in the area. More than half the people on this mountain had one just like it.

Riley zipped up her backpack, or tried to, but the ragged zipper caught. This didn't slow her down. She merely hugged the thing to her chest and took off, and in less than ten seconds, was swallowed up by the woods.

Matt shook his head and went back to the station, but he didn't sit more than thirty minutes behind his desk before he was called back out. Being supervisor of the district required him to wear many hats: firefighter, EMT, cop, S&R. Over the next several hours, he used the S&R hat to rescue two kayakers from the Shirley River, which at this time of year was gushing with snow melt. Finicky and dangerous, the river had been closed off to water play. But the kayakers had ignored the warning signs and had gone out anyway, then got stuck on the fast rushing water.

It took Matt, his rangers, and an additional crew from the south district to get the kayakers safely out of the water. Two rangers were injured in the rescue, but even after all that, the kayakers refused to leave, saying they had the right to do as they wanted on public land.

Matt ended up forcibly evicting them for violating park laws, and when they argued, he banned them for the rest of the season just because they were complete assholes.

Sometimes it was good to wear the badge.

Now down two rangers, he went on with his work. He assisted in the daily reporting on the condition of the trails, tracked the movement of various wildlife as required by one of the federal conservation agencies, then checked on the small forest fire that was burning on the far south end—which was thankfully 95 percent contained, which was good. By the end of his shift, he was hot, sweaty, tired, and starving. But before he left the area, he took the time to drive by the campsite where

Riley had said her family was staying to check the registers. Easy enough to do, it was early in the season, and the snow had barely melted off in the past few weeks. He had four sites booked at this time, and only one of those sites had been booked by a family.

When he pulled up, that family was standing around their campfire roasting hot dogs and corn on the cob. His mouth watered. He'd had a sandwich hours and hours ago, before the river rescue.

The campers didn't have a teenage daughter.

Which meant that his dinner was going to have to wait. Turning his truck around, he headed back up the fire road to the site of the illegal campfire, where earlier he'd found the teen girl.

The fire was still out and still emitting residual warmth. Huddled up as close as she could get to it in the quickly cooling evening sat Riley.

She took one look at him and leapt to her feet.

He pointed at her as he got out of his truck. "Don't," he warned. "I'm not in the mood for another run through the woods." He was tired as shit and hungry, dammit.

"What are you doing here?" she asked, still as a deer caught in headlights, though not nearly as innocent as any Bambi.

"That's my question for you."

"I have rights," she said.

"You lied to me."

Her eyes flashed. "You weren't going to believe anything I told you!"

"Not true," he told her. "And for future reference, lying to law enforcement officers isn't a smart move. It makes them not trust you."

"Oh, please." Her stance was slouched, sullen. Defensive. "You didn't trust me before I even opened my mouth."

"Because you *ran* from me."

"Okay, well, now I know. You don't like running or lying. Jeez."

"I don't like attitude either," he said.

She tossed up her hands. "Well, what *do* you like?"

"Not much today. Where's your family, Riley?"

"Okay, fine, I'm not with my family. But you saw my ID. I'm eighteen now. I'm on my own."

"Where did you come from?"

"Town."

Well wasn't that nice and vague. "What are you doing in town?"

"Visiting friends."

He sighed. This conversation was like running in circles. "What friends?"

"I watch all the cop shows, you know." She crossed her arms. "I don't have to tell you anything."

Christ. "Fine." He gestured back to his truck. "Let's go."

"Wait—What?" Her eyes got huge, and she scrambled back a few feet. "You can't arrest me."

"Have you done something arrest worthy?" he asked.

"*No.*"

"Then you're not getting arrested. I'm driving you into town. To your *friends*." And then he planned to call his friend Sheriff Sawyer Thompson to run her ID to see if she was a person of interest or reported as missing.

She looked away. "I don't need a ride."

"You're not sleeping out here tonight. Get in the truck."

She threw her backpack into the truck bed with

enough attitude to give him a starter headache. Then she climbed into the passenger seat and slammed the door.

Matt drew a deep breath and walked around to the driver's side. He drove her attitude-ridden ass into town, wondering what it was with him and stubborn females this week.

In the heavy silence of the truck cab, Riley's stomach grumbled. She ignored both it and Matt, keeping her face firmly turned toward the window. But by the time they drove down the main drag of Lucky Harbor, her stomach was louder than the venomous thoughts she was sending his way.

"Where to?" he asked.

"Here's fine."

Here was the corner where the pier met the beach. "Your friends live on the pier?" he asked dryly.

"I'll walk to their place." Her stomach cut her off with yet another loud rumble.

Matt sighed and pulled into the pier parking lot.

Riley immediately reached for the door handle but Matt gripped the back of her sweatshirt. "Not so fast."

She stiffened. "I'm not thanking you for the ride with anything that involves me losing my clothes."

Jesus, he thought, his gut squeezing hard. "I'm not looking for a thank-you at all, but I'm not dropping you off on the damn corner. I'm taking you into the diner to feed you."

She stared at him. "Why?"

"Because you're hungry. And no," he said before she could speak again. "I don't expect a thank-you for that either."

Like a cornered, injured, starving animal, she didn't so much as blink, and he felt the punch of her mistrust more forcibly than he'd felt Ty's right uppercut this morning.

"I don't have any money," she finally said.

"You're not going to need any."

This produced another long, unblinking stare.

In the silence, his own belly grumbled. "Let's go."

Her eyes swiveled to the diner on the pier's corner. "What kind of place is called Eat Me?" she asked, unwittingly cementing what he'd suspected all along.

If she hadn't known the name of the only diner in Lucky Harbor, she hadn't come from town. She didn't belong here any more than she'd belonged out on the mountain. And he knew what that likely meant, he'd seen it all too often in Chicago. Homeless teens, a rising phenomenon that no one had yet come up with a solution for. She was either a runaway, abandoned, or a juvenile delinquent dodging the authorities. "The food's good," he said. "And I'm starving. So are you."

The girl seemed to fold in on herself. "I'm not cleaned up good enough for a fancy place like that."

Eat Me was just about the furthest thing from fancy he'd ever seen, but he gave her a cursory once-over. "You look fine."

"But—"

"Now, Riley."

She slammed out of his truck and grabbed her backpack, hugging it tight to herself.

Matt almost told her to stop abusing his door but he thought back to all the times his dad had yelled at him for doing the same thing and kept his mouth shut. He refused to turn into his father. Not that there was anything wrong with his dad's parenting skills, but it was unnerving to hear himself become that guy.

As he opened the diner's door for her, he said, "The waitress is a friend of mine. Be nice."

"Friend or *friend*?"

Ignoring that, he nudged her to a booth, not happy that under the harsh fluorescent lighting, he could see a fist-sized bruise on her jaw.

Amy was several tables down, serving from a large tray and clearly babying her wrapped wrist. She was wearing a black sundress with her kick-ass boots, topped off by the ever-present pink Eat Me apron. Just looking at her short-circuited his brain.

She turned her head and met his gaze, revealing nothing. She was good at that, too good. But two minutes later, she came by their booth with two sodas, and Matt smiled at her.

Amy didn't return the smile but her gaze dropped to his mouth, and he knew she was thinking of their last kiss up against her door.

Worked for him, since he'd pretty much done nothing but.

Riley picked up the tension between them, Matt's smile and Amy's lack of, and cracked a small snarky smile. "Thought you said she was your girlfriend," she said to Matt. "She doesn't appear to like you much."

Amy gave Matt a long look.

Matt didn't bother to sigh. "Thanks," he said to Riley. "Thanks a lot."

The girl flashed her first real smile.

Not Amy. Her eyes narrowed in on Riley like a hawk. "Hey, you're the one who was watching me through the bushes on the mountain."

Chapter 7

Chocolate does a body good.

Amy couldn't believe it. She stared at the teenager who was still wearing the blue sweatshirt. Her face was dirtier than it'd been the other day, and her eyes were bright with false bravado and pride. Behind that lurked fear, plain and simple. There was a bruise on her jaw, too. Someone had hit her, and at that knowledge, Amy's gut squeezed.

"Amy, this is Riley. Riley, Amy." Matt met Amy's gaze. "Riley's hungry, and I'm my usual starving."

"No problem." Amy set a menu in front of the squirming, skinny Riley. She hadn't bothered to bring one to Matt. He knew everything they served.

Matt tapped on Riley's menu. "Whatever you want." Then he rose, and moving with his usual quick efficiency, took Amy's arm in a firm grip. "A minute?"

She opened her mouth to tell him she was swamped, but he met her gaze and she saw something in his— exhaustion. She let him direct her into the back hallway just outside the bathrooms. "You okay?" she asked.

There was a beat of surprise from him, then finally, he nodded. He was either fine or he didn't want to discuss it. "What is she doing here with you?"

He didn't answer the question, and by the way he was looking at her, she knew that wasn't what he'd brought her back here to discuss. She had no idea what that might be.

"I've been thinking about you," he said.

Not expecting that, or the punch of emotion the words brought, Amy stared into his light brown eyes. He hadn't even touched her, and that now familiar zing ran through her, from the very roots of her hair to her toes, and then straight back to every erogenous zone she owned—of which there appeared to be more than she remembered.

Not appearing to be bothered by the zing in the least, Matt put his hands on her hips and gently bumped her back a step, up against the wall.

Not only wasn't he bothered, she could feel that he liked the zing.

A lot.

There was nobody else in the hallway, so when he leaned in and kissed her, no one heard her soft murmur of surprise.

And arousal.

He gave her no tongue, nothing but his firm, warm lips, but the kiss wasn't sweet, not by a long shot. Nope, this kiss had purpose, and that purpose was to remind her exactly how explosive their chemistry was. In that moment, there was nowhere else she'd rather be, and she showed him by pressing close and deepening the kiss.

There wasn't much give to Supervisory Forest Ranger Matthew Bowers's body, not a single inch—except for his

mouth, his very giving mouth. Not until her knees had dis-
solved and she was grasping his uniform shirt in her sweaty
fists to keep herself upright did he break free, pulling back
just enough to meet her gaze. He murmured something that
sounded like "every fucking time," then gave a low laugh
and shook his head, as if he couldn't quite believe it either.
Once more he brushed his mouth across hers, a lighter
caress this time, slowing the pumping blood slightly.

And then as if nothing had just happened, he spoke.
"Found the girl in an illegal campsite. I think she's living
out there. Has an ID that claims she's eighteen. I want to
have Sawyer run the address and check her out, but first
I want to feed her."

Aw. Aw, dammit. How the hell was she supposed to
keep her distance when he kissed like that *and* had a soft
spot for a teen in trouble? "She's not from around here?"

"I don't know. She lied to me about camping with her
family, and now she's saying she's here in town visiting
friends, but she's lying about that, too. I'd like to take her
back to where she belongs, if I could figure out where
exactly that is."

Amy grimaced.

"What?"

"Not everyone lives a fairy-tale home life," she said,
painfully aware of what the girl might be trying to stay
away from.

Matt's eyes and mouth were grim, suggesting that he
understood that all too well, perhaps more than Amy gave
him credit for. "Yeah," he said. "I know. I thought maybe
you could help me figure her out a little."

Amy went still, staring up at him. He looked at her
right back. Steadily.

He wasn't kidding. "Oh no," she said. "No, no, no."

"Why not?"

"Because what do I know about teenage girls?"

"You remember being one, right?"

Yes, far more than she wanted to admit. Like Riley, she'd ended up on her own at too young of an age. Looking back, it was a miracle that she'd made it relatively unscathed, not to mention alive. "I really don't have time for—"

"Just soften her up a little," he said. "I want to help her but she's not overly fond of me, and I think she might be in some sort of trouble."

"What kind of trouble?"

"I don't know." He ran a hand over his face, as if he was bone-tired and barely keeping himself awake. And hell if that didn't soften her, too.

"Just get what you can out of her," he said, sensing her capitulation, not too tired to press his advantage. "That's all. A few minutes."

"And why me exactly?"

He ran a callused finger along her temple, making her shiver. "Because you have a way with people."

She choked out a laugh. Her way with people was usually to piss them off. "If I'm your best bet, you're the one in trouble."

He gave her a searing look that promised he was not only *in* trouble, he *was* trouble, and that he'd be worth every second of it. But his next words quickly doused any inner fire.

"I think she's been abused," he said quietly. "She doesn't like to be touched. And when I brought her here to feed her, she assumed I'd demand sex as payment."

Amy's gut clenched hard, but she nodded and then tried to move past him to go back to the dining area. Matt wrapped his fingers around her wrist, stopping her. "Hey." He dipped down a little to see directly into her eyes. "You okay?"

"Of course." Wasn't she always? She tugged, giving him a level look when he didn't immediately let go. Her patented "don't make me kick your ass" look. "I have to get back to work. Jan doesn't pay me to stand around and kiss her customers."

That alleviated some of the strain from his eyes, and he smiled. The kind of smile that made her want to kiss him some more. "You kiss a lot of customers?"

She gave him a push. He knew damn well he was the only one. And despite what she'd said about needing to get back to work, she didn't go directly back to her tables. She took a moment and a deep breath. There was a lot going through her. She'd been serving a big table when that first prickle of awareness had raced up her spine, settling at the base of her neck, followed by a rush of warmth, and she'd known.

Matt had come into the diner.

Nothing unusual, really. He came in a lot. Tonight he'd been later than usual, which meant he'd had an especially long day. Shaking it off, she moved to the drink dispenser to get him another soda.

Jan was there, checking the ice machine. "Look at you jump for him," she murmured. "Never figured you for the kind to jump for a man."

"I'm not jumping for anyone."

Jan sent her a knowing smirk, which was both annoying and embarrassing. So she knew Matt would be thirsty after a long day and that he'd want a refill, so what? Matt was hugely popular in town. *Everyone* knew what he drank, and how much.

And yeah, okay, she'd followed him to the back when he'd wanted to talk. That had been business.

Sort of.

She shifted so that she could see him in the booth with the girl, soaking up the sight of him in his uniform, slightly dusty, a lot rumpled. Armed. Clearly weary, his long legs were sprawled out in front of him, his broad shoulders back against the booth. He'd probably been outside all day, his tanned features attested to that, but somehow he'd still smelled wonderful.

Which only annoyed and embarrassed her all the more, because she really needed to stop noticing how he smelled. Rolling her eyes at herself, she went to his table to take their order.

"I'll have the usual," Matt told her, and looked at the sullen teen across from him, who was meeting no one's eye. "Riley?"

"I don't care."

Matt sighed and turned to Amy. "Make it two of the usual."

"His usual," Amy informed Riley, "is a double bacon blue burger, fries, non-stop refills of Dr. Pepper, and a piece of pie. And by piece, I mean a quarter of an entire pie. You up for all that?"

Riley's mouth had fallen open, but she nodded.

Amy went back to the kitchen. Jan was there with Henry, their cook. Henry was ten years younger than Jan and born and bred in Lucky Harbor. He'd been a trucker for two decades before going to culinary school in Seattle. He claimed cooking had healed his soul. It certainly had healed Eat Me, which had been floundering since they'd lost their last cook, Tara Daniels, to the Lucky Harbor B&B.

Jan was at the pie case dividing the only remaining half of apple pie into three pieces. Amy stuck Matt's order into Henry's order wheel, then reached in past Jan and snagged the biggest piece of pie.

"Hey," Jan said. "I was going to serve that piece."

"There's still two left."

"Yeah, but you took the biggest one."

"It's for Matt," Amy said. She grabbed the second-to-last piece as well. "And this is for the girl who's with him."

"Why is Matt's piece the biggest one?"

"Because you cut it uneven."

"Yes, but why is *his* piece the biggest?"

"He tips the best," Amy said.

Jan stared at her, and then cackled, slapping her thigh in rare amusement. Henry joined her.

"Hey," Amy said, insulted, "it's true." Well, at least partially true. Matt did tip better than any of her customers. "He likes the pie."

"Girl," Jan said, "he likes you."

Amy ignored this, even as the words brought her a ridiculous shiver of pleasure. This was immediately followed by denial. Matt didn't know her, not really. Sure, he was attracted to her. She got that, loud and clear. And that was 100 percent reciprocated. But as for him *liking* her? She'd never really cared what anyone thought of her before, so it was disconcerting to suddenly realize she cared now. She set the pieces of pie aside, pointed at Jan to leave them alone, then made two dinner salads.

"There aren't any salads on his order," Jan said.

"What, you writing a book tonight?"

Jan cocked a brow.

"The girl's a runaway. She needs greens," Amy said.

"Hey, I don't care if she's the president of the United States. Somebody better be paying for those salads."

"You won't be shorted," Amy assured her and brought the salads to Matt's table.

The expression on his face was priceless as he stared down at the plate, looking as if maybe he'd swallowed something sour. "I don't like salads," he finally said.

"Why not?" Amy asked.

His brow furrowed. "Because they're green. I don't like anything green."

"Me either," Riley said, and pushed her plate away.

Amy put her hands on her hips and faced Matt. "Salads are healthy. And," she added with a meaningful look and a hitch of her chin towards Riley, "for people who aren't eating regular meals every day, they can be a critical addition to a diet."

Matt stared up at her, six feet plus of pure testosterone. She knew that, in general, he did as he wanted, and she figured he'd been doing so for a damn long time. But he'd asked for her help, and even if he hadn't, she wanted this girl to eat a frigging salad. The silent battle of wills lasted for about five seconds, and then Matt gave a sigh, picked up his fork, and stabbed at the lettuce with little enthusiasm.

Amy turned to Riley, who was staring open mouthed at Matt, clearly shocked that he'd caved, that he was going to eat the salad just because Amy had asked. Or *told*.

"You, too," Matt said to Riley, jabbing his fork in the direction of the girl's salad.

"But—"

"No buts," Matt said. "Amy's more stubborn than a mule. You're best off just doing what she asks or it's like beating your head against a brick wall."

Amy opened her mouth but decided to let that one go.

Riley sized her up for a beat and then blew out an exaggerated breath that spoke volumes on what she thought of being told what to do. Still, she began eating her salad.

Satisfied, Amy leaned against the outside of the booth, grateful to take some of the weight off her feet for a minute. For all Riley's bitching, she was inhaling the salad like she hadn't eaten in days. And hell, maybe she hadn't. "So where are you from?"

"Around," Riley said.

Well if that wasn't downright helpful. "You enjoy the mountains?"

"Yeah," Riley said around a big bite of lettuce. She was carefully avoiding the cucumbers as if they were poisonous snakes.

So was Matt.

"I'm going back up there to do some more exploring tomorrow morning, since I don't have to work until late afternoon," Amy said. "How long did you say you were camped out there?"

Riley went still, obviously shutting down. "I didn't say."

Amy nodded and met Matt's gaze, which was warm and fixed on her. She didn't want to think about why that made her feel warm in return, so she left them and went back to the kitchen. When the food was ready, she brought out the order, setting down Riley's plate first. "You might want to—"

Riley began inhaling the burger and fries with vigor.

"—Take it easy," Amy continued. "Too much on an empty stomach isn't good."

Riley didn't slow down.

Matt moved over and patted the place next to him, and Amy caught Jan's eye to let her know she was taking a quick break before sitting. "You been on your own for a while," Amy said.

Riley shrugged.

"When I was living on my own," Amy said, "it was a jar of peanut butter and raw ramen noodles for the week. Used to be able to get those for like nineteen cents each."

Riley was halfway through her burger already. "On grocery Tuesdays, you can get other stuff cheap, too."

"Grocery Tuesdays?" Matt asked.

Riley lowered her gaze and hunched over her food, like she'd accidentally imparted a state secret.

Amy's throat tightened and she looked at Matt. "It's when some of the grocery stores throw out their older stock to make room for the new stock."

Matt's gaze slid back to Riley, but he didn't say anything more.

From the kitchen, Henry dinged the bell, signaling that Amy had another order ready. She sent Matt a did-the-best-I-could look and walked away. It was what she did with problems. Walk. Teenage life sucked? She walked. Her mom's new husband giving her trouble? She walked. Her own guy trouble? She walked. It was her MO.

But this time, for the first time, she wasn't proud of it.

•   •   •

Matt watched Amy go, something new unfurling in his gut as certain things began to click for him. She didn't like being approached unexpectedly, or startled. She'd once survived on peanut butter and ramen. And she was slow to trust.

At some point in her life, things had been bad, possibly worse than he could imagine. It wasn't any of his business, and it certainly wasn't his job, but that didn't stop him from aching for her and Riley both. Amy didn't want his sympathy. He knew this. Riley didn't want his sympathy either, but she was in trouble. He knew it deep in his gut. He'd like to help but he held no delusions on his ability to do that for either of them.

He didn't have a great track record when it came to fixing people's problems. In fact, he had a downright shitty record when it came right down to it. He turned his attention to Riley. Clearly she was on the run, maybe from someone abusive, or at the very least, she'd been sorely neglected. She'd practically licked her plate clean, eating everything except for the cucumbers. Couldn't blame her there. "Better?"

She answered with a nod, though she did smile when Amy delivered the pie. The way to a woman's heart… dessert. Good to know.

Riley waited until Amy moved onto another booth. "Your piece is bigger," she said.

"So?" Matt said. "*I'm* bigger."

"Yeah, that's not why your piece is bigger."

Matt ignored this. When they'd finished, he paid the bill. The salads hadn't been on it, which meant that Amy intended to pay for them out of her own pocket, so he made sure his tip covered the cost plus, then led Riley back to the parking lot. He could feel her anxiety level rising. "You have two choices," he said. "You can tell me where your friends live so I can drop you off there, or I can run your ID and figure out your secrets."

He was going to do that anyway, but she didn't have to know it.

"I'm of age," she said. "I don't have to give you my friends' address."

"Don't have to...or can't, because there are no friends?" he asked.

She stared at him, the silence broken by the sound of someone clearing her throat.

Amy. She was standing in the parking lot, purse slung over her shoulder, keys in her hand. "I got off early," she said. "I have a spare bedroom, Riley. It's the size of a piece of toast, but it's all yours for the night if you'd like."

"No," Matt immediately said. It was one thing for *him* to get involved with a troubled teen they knew far too little about, another entirely for Amy to do it for him.

"No," Riley said, echoing Matt. "I couldn't do that. But thanks. I just want to go back to the woods."

"You're done with the woods," Matt said. "No more illegal camping. It's not safe, and I can't have you out there."

"And besides, you don't *have* to camp," Amy said to Riley. "Just come to my place. You'd get a hot shower and a roof."

Matt opened his mouth, but Amy gave him a small head shake. To Riley, she gestured toward her car, and to his surprise, Riley got into it.

Amy turned to him, her expression one of grim

determination. He could see that Riley had stirred something inside of her. Protectiveness, certainly, but memories too, and it didn't take a genius to see that those memories made her sad.

His fault. "Amy—"

"I'm doing this," she said.

Clearly, whether he liked it or not. And for the record, he didn't. "When I asked for your help, I didn't mean for you to—"

"I know. But I can't leave her here, Matt. I just can't." There was something in her voice, something that twisted the knife deeper within him. "We'll be fine," she murmured, and slid behind the wheel of her car. He stepped between her and the driver's door before she could shut it, crouching at her side. "Be careful."

"Always am."

He paused, but he had no further reason to detain them so he stood and backed up, watching her drive off. He didn't feel good about this, about sending a possible juvenile delinquent home with the woman he had a thing for. He wasn't sure what kind of thing exactly, but it didn't matter at the moment. This was his doing, and if something went wrong, he wouldn't be able to live with himself.

So he followed them. He parked on the street outside of Amy's building and watched them go inside together. A minute later, the lights came on. While he watched from his truck, he called Sawyer, requesting a search for a missing persons report on one Riley Taylor.

If Riley Taylor was even her real name...

While he waited to hear back, Matt spent the time keeping an eye on the building, and maybe playing solitaire on his phone.

When Amy knocked on the driver's window, she nearly gave him a coronary.

"If you're not going home," she said through his window, "you might as well come in."

She'd showered and was wearing an oversized T-shirt and tiny booty shorts that revealed her mile-long legs. Her hair was wet, her long, side-swept bangs falling over one eye. She smelled like shampoo and soap—and warm, soft woman. He followed her up the stairs, watching her ass in those short shorts. She could've led him right off a cliff and he'd never have noticed.

Her place was a tiny two bedroom, emphasis on the tiny. The living room, kitchen, and dining room were all one room that was not much bigger than his truck. Small as it was, it was also cheerful. Sunshine yellow paint in the kitchen, bright blue and white in the living room. Clearly the place had come like this because he was quite certain that Amy wouldn't have picked such vibrant colors. Amy was a lot of things—smart, loyal, fiercely protective, beautiful, edgy—but not exactly cheerful.

Proving the point, she gave him a blanket, a pillow, the couch, and a long look that he didn't even try to interpret. "Thanks," he said.

She nodded and turned away.

Then turned back.

Their gazes caught and held for a long moment, and the air hummed with hunger and desire. Fuck it, he thought, tossing the blanket and pillow down, but just as he stepped toward her, she hightailed it into her bedroom.

Smart girl.

Two hours later, he was still tossing and turning on the couch that wasn't wide enough for his shoulders and about two feet too short. What the hell was he doing here? Thinking of sex, that's what he was doing. Sex with Amy, which he was no longer sure was a good idea.

In fact, he was pretty damn sure it was a *bad* idea now that he suspected Amy had an extremely rough past. A past he'd likely stirred up for her by bringing Riley into her life. He needed to stay the hell away from her, that's what he needed to do. She didn't need the complication.

Getting comfortable was impossible, so he sat up and put his feet on the small coffee table. Slightly better. Count sheep, he told himself, but when he closed his eyes, sheep wasn't what came to mind.

Amy came to mind. Amy, straddling him.

Naked.

Damn if that wasn't a hell of a lot better than sheep. But it wasn't exactly conducive to falling sleep, so he rose, thinking a kitchen raid might work. A rustle warned him that he wasn't the only one awake just as he collided into a willowy, warm body that his own instantly recognized. *Amy.* Catching her, he dropped backward to the couch, taking her with him.

She landed sprawled over the top of him, all soft, tousled woman, her breasts rising and falling against his chest with every breath. "You okay?"

Apparently she was, because she fisted both hands in his hair and kissed him, a really deep, wet, hot *holy shit* kiss. Yeah, this. *This* was what he'd needed all fucking day long. It was perfect.

She was perfect.

Instantly hard, he rolled to tuck her beneath him, spreading her legs with his to make room for himself, pressing into her so that he was cradled between her thighs. It was dark so he couldn't see much, but he sure could feel. And what he felt just about stopped his heart. She appeared to be wearing an oversized shirt, panties, and nothing else, as he discovered when his hands slid beneath the shirt to cup her bare breasts.

Amy gasped his name, and he went still, realizing he had her pinned beneath him, a perfect breast in each hand. And he wanted to keep kissing her, keep touching her until she was too hot to stop him. Even the thought revved him up. But Jesus, he'd forgotten the reason he was even here—Riley was in the next room. With a Herculean effort, he managed to let go of Amy and rise to his feet.

The distance didn't help. Nor did the sight of Amy still sprawled on the couch trying to catch her breath. Her shirt had risen up, her cute little panties looking very white in the dark of the room. He wanted in those little panties. Wanted that more than his next breath.

Not happening. Snatching up the pillow and blanket, he strode to the door. "I'm going to sleep in my truck."

A lie. He wasn't going to sleep at all.

"I thought the truck was uncomfortable," she said.

Yes, and so was a hard-on. He'd just have to live with it.

Chapter 8

The best things in life are chocolate.

Amy got up early. She had until four this afternoon to try to get up to Sierra Meadows and back. *Try* being the key word. She wasn't at all sure she had any confidence in her ability to do so, but she had to try.

She had some hope to get to.

She was deciding whether or not to leave Riley a note or wake her up when the teen staggered out of the spare bedroom. She was wearing the same ratty jeans as yesterday but a different shirt, this one strategically torn in some sort of misguided teenager sense of fashion.

"Sleep okay?" Amy asked her.

"Yeah." Riley looked out the kitchen window. "The cop's gone."

Yes, Matt was gone. She'd heard him leave before the crack of dawn. She'd been lying in her bed awake, hot, aching, remembering what his hands had felt like on her when she'd heard his truck start up and drive away. "And he's not a cop. He's a forest ranger."

"Same thing."

Pretty much, Amy agreed. And she recognized some of the authority issues in Riley's voice well enough since she'd always had her own to contend with. "Listen, I'm going up to Sierra Meadows. Feel free to stay and catch up on some sleep. There's food, hot water...TV."

Riley looked around, her wariness showing. "I don't know."

"No one will bother you here. Is that what you're worried about? Because if someone's bothering you, maybe I can help—"

"No," Riley said quickly. Too quickly. "I don't need help. I'm fine."

Amy's heart squeezed because she'd been there, right there where Riley was, terrified and alone with no one to turn to. Well, actually that wasn't quite correct. She'd had people to turn to, but she'd screwed that up, so when she'd needed help, no one had believed her.

"You're safe here," Amy said.

Riley nodded, and Amy felt relieved. Maybe she'd stay and be safe for the day, at least. "Is there someone I can call for you, to let them know where you are?"

"No."

Well, that had been a long shot.

"I left out some spare clothes if you're interested," Amy said. "There's some food in the fridge, but not much. If you walk down to the diner later, I'll make you something to eat, whatever you want."

"Why?"

Riley wasn't asking about the food, and Amy knew it. What she didn't know was how to answer, so she went with to-the-bone honesty. "Because I know how it sucks to not know where your next meal's going to come from. You don't need to feel that, not today anyway."

It took Amy two hours to get up to Sierra Meadows, made easier by the fact that now she knew where to go. Lungs screaming, huffing like a lunatic, she climbed to the same spot where only a few nights ago she'd teetered and then fallen, sliding down on her ass in the inky dark.

There was no fog now so she could see, and the view was breathtakingly gorgeous. The sun poked through the lush growth, dappling the trail. Far below, down in the meadow, the steam rose from the rocks as the sun hit the dew. Making her careful way down the steep incline to the meadow floor, she walked through shoulder-high grass and wildflowers to the wall of thirty-foot prehistoric rocks on the far side. The meadow was a lot longer than it appeared from above, and there was no path, so this took another half hour. Finally she stood before the towering rocks, feeling quite small and insignificant.

Heart pounding, she slowly walked the entire length of them. Names and dates had been carved into the lower stones by countless climbers before her. Not needing to read her grandma's journal, Amy followed the right curve as far as she could and found the last *huge* "diamond" rock. There were rows of initials, and she painstakingly read each and every one, looking for the RB and SB that was Rose Barrett and Scott Barrett. It took her another thirty minutes to decide they weren't there.

Frustrated, she sat in the wild grass and stared at the rock. To give herself some time to think, she pulled out her sketch pad and drew the rocks. She needed to start back soon but she was hesitant to leave without answers. She looked at the rocks again and let out a breath.

Then she reached for her phone and called the one person who could help her.

"Hello?"

Amy went still at the sound of her mom's voice.

"Amy?"

Amy cleared her throat, but the emotions couldn't be swallowed away. Guilt. Hurt. Regret. "How did you know?"

"You're the only one who ever calls and says nothing. Though it's been a few years." Her mom paused. "I suppose you need something."

Amy closed her eyes. "Yeah."

Now her mother was quiet.

"I'm in Lucky Harbor," Amy said. "In Washington State."

More silence.

"Following grandma's journal."

This got a reaction, a soft gasp. "Whatever for?" her mom asked.

For hope and peace, Amy nearly said. *To find myself . . .* But that was all far too revealing, and her mother wouldn't believe it anyway. "Her journal says they left their initials on the mountain, but there's no RB and SB for Rose and Scott Barrett anywhere that I can see."

Nothing.

"Mom?"

There was a sigh. "It was all a very long time ago, Amy."

"You know something."

"Yes."

Amy wasn't breathing. "Mom, please tell me."

"You're looking for the wrong initials. You should be looking for RS and JS. JS is for Jonathon Stone." Her mom paused. "Your grandma's first husband."

Amy felt her heart stutter. "What?"

"Rose ran away when she was seventeen, you knew that. She eloped."

She hadn't known *that*. "With Jonathon Stone."

"Yes. Their families didn't approve. Not that Mom ever cared about what people thought. You're a lot like her in that regard..." Amy's mother sighed again, and when she spoke this time, there was heavy irony in her voice. "The women in our family don't tend to listen to reason."

Amy ran back to the rock and searched again. It didn't take but a minute to find it, the small RS and JS together. She pressed a hand to the ache in her chest. "No," she agreed softly. "We don't tend to listen to reason."

There was another awkward pause, and Amy had this ridiculous wish that her mom might ask how she was. She didn't. Too much water under the bridge. But she hoped there was enough of a tie left to at least get the answers she wanted. Needed. "What happened to Jonathon?"

"It's a sad story," her mom said. "Jonathon was sick," her mom explained. "Lung cancer, and back then it was even more of a death sentence than it is now. Jonathon had a list of things he wanted to do while he could. Rock climb the Grand Canyon. Ski a glacier. See the Pacific Coast from a mountaintop..."

The Olympic Mountains. Where Amy currently sat. "Did he get to do those things in time?"

Her mom was quiet, not answering.

"Mom?"

"You haven't called me in two years. Two years, Amy."

She sighed. "Yeah."

"It'd have been nice to know you're alive."

The last time Amy had called, her mother had been having marital problems with husband number five— shock—and she'd wanted to play the place-the-blame game. Amy hadn't wanted to go there. So it'd been easier not to call. "What happened to Jonathon, Mom? And do you know where it was exactly that Grandma Rose ended her journey? Her journal is clear on the first two legs of their trek in the Olympic Mountains, but it's vague on the last stop." Where Rose had found heart... "Do you—"

"I'm fine, you know. Thanks for asking."

Amy grimaced. "Mom—"

"Is this your cell phone? This number you called me from?"

"Yes," Amy said.

"You have enough minutes in your phone plan to make a few extra calls?"

"Yes."

"Good. Call me again sometime, and you can ask me another question. I'll answer a question with each call. How's that sound?"

Amy blinked. "You *want* me to call you?"

"You always were a quick study."

"But—"

Click.

Amy stared at the phone. This was almost too much information for her brain to process. Her Grandma Rose had made this journey when she'd been seventeen years old. *Seventeen.* And she'd been a newlywed, in love with someone who'd died young and tragically.

How had that brought her hope? Or peace? Or her own heart ... ?

Amy pulled out the journal. She'd read it a hundred times. She knew that there was no mention of Jonathon. Just the elusive and misleading "we."

It's been a rough week. The roughest of the summer so far.

Well, that made sense now. Jonathon had been sick. Dying. Amy flipped to the next entry.

Lucky Harbor's small and quirky, and the people are friendly. We've been here all week resting, but today was a good day so we went back up the mountain. To a place called Four Lakes this time. All around us the forest vibrated with life and energy, especially the water.

I never realized how much weight the water can remove from one's shoulders. Swimming in the water was joy. Sheer joy.

I could hear the call of gulls, and caught the occasional bald eagle in our peripheral. The sheer, vast beauty was staggering.

Afterward, we lay beneath a two-hundred-foot-tall old spruce and stared up through the tangle of branches to the sky beyond. I'd always been a city girl through and through, but this ... out here ... it was magic. Healing.

I carved our initials on the tree trunk. It felt like a promise. I had my hope, but now I had something else, too, peace. Four Lakes had given me peace.

A little shocked to find her eyes stinging, her knees weak with emotion, Amy sank to the grass, emotion churning through her. As odd as it seemed, she'd found the teeniest, tiniest bit of hope for herself after all. Maybe her own peace was next...

"Phone's for you!" Jan yelled to Amy across the diner. "You need to let people know that I'm not you're damn answering service!"

Amy had gotten to work on time, and though she was still reeling from the afternoon and all she'd learned, she managed to set it aside for now. That was a particularly defined talent of hers. Setting things aside. Living in Denial City.

For now, she had to work; that's what kept a roof over her head and food in her belly. She had no idea who'd possibly be calling her here at the diner, but she finished serving a customer his dinner and then picked up the phone in the kitchen. "Hello?"

Nothing but a dial tone. She turned to Jan. "Who was it?"

"Some guy." Jan shrugged. "He wanted to talk to the waitress who'd been seen with the runaway teen."

Amy went still. "And you didn't think that was odd?"

Jan shrugged again. Not her problem.

Amy had a bad feeling about this, very bad. To save money, she'd never gotten a landline at her apartment. This meant she couldn't check on Riley, which she felt a sudden real need to do. "Going on break," she said.

Jan sputtered. "Oh, no. You just got here an hour ago."

Amy grabbed her keys. "I'll be back."

"I said *no*." Steam was coming out of Jan's ears. "You've got a room full of hungry people."

Amy understood, but there was a sinking feeling in her gut that Riley needed her more. "Sorry." She headed out the back door as Jan let out a furious oath.

There was no Riley waiting at home.

And no note.

No nothing, though the clothes Amy had set out for Riley were gone. Unhappy, Amy left Riley a sticky note in case she came back, then returned to work, eyeing the door every time someone came in.

But Riley never showed.

At the end of Amy's shift, Mallory and Grace arrived. Amy waved them to a booth, grabbed the plate of brownies she'd been saving as well as the charity jar from the counter, and joined them. She plopped down, put her feet up, head back, and sighed out a very long breath.

"Long day?" Mallory asked sympathetically.

Amy looked at Mallory. "*You*, I'm not talking to."

Mallory winced, guilt all over her face, clearly knowing Amy was referring to the Matt-to-the-rescue episode.

Amy popped the lid off the money jar and pulled out a wad of cash, 100 percent of which would go directly to the teen center at the local health services clinic that Mallory ran. "Two hundred and fifty bucks. Even if I am mad at you."

"Luckily you're not the type to hold a grudge," Mallory said sweetly, taking the money.

"I hope we're going to talk about guys," Grace said, picking out a brownie. "I'm in the middle of a man drought, and I need a thrill. I plan to live vicariously through you two."

"Ask Mallory here to set you up," Amy said dryly.

"Actually," Mallory said, ignoring the jab, "there're

plenty of single guys around here. My brother's newly single. Again."

"Yes but he's a serial dater," Amy said. "Even I know to stay away from serial daters."

"Even you?" Mallory asked.

"I don't date." But she did, apparently, lust after sexy forest rangers who shared their tents and last Dr. Pepper.

"Why?"

Amy shrugged. "Not my thing."

"Again," Mallory said. "Why?"

"I don't know. I guess because I haven't had much time for that sort of thing."

"That sort of thing?" Mallory repeated. "Honey, *every* woman has enough time for love. It's what makes the world go round."

"No, that's chocolate. And of course you think love makes the world go round. You're getting lucky every night with Ty."

Mallory grinned. "True." Her smile faded. "Tell me the truth—how bad did I screw up by sending Matt to the forest?"

"Yes!" Grace whooped and pumped her fist. When Amy and Mallory stared at her, she winced. "Sorry. It's just that we're really going to dissect Amy's life instead of mine." Happy, she stuffed a brownie in her mouth.

Mallory was looking expectantly at Amy, who gave in with a sigh. "It's not your fault," she admitted, digging into her own very large brownie. "I'm the idiot who got lost on the mountain. Matt helped me out. And then, because of a stupid *tree*, we ended up camping out overnight."

They both gasped, Mallory in delight, Grace in horror. *"With no electricity?"*

Mallory laughed. "They spent the night together and *that's* what you want to know? About the lack of electricity?"

"Hey," Grace said, "a woman's morning routine is complicated enough *with* electricity."

"We didn't sleep together," Amy said, then grimaced. "Well, at least not until I fell down a ravine trying to find a place to pee in private, sprained my wrist, cut my leg, bruised my ass *and* my ego, and had to be rescued *again*." She waved her bandaged wrist for their viewing pleasure.

Mallory's eyes were wide. "You fell down a ravine going to pee, and he rescued you? Were your pants still around your ankles? Because that's not a good look for anyone."

"*No*," Amy said. "My pants were *not* around my ankles. But your concern is touching." She kicked Mallory, who was snorting with laughter. "And how would that have been funny?"

"Oh, trust me, it would have been. Come on, this is the stuff that chick flicks are made of—the classic meet-cute, you know? *And* a story for your kids someday."

"There will be no kids!"

Mallory licked a brownie crumb from her finger. "I'd suggest that good girl lesson number five should be to keep your pants *on* during a first date, but the truth is I can't really talk in that regard since I slept with Ty on our first date."

"Actually," Amy said, "technically, you slept with Ty *before* your first date. And fine, if you must know my pants weren't down when I fell but they might have come down shortly thereafter."

Grace and Mallory gasped in delighted tandem.

"Get your heads out of the gutter," Amy said. "I had a cut on my leg, and he had to doctor me up."

"Of course," Grace said dryly, and then leaned forward, brownie forgotten. "What kind of undies were you wearing, a thong or granny panties?"

"What does that matter?"

"Oh, it matters," Mallory said.

"I can't remember," Amy lied.

From the next booth over, a face popped up. It was Lucille, local art gallery owner and all-around gossip extraordinaire. She exited her booth and stood in front of the Chocoholics, a smile on her face. She wore eye-popping lime green sweats today with Skechers tennis shoes that gave her four-foot-nine-inch frame an extra few inches. Her steel-gray bun gave her a few more. She shoved a twenty into Amy's now empty charity jar while sliding her dentures around some. "What's this I hear about panties and Ranger Hot Buns?"

Both Mallory and Grace pointed at Amy like the Two Stooges.

Good friends.

Amy pulled the entire plate of brownies toward herself. "Good girl lesson number six—don't be traitors." She looked at Lucille. "I had a little trouble out on the trail and got some assistance. End of story. Nothing more to report."

"But he rescued you from the latrine," Lucille pressed. "I don't suppose you have a pic?"

"No!" She didn't need a picture. Everything that had happened, from being rescued to the feeling of lying in Matt's arms, was engrained in her brain.

"Well, jeez," Lucille said. "No need to get your

panties in a twist." She paused. "But if you *did* get your panties in a twist, what kind of panties would they be? You know, for accuracy in reporting's sake?"

Amy narrowed her eyes at her, and Lucille backed away. "Oops, look at the time—I've gotta skedaddle."

When she was gone, Mallory eyed the brownie plate.

Amy tightened her grip on it. "Don't even think about it."

"Forget the brownies. What happened with Ranger Hot Buns?" Grace demanded to know.

"We shared his tent," Amy said. "Nothing happened." Well, nothing except for some pretty amazing kisses...

"Let me get this straight," Grace said in disbelief. "You slept with Matt Bowers, the hottest guy in town, and nothing happened? Are you kidding me? That's a crappy story."

"Matt's pretty hot," Mallory agreed. "But I wouldn't say he's the *hottest* guy in town. Because Ty's pretty damn hot. I mean think about them, side by side..."

There was a beat of silence as the three of them thought about the incredible hotness that was Ty and Matt, side by side. Amy let the image sink in and shivered, which she covered by stuffing another big bite of brownie into her mouth. There were certain things she knew for sure. When in doubt, eat chocolate. When stressed, eat chocolate. When in doubt *and* stressed, eat chocolate. *Especially* when that doubt and stress were related to a man and her feelings for said man.

"Did you at least dream about all the things you would do to him?" Grace asked. "Cuz that's what I'd have done."

Hell, yes, Amy had dreamed about all the things she'd

like to do to Matt. Repeatedly. Not the point. "Yesterday he found a homeless teen up where we camped and brought her here to the diner. We fed her and then took her to my place so she could have a bed and a hot shower."

"We?" Mallory asked. "You took Matt home with you as well?"

"He showed up on his own. I found him outside my house keeping watch." She shook her head. "Not sure what that was about, to be honest."

"I bet he wanted to make sure you were okay," Mallory said.

Amy laughed, and Mallory and Grace exchanged a telling glance. "I'm *always* okay," Amy said. "Probably he didn't trust me not to screw it up."

"Honey." Mallory covered Amy's hand with her own. "Why wouldn't Matt trust you?"

Because no one ever had. But that was before, she reminded herself, before she'd worked so hard at growing up and separating herself from the past. She needed to remember that.

Mallory squeezed her hand. "Can I ask you something?"

"No, you can't have another brownie. They're all mine now."

Mallory smiled but shook her head. "Why would you give Riley a chance and not Matt?"

"What are you talking about? Matt's never wanted a chance with me."

"Oh, please." Mallory gave her a get-real look. "The guy comes into the diner only when you're working. He sits at *your* table, and he watches you the same way that Ty watches me."

"Yeah, and how's that?" Amy asked.

"Like you're lunch."

Amy squirmed a little bit because deep down she knew it was true. She'd caught him at it. It never failed to evoke a multitude of emotions, not the least of which was an undeniable lust in return, but also something deeper and far more complicated than sheer desire.

And that's what made it so uncomfortable. That's what scared her.

"So I'll ask you again," Mallory said quietly. "Why not give him a shot?"

It was a question for which Amy didn't have the answer.

Chapter 9

A balanced diet is a chocolate in each hand.

Matt knew he had a reputation for being laid-back and easygoing. He wasn't sure that either of those things was exactly true, but part of the appearance came from being prepared for anything at any time.

This ability had been honed in the military and then on the streets of Chicago. If a guy could survive warfare and SWAT, he could survive anything. Certainly one willowy, enigmatic, tough-nut-to-crack brunette named Amy Michaels.

He wanted to see her again. He'd resisted for two days now, but then he caught sight of her at the front counter of the ranger station. His office was down a hallway so she hadn't seen him, but he'd seen her just fine. After she left, his junior ranger manning the desk had said she'd asked for a map to Four Lakes.

Matt had known she'd gone back up to Sierra Meadows the other day. He'd seen her there, amongst the diamond rocks, sketching. It'd taken all he'd had to leave her to the privacy she'd obviously wanted.

But why was she suddenly out on the mountain on her days off, hiking alone? He didn't know, but he wanted to, so he made it a point to patrol today instead of trying to conquer the mountain of paperwork in his office. Just as well since he'd been taking a ribbing all morning for a certain Facebook post that had gone up the other day, something about how he'd added two new duties to his job description: rescuing maidens and playing doctor.

His staff had loved that. So had Josh and Ty, both of whom had called him with the news like two little girls, the fuckers. Matt could only imagine what Amy thought of it.

He found her just where he thought he would, up at Four Lakes. What he hadn't expected was that she'd be about fifteen feet up a huge five-hundred-year-old spruce at the base of the first of the four lakes, which were connected by little tributaries.

Amy was holding a sketch pad and was talking either to herself or to the tree.

"If you fall," she was saying, "you know who's going to come get you, right? And just your luck, you'll break your fat ass this time..."

"Your ass isn't fat," Matt said, staring up at the long, toned leg hanging down. "It's perfect. And what the hell are you doing up there?"

She went still, then leaned over a branch and peered down at him. "I'm not lost."

"Good. But that doesn't answer my question."

This was met by silence and a rainfall of pine needles as she began to climb down. Her backpack dropped to the ground and then the sketch pad. Then those long legs came within reach, so Matt grabbed her around the waist and pulled her out of the tree. "Hey there, Tough Girl."

"Hey." Her warm body slid down every inch of his, and there was a moment just before her feet touched the ground where he'd have sworn she even nestled into him.

Or maybe that was his imagination, because then she stepped free. She was wearing jeans shorts, emphasis on short, and a V-neck tee that was loose enough to be hanging off one shoulder, revealing a bright blue bra strap. She had a scratch on her jaw and a smudge of dirt across her forehead. "The tree's taller than I thought," she said.

"What were you looking for?"

"Nothing important."

Nothing important, his ass. She wasn't the type of woman to climb a tree just for the hell of it. But if he knew anything about her, it was that he couldn't push for answers. He needed a diversion for now, then he'd work his way back to the subject at hand. "How's Riley?" He'd heard back from Sawyer that the teen wasn't a missing person, or even a person of interest, so there'd been no legal reason to interfere in her life again. But he wanted to know that she was okay.

"I haven't seen her after the sleepover," Amy said. "I know you were worried about her, and also about me taking care of her, but she's gone. I'm sorry."

Unable to stop himself, Matt stroked a strand of hair out of her pretty eyes. "I was never worried about you taking care of her."

"Maybe you should have been."

"Why?" he asked, confused.

"Well, it's not like you know me, not really. I could be a horrible person, who's done horrible things."

"I know enough," he said firmly.

"But—"

He put a finger on her lips. She stared at him for a long beat, as if taking measure of his honesty. Or maybe she was deciding on a way to kick his ass for shushing her. Then her gaze dropped to his mouth, and he hoped she was remembering how good it felt on hers.

Because that's what he was remembering. Ducking a little, he cupped her jaw and eyed her newest injury—the scratch. It could use some antiseptic. He ran his other hand down her arm to her wrapped wrist. "How is this doing?"

"Better."

He shifted his hand to her leg, his fingers brushing bare skin thanks to the shorts, before landing on the bandage there. "And your thigh?"

She didn't answer as quickly, and when she did, her breathing wasn't as even as before. "Better."

"And your..." His hand slid around now and cupped her very sweet ass.

She choked out some reply and gave him a shove to the chest that made him grin. Turning, he scooped up her sketch pad for her. Before he could open it, she snatched it from him and shoved it into her backpack. "Thanks," she said.

He watched her fiddle with her stuff a moment. She was clearly waiting him out, assuming he'd move on.

She was wrong. "So are you going to tell me what you're doing out here?" he asked. "Or maybe you were hoping to find *me*."

She laughed. "Nice ego. But no. Not hoping to find you."

"Ouch."

"Yeah, I'm sure you're crushed." She zipped her backpack. "My grandma came here one summer, a long time ago. She used to tell me stories about the places she hiked to and the things she'd seen."

"It's a pretty unforgettable place," he said.

"Her stories were my fairy tales growing up. Her trip out here was important to her. It changed her life."

"Are you looking to change your life?" he asked quietly.

She shrugged. "Maybe. A little."

"Why now?" he asked.

"What do you mean?"

"Your grandma died when you were twelve, right?"

"Yes," she said, looking surprised that he remembered. "And then I went to live with my mom and her new husband. Until I was sixteen."

He waited but she didn't go on. "What happened when you were sixteen?"

Some of the light went out of her eyes, but then she turned her head from him pretty quickly. She looked out at the water.

Okay, so this wasn't up for discussion. He stood at her side and looked out at the first lake as well. There were wet prints on the rocky shore. She'd gone swimming. He'd have liked to see that. "So...where did you go at sixteen? Is that when you traveled around?"

"Yes."

"What did you do with yourself?"

"I grew up," she said flatly. "That took a while. And then, finally, I ended up out here in Lucky Harbor."

"To recreate your grandma's journey. To change your life."

"Yes." She paused, clearly weighing her words. "She wrote in her journal that out here she found...things."

"Things."

"Hope. Peace." She paused, grimacing as if she was embarrassed. "Her own heart. Whatever that means."

"In a tree?"

She gave a little laugh and told him about the initials at Sierra Meadows, about Jonathon, his illness, and how Rose had found hope there at the base of the diamond rocks.

"And what about you?" he asked. "Did *you* find hope?

She looked into his eyes, and the air seemed to crackle between them. "I found something," she said softly. She held his gaze for another beat and then turned back to the water. There was a light breeze now, rippling the surface of the lake, raising whitecaps.

"What did Rose find here at Four Lakes? Peace?"

"Apparently. Her initials are on the tree trunk, up about twenty feet. I think she saw Jonathon swimming and feeling stronger, and she realized that they could fight the illness. And before you ask, I don't know where she found her heart. The journal entries aren't as clear when it comes to the last leg of her trek, something about going around in a circle." She was quiet a moment. "Out here, it's unlike anything I've ever seen. No buildings, no people. People always say the city is a scary place, but to me, this is scary. It's big."

He nodded. He knew exactly what she meant. In the city, there was always something right in front of you. A car, a building, people. Out here there was nothing but space, wide open space. "It's just different from what you're used to."

"Very," she agreed on a low, throaty laugh. "And it takes my breath the way the mountains cut into the cliffs and valleys. Everything's so tough and rugged."

"Like the people who roam here." He got a smile out of her for that one. He wanted to ask her more about her past but knew she wasn't ready to tell him. And he didn't need to know, he reminded himself. This wasn't a relationship.

She picked up a smooth, round rock and tried to skim it across the water, but it plopped instead. "When you saw me on the trail that first time," she said, "I was having trouble locating Sierra Meadows and the wall of rocks there."

He picked up a rock, flatter than the one she'd used. "You could have told me." He skimmed the rock across the surface of the lake six times.

"Show-off," she said. "And I didn't want help. But then I fell down that ravine and found the meadows by accident. Four Lakes was *much* easier to find. The tree though..." She sent it a look. "Not so much."

He eyed the entire stand of trees around them, at least ten. "How many did you have to climb before you found the right one?"

She rubbed at the scratch on her jaw. "Five. Not bad odds for a city rat."

"Did you find peace?"

"No. I found sap, and the will to never climb another tree again."

He smiled. "I bet."

"But I enjoyed the day," she said with some surprise. "It made me want to have more days like this one."

He met her gaze. "Maybe *that's* peace."

"I don't know." Her expression was more open than he'd ever seen it, and he felt a surge of something swell in his chest.

Not good.

Not good at all.

She rubbed at her scratch again, and he brushed her hand away, then bent and kissed her jaw just above it.

She sucked in a breath and went still. Then she turned her head so that their mouths were lined up, a fraction of an inch apart. "What are you doing?"

"Kissing your owie and making it better. Consider it just another of the services I provide."

"Maybe I should see a list of these services," she said.

"For you, anything goes."

Her smile faded, and her eyes went very serious, though she didn't step back from him. Her warm breath commingled with his. It was an incredibly erotic feeling, alone on a mountaintop, surrounded by hundreds of thousands of acres of wild land, standing toe to toe.

Mouth to mouth.

Sharing air.

"Matt?"

"Yeah?"

A sigh escaped her lips. "I really want to sleep with you, but..."

"Damn," he said. "That was a great sentence right up to the 'but.'"

"But," she repeated firmly, then hesitated and blew out a breath, "I have...qualms."

"Tell me."

"Okay. The thing is, I think the sex would be good—"

"Good? Try off the charts."

She acknowledged that with a nod. "Yeah, probably."

Definitely.

"But..."

He sighed. The "but" again.

"*But*," she repeated, "if you want anything more than that, I'm not interested."

Wait—What? Had he heard her correctly, or just projected the words he'd want to hear?

She was waiting for a reaction, and it was just so unbelievable, and unbelievably perfect, that he laughed out loud.

Chapter 10

*Flowers and champagne might set the stage, but
it's chocolate that steals the show.*

Amy stared at Matt as he started laughing and felt her
eyes narrow. "I'm sorry, but how exactly is the idea of us
having sex funny?"

He laughed some more, looking quite gone with
amusement, and it pissed her off. He made a clear effort
to control himself, but it was too late. She was over it, and
over him. And embarrassed to boot. "You think because
I'm a woman I'd automatically want more than just sex?
Well guess what Ranger *Hot Buns*—" She took a beat to
enjoy his wince. "Women want just-sex as much as any
guy." *Some more than others. Some had suppressed their
urges for far too long and were fire rockets just waiting to
go off.* "So welcome to the twenty-first century," she said.
"Where women *like* just-sex."

For some reason, this set him off again, and she
pushed him. He didn't budge, though, so she pushed him
again, or at least she meant to. But her brain scrambled

the signal, and her hands fisted in his shirt. "I ought to shut you up."

This got his attention. "Yeah," he said, hands sliding to her hips, "shut me up."

"Fine." She shut him up with one hell of a kiss. By the time it ended, she was plastered up against his hard body, her own humming. The force of his personality came through every touch of his rough, callused hands, exuding heat and the promise of unbelievable ecstasy. "Not laughing now, are you?" she said.

"Hell, no." He came at *her* this time, and she found herself melting into him like suddenly there was no invisible line in the sand between them, nothing but this incredible pleasure, pleasure she couldn't remember ever getting out of a simple kiss before.

Problem was, nothing about Matt was simple. Not for her. His arms held her close, and the scent of clean, warm male was making her heart pound. Her head was overrun with wicked thoughts involving her tongue and every inch of his body. Unable to help herself, she nipped at his throat.

"Amy." His voice was thrillingly quiet and gruff as he ran his lips along her jaw. "Don't promise what you don't want to deliver."

Turning her head, she cupped his face and pulled it closer. He let out a sound and sucked hungrily on her bottom lip. And while his mouth and tongue were very busy, so were his hands, gripping her hips.

"I rarely make promises," she told him. "But when I do, I deliver." She nibbled at his ear next, then, when he groaned, did it again.

A phone vibrated, Matt's, but he ignored it. Whoever

it was called back again immediately. Swearing quite creatively, Matt yanked the phone off his service belt. "Busy," he said and shoved it into his pocket.

"When do you get off?" Amy asked.

"If we're not careful, in less than ten seconds."

She looked down at the hard-on threatening the zipper of his uniform trousers. "I meant off work."

He once again pulled his cell phone and looked at the time. "Twenty minutes."

She bit her lip and looked around them. There was the lake and a lovely area of wild grass, but it might be full of the creepy crawlies he'd mentioned the other night.

Reading her mind, he smiled but shook his head. "Not here. Not the first time."

"There's only going to be one time." That was all she needed to take the edge off. The fact was, it'd been so long. Too long. She hadn't realized how much she missed the feel of a man's body against hers, how much she needed an orgasm that wasn't a self-serve. And she wanted that without the pomp and circumstance, without planning, without anticipation. She wanted it now, wanted the sweet oblivion, the little bang, and then she'd go back to her day. "You've never done it in the great outdoors?"

"That's not where *we're* doing it," he said firmly.

"Hmm." She ran her finger down his chest, hoping to infuse some of her urgency to him.

He caught her wandering hand in his. "*Hmm* what?"

"Didn't peg you for a prude."

His eyes narrowed dangerously at the implied insult to his manhood, and he tightened his grip on her. "You're going to take that back in a little bit."

She had no idea what it said about her that this ridiculous display of alpha-ness brought her a delicious shiver of anticipation. "Yeah?"

"Oh, yeah. Where's your car?"

"At the trailhead," she said. "Your truck?"

"On a fire road, a quarter of a mile from here."

Not too far...

He read her expression, and his own went dark, further quickening her pulse. "I live close." His hand slid into her hair, tipping her head up to his. "If we leave now, I'll be off the clock by the time we get to my cabin."

"Yes," she breathed. His gaze tracked to her mouth, which he gave one quick, hard kiss before leading her to his truck.

The drive took them up old Highway 20, then down a narrow, curvy road. Amy caught sight of the occasional cabin, but not much else. When the road ended, Matt kept going, on a dirt road now, which opened up to a small clearing, and then his house.

"Two minutes left," she said, staring at the rugged cabin in front of her. It was way off the beaten path, which suited him. So did the inside. The ceilings were open beamed, the floors scarred hardwood. Everything was wood accented, including the big, comfy looking furniture and the frames of the pictures on the walls of the Northwest Pacific landscape.

Amy felt a little ping deep in her chest. Not of jealousy, but envy. Matt had found his place in this crazy world. He knew who he was and what he wanted. And he'd gotten it for himself.

Someday soon, she promised herself. She was working on doing the same.

"Want a drink?" he asked. "Something to eat?"

The tension between them was so palpable she could taste it. "No." She was here for one thing, and it was nourishment of a different nature altogether. With any luck, they'd do this and get each other out of their system. Then maybe she could go back to concentrating on why she was in Lucky Harbor—following Grandma Rose's journey. She dropped her backpack to the floor.

He tossed his keys to the coffee table.

"No getting attached to me," she said, hands on hips. "Cuz I'm not going to get attached to you."

He gave her a smile. "Can you resist?"

"Yes," she said firmly. It was her specialty. She shrugged out of her sweater and let it fall on top of her backpack.

His eyes heated.

She bent to undo her boots, but he said, "I have fantasies about those boots," so she left them on and pulled off her top.

His gaze drifted warmly over her, heating her in the places yearning for his hands and his mouth.

"You're lagging behind," she said.

He unholstered his gun and set it on the coffee table. Next to that went his utility belt. He kicked off his boots. Then before he got to anything good, he stepped toward her.

"More," she said.

"Oh, there's going to be a lot more." His voice was husky with the promise of it. "But I want you in my bed." He took her hand and tugged her into him. Then he slid his other hand up her back and into her hair, holding her for his kiss. It was slow and romantic. And not what she wanted. So she broke away and went for the button on his uniform cargo pants. She'd long ago learned that to get what she wanted from a man, all she had to do was get him naked.

Luckily this time what she wanted and what this man wanted were perfectly in sync. She got his button popped, his zipper down, and slid her hand inside, wrapping it around his glorious, hard length.

He made a sound that was pure male hunger before stopping her. "Bedroom," he said again firmly, and gave her a nudge to the hall.

She nudged back and pushed him up against the wall, just to the side of his fireplace. He'd asked if she wanted something to eat, and she did. "Dessert first," she said. "Always."

His mouth curved. She was amusing him. Turning him on, too, the proof was hard against her belly. Her body responded to that, and she kissed him, long and deep as she unbuttoned his shirt. God, his torso. Hard. Ripped. She wanted to lick him, and started in the dip at the hollow of his throat.

His groan reverberated in his chest, and in response, the blood pounded through her body. His hands were on her, everywhere. One glided down her back to her bottom, the other cupped a breast, his thumb teasing back and forth over her nipple. He murmured her name as his body shifted, and she knew he was about to take the control from her. So she dropped to her knees on the fireplace rug and took it first, slipping her hands back inside his open pants, freeing him so that she could run her tongue up his hot, silky erection.

With an inarticulate growl, his head thunked back

against the wall and again his hands slid into her hair. She could feel the fine tremor in his legs, and that turned her on. He was the epitome of a strong and dominant male, and she had him weak at the knees at one touch of her tongue, so she gave him another. And another...

"Jesus," he gasped. "Jesus, Amy. We've got to slow down."

She didn't, and he lasted only a few minutes more before swearing roughly and creatively, his fingers tightening reflexively in her hair. "Keep that up, and I'm going to come."

She wanted him to. Making him lose control was really working for her, and when they were done with this, she was going to take him apart in a different way.

"Christ. Amy—"

She kept going, taking him through what sounded like a very happy ending. She was still enjoying the little aftershocks running through his big, powerful body when he dropped to his knees and pulled her into his lap. He unhooked her bra and bent her back over his arm, sucking a nipple into his mouth, hard.

With a gasp of pleasure, she gripped his head. Not to pull him away but to keep him there. God yes, right there. A minute later, she realized he'd somehow peeled her out of her shorts and panties as well. In only her boots, he adjusted her so that she was straddling him right there on the floor. His hand traveled down her torso, between her open thighs, his long fingers playing slip and slide.

Pleasure swamped her, making her cry out. She never cried out. Shocked at the hurry-up noises she was making, she bit his shoulder to shut herself up.

Matt hissed in a breath but kept stroking her with

those talented fingers, in and out, in a rhythm that became her center of gravity. He commandeered her mouth as well, kissing her hard and deep, reducing her to a gasping, panting, pleading mass until, unbelievably, he sent her flying. She came back to herself to find him still idly stroking her core, his mouth soft and gentle. "Round one," he said silkily, "is a tie." Then he laid her out on the rug, holding her still when she wriggled, trying to get on top.

She was always on top.

But he shook his head, a smile curving his mouth, a very wicked smile. Lowering his head, he kissed his way down her body, stopping to pay special homage to each breast, and then her stomach, playfully tugging her crystal belly button piercing with his teeth before moving lower.

"Matt. Matt, wait—"

He didn't listen to her any more than she'd listened to him a few minutes ago. With his broad shoulders holding her legs wedged open, he took all her power away with one perfectly placed stroke of his tongue. Reduced to a whimper, she slapped her hands down on the rug on either side of her hips as he sucked and nibbled and drove her straight out of her ever-loving mind.

It was a shockingly short drive, and this time she came back to herself, boggled. Normally she had to concentrate to climax at all, and yet he'd given her a twofer, so effortlessly she hadn't even known what hit her. She didn't know whether to thank him or be embarrassed. "Well." She rose up on her elbows and eyed the room for her clothes, which were scattered. Except for her boots. Those she was still wearing. "I'm going to need a ride."

He rose up, too, still between her legs. His smile deepened, turning positively wicked. And unbelievably, she felt her body react.

Again.

"Yes," he said. "I believe I can give you a ride." Stripping out of his remaining clothes with a few economical motions, he then turned his attention to her boots, pulling them off for her. When they were both bare-ass naked, he scooped her up and kissed her, his tongue sweeping and sucking and stroking in demand.

And damn. Damn, she couldn't hold back her breathless moan, because good Lord the man knew how to use his mouth, stirring up emotions during an act that should have been only a physical release, and he did it effortlessly. She tried to pull back to think about that, but he had a good hold on her, and next thing she knew, they were on the move to his bedroom.

He set her down on a huge bed, then before she could scramble away, he stretched his body over hers.

And let's face it, scrambling away would have been tricky without any bones left in her body.

He produced a condom, and in the next instant, thrust inside her, and oh, God, the pleasure, the panic... Because she knew. She knew it even as she cried out and clutched him closer to her that she was in the worst sort of trouble now.

Because this wasn't just a physical release at all.

Not even close.

"Look at me," he said.

With effort, her eyes fluttered open, and she focused in on his face, transfixed by the expression of pure ecstasy etched on his features. She had no idea what it was with her, whether it was the eroticism of what they'd already done to each other, or that she could still taste him on her tongue, or maybe it was just the incredible feel of him so hard, so deep within her, but she wanted him with a desperate need she hadn't even known she could feel. Bringing her legs up, she wrapped them around his waist, whimpering when he slowly withdrew only to push back inside her.

"Good?" he asked.

She didn't answer. *Couldn't*, she was drowning in the sensations. He ran his hands down her arms until their fingers were entwined, then drew them up above her head, securing them there.

That brought her out of herself a little. She arched into him, trying to tug free but he held her down as he nudged his hips, giving her a slow, glorious thrust. Another cry was torn from her lips, and she couldn't quite understand what was happening. He was claiming her completely—heart, body, and soul in the most primal, raw way she'd ever allowed. And as he did, his eyes held hers prisoner in the same way he held her body, watching as her body writhed under his ministrations.

Branding her as his.

It was too much, and she tugged hard. "No."

He immediately let her hands loose, a frown of concern forming, but before he could say a word she rolled him, knocking him flat to his back. Holding *him* down now, she mirrored his actions, running her hands up his arms until their fingers were linked over *his* head.

Ha.

His hooded eyes searched hers for a long beat before he gave her a sexy smile. "Better?"

"Much," she said, and the next sound out of either of them was two shuddering breaths of pleasure as she lifted up before sinking back down on him.

Matt's groan was rough and heartfelt, and he let her do as she wanted, as she needed, which was to ride him hard and fast, every thrust sending electric heat sparking and crackling along each nerve in her body. And in the end, when they'd both shattered and she'd sagged boneless to his chest, when he'd gathered her in and pressed a sweet, tender kiss to her damp temple, she realized the truth.

When it came to Matt Bowers, she had no control at all.

An hour later, Matt stood in the dusty staging area at the trailhead, watching Amy drive off. He'd taken her to her car as she'd asked, and she'd left him so quickly his head was still spinning.

Seemed what they'd shared had gotten a little too close for comfort back there in his cabin, and apparently, Amy wasn't all that fond of that.

Well she could join his damn club. He'd come here to Lucky Harbor to get away from everyone, *not* to get too close for comfort ever again.

Something else he'd failed at.

"Remember," she'd said back in his bed, bare-ass naked, tousled, and gorgeous. "That was just sex."

He'd nearly asked if she'd been reminding him—or her. But she'd had an emphatic look on her face, making it clear that *she* was in no danger of wanting more.

The drive to her car had been made in silence. Hard to tell if it'd been good or bad silence since his woman-radar had been broken ever since Shelly had packed her shit and walked right out of his life.

Actually, she'd run.

He shook his head but it was no good. His brain was still scrambled. Amy had scrambled it good with the best blow job he'd ever had. Then she'd ridden him like a bronco, detonating any brain capacity he might have managed to retain. She'd taken him her way, all the way, clearly not liking being vulnerable, just as clearly needing to be in charge.

Which had been new and...interesting.

It sure as hell would be hard to argue that he hadn't had a great time. It'd been the kind of sex that every guy dreamed about, down and dirty, mindless.

No strings attached.

And isn't that exactly what he'd wanted from her?

Chapter 11

So much chocolate, so little time.

The next day, Amy worked at the diner. It was a slow, uneventful shift, made even slower due to a daylong downpour. The pier was empty as the rain beat down on the entire Washington coast, and the diner remained empty, too. This left Amy with way too much time to think.

Not a good thing when she kept flashing to the memory of Matt in bed moving over her, his voice a sexy, erotic whisper in her ear, their bodies slick with sweat, their limbs entangled. Every time she replayed it, she felt a tingle in spots that had no business tingling while she was serving customers.

It'd been so long since she'd been with someone. That's what she told herself. Years long, in fact, since an ugly night in Miami years ago now, when she'd landed into yet another rough situation that she almost hadn't gotten out of. Just another case of a guy wanting more than she wanted to give. She'd forgone sex completely after that.

But it had been different with Matt, so different than anything she'd ever shared before. Sex with him had meant intimacy, and she hadn't been prepared.

Not even close.

To take her mind off Matt, she used her break to hole herself up in the tiny back office of the diner and pull out her cell phone. She wanted to plan the last leg of her grandma's journey, but she was at a bit of a loss.

Call me again sometime, and you can ask me another question. I'll answer a question with each call. How's that sound?

Her mom's words were echoing in her head. They'd had such a tempestuous relationship, always, from the day Amy had gone to live with her at age twelve, to the day Amy had walked away at age sixteen. But hindsight was twenty-twenty, and Amy could admit that she wasn't blameless, that she'd had a big hand in how things went down. Facts were facts, and Amy had been a liar. A petty thief. A girl who'd wielded her burgeoning sexuality like a magic wand.

A nightmare.

And she'd walked away without looking back, without even considering how her mom might feel. Not caring...

Amy let out a shaky breath and hit her mom's number. The phone was answered quickly, with a breathless, "Amy?"

"Yeah, Mom. It's me."

There was a silence, and Amy grimaced, feeling unwanted and stupid. And God how she really *hated* feeling stupid. She shouldn't have done this; she shouldn't have—

"I'm glad you called."

Amy sucked in another breath. "You are?"

"You surprised me last time. I didn't get a chance to ask you if you're okay."

Amy's chest physically hurt. She didn't do this, this emotional stuff. And yet it seemed like lately that was all she was doing. "I'm okay. You?"

"Good. I'm...single again. I just wanted you to know that."

Probably the closest thing to an apology she was going to get.

"You still in Lucky Harbor?" her mom asked. "Do you have a place? An address?"

"Yeah." Amy cleared her throat and gave her the apartment address. "You said I could ask you a question."

"Yes."

Amy drew a deep breath. "Do you know where Grandma Rose ended her journey exactly?"

"I'm sorry," her mom said with real regret. "I don't. All she ever told me was that in the end, she went full circle."

Full circle. Same thing the journal had said. Disappointment clogged Amy's throat, thick and unswallowable. "Oh. Okay, well, thanks. I've got to get back to work."

"Will you call again?"

Amy closed her eyes. It'd been a long time since she'd ached for someone's approval. A damn long time. Since her Grandma Rose's death probably. Amy had told herself a million times that she'd outgrown needing acceptance. Would she call again? Honestly, in that moment, she had no idea. "I have your number," she said carefully.

"Okay."

"And Mom?"

"Yes?"

"You have my number now, too."

At the end of her shift, Amy gathered the trash and left out the back door. She dropped it in the Dumpster on her way to her car and nearly tripped over Riley in the alley. "Hey," Amy said, surprised. "What are you doing?"

But the answer was clear. It'd been pouring steadily, relentlessly, all afternoon, and Riley had been rained out of wherever she'd been staying in the woods. She was wet through and through, huddled up against the wall on the stoop. "You okay?" Amy asked.

Looking miserable, Riley nodded.

"Come on, I'll give you a ride."

Riley didn't ask where, or even bother to argue, which told Amy exactly how wet and cold the teen was. Once they were inside Amy's piece-of-shit car, Riley sidled up against the heating vents, rubbing her arms over the long-sleeved tee that Amy had given her. "You know, if you'd stayed at my place, you'd be warm and dry right now."

"Didn't know how long I could stay."

Amy's heart squeezed. "How about until something better comes along?"

Riley was huddled into herself, shivering, and didn't answer. Amy understood that, too. When Amy had been that age, nothing better *ever* came along. Amy pulled out of the diner parking lot and drove home. They climbed the stairs in silence, and inside she nudged Riley toward the bathroom for a hot shower. By the time the water turned off, Amy had pulled out another spare outfit from her own meager stash for Riley.

They ate grilled cheese sandwiches at the small kitchen table—Amy's go-to comfort food. Riley inhaled every last crumb. "Thanks," she said when they were done. She was looking a whole lot less like a drowned rat now. Her hair was drying in soft, natural curls, and with her face clean, Amy realized just how pretty she was. "Got a call about you the other day," she said. "A hang-up, actually." She told Riley about the phantom phone call she'd received at the diner.

Riley didn't say a word but went pale.

Amy frowned at her. "What is it? You know who called?"

Riley shrugged.

"You want to talk about it?"

"No."

Well there was a surprise. "You know you don't have to live like this, on the run, right?" Amy asked. "You could get some help, make some roots. Stick around."

"I don't have any money."

"So get a job."

"I'm not good at anything."

"Well, that's not true. For instance," Amy said, "you're a great conversationalist. And such a sweet, sunny, friendly nature, too."

Riley had the good grace to grimace at the gentle teasing.

"Look," Amy said, "you could bus tables at the diner. You won't get rich or anything, but you could support yourself. There's a lot of freedom in that, Riley."

Riley remained quiet while staring at her empty plate.

"And as a bonus, you could eliminate the sitting in the rain bit entirely, fun as that probably was. And with all your spare time, you could get good at whatever you want to be good at. You could go to school, or whatever you want."

Riley looked at her. "What are you good at?"

"Drawing."

"I suck at drawing."

"So you'll find something you don't suck at," Amy said. "Something for you. It's all about choices and decisions."

"I usually choose to make really bad decisions."

Amy laughed softly in sympathy. "I hear you. I happened to major in bad decisions myself. But I'm working on it. Part of that comes from stopping the cycle, getting some good sleep and decent food in your system so you're not reacting off the cuff. Stay here tonight."

Riley shrugged.

"Yes or no."

Riley looked out the window, where the rain was still pouring down. She sighed. "Yes."

"Now see? There's a good decision."

The next day, Matt was hanging off the North Rim, forty feet above ground, holding onto the granite with only his fingers and toes.

Josh was at his right and a foot or so below him.

It was a race to the top, with the loser buying dinner. Josh had bought the past four meals in a row, which he'd bitched about like a little girl, claiming that the finishes had been far too close to call.

Bullshit. Matt had won fair and square, though granted he'd only done so by an inch or two. But a win was a win.

"Move your lady-like fingers," Josh groused when

Matt reached out far to his right for a good finger-hold. "You're in my way."

Matt didn't move. The sun was beating down on his back, and he felt sweat drip down the side of his jaw. "Hey, Josh?"

"Yeah?"

"Which lady-like finger am I holding up now?"

Josh took in Matt's flipping him the bird and *tsk*ed. "Rude."

"You want rude? I'm having everything on the menu at Eat Me tonight, on *your* dime."

"Fuck you," Josh said. "I'm not buying you everything on the menu."

"Is that what you say to the ladies?"

"The *ladies*," Josh said with a grunt as he pulled himself up another few feet, "can have anything they want."

Matt eyeballed the ledge above him and tried to figure out the best way to get there. "Fine. If you don't want to buy dinner, you're going to have to beat me to the top."

Apparently getting a second wind at the thought, Josh pulled himself up another few feet. This put him in the lead. Matt wasn't too worried. There were still a few feet to go, and Josh was breathing hard. "You're sucking some serious wind, Doc. You need to get in the ring before you go soft like...like a doctor."

Josh snorted. There wasn't an ounce of fat on his large six-foot-four-inch frame, and they both knew it. People teased him that he was like a bull in a china shop, but the truth was, Dr. Josh Scott was so highly regarded as a doctor that he had to turn patients away.

And for all his big talk, Josh turned away the women, too.

"When's the last time you even got any?" Matt asked.

Josh slid him a look behind his dark sunglasses. "You want to swap stories?"

"Do you even have a story to swap?"

Josh let out what might have been a sigh. "Been busy."

"No one should be that busy, man."

"My practice is swamped. And Anna's been acting up. And Toby . . . he needs me at home."

Josh had sole custody of his five-year-old son, Toby. He'd also taken in his younger sister after their parents died six years ago. Anna was twenty-one now and hell on wheels, literally, having ended up in a wheelchair from the same car accident that had killed their parents. She'd spent her teen years dedicated to making Josh insane, and she'd nearly succeeded, too. It'd be a lot for any guy to handle, but with Josh's job, it'd been nearly impossible.

"So you and Amy finally did it, huh?" Josh said.

Matt nearly fell off the face of the mountain. "Who told you that?" he demanded, once he'd recovered his hold and had secured himself so that his own death wasn't imminent.

Josh dipped his head to eye Matt over the top of his sunglasses, mouth curving. "You. Just now."

"Shit." He had nothing else to say. Mostly because he didn't *know* what else to say. What'd happened between him and Amy had been . . . hot as hell. But it was also still bugging him, how much she'd hidden behind the act itself. How much she hid in general.

Pot, kettle. He knew this. He hated this. He'd called her earlier to check on her, just to see if she was okay. According to her, she'd been fine. She'd also steered clear of a real conversation, other than to tell him that Riley was back and staying with her.

"So you and Amy, huh? Funny."

"How's that funny?"

Josh shrugged. "She always acts like she hates you."

"Turns out there's a fine line between hate and lust," Matt muttered.

Josh slid him another look. "You've wanted her forever. You should be grinning like an idiot. It wasn't good?"

He'd done his share of grinning like an idiot. And it'd been good. Hell, if it'd been any better, they'd have gone up in flames. But—

"*Yes!*" Josh yelled in triumph, because while Matt had been thinking too much, Josh had used his gorilla arms to reach the ledge. With a whoop, Josh collapsed on the plateau like a limp noodle, lying there gasping. "I *finally* beat you."

Matt rolled over the ledge. "Fluke. Just a one-time fluke."

Josh came up on an elbow, sweaty and dirty and grinning. "*Everything* on the menu. I want everything on the menu."

"Fuck." Matt stared up at the sky, also gasping for breath. "Fine. But I'm not putting out afterward."

Amy would have liked to be studying a map and planning her next leg of Grandma Rose's journey. But nope. She was working. She was *always* working, it seemed.

And as a bonus, it was raining again. Or still. But Jan had put out a buy-one-entree-get-one-free Facebook post, and now, for the dinner rush, Eat Me was packed. The crowd was rowdy, but Amy had learned she could serve and daydream at the same time.

The call to her mom hadn't yielded much help, and Amy still had no idea what the third and last leg of Rose's trip had been. All she knew was that Rose had found her heart. Giving up a bathroom break, Amy pulled her grandma's journal from her purse, and in a back corner of the kitchen, flipped through it.

It's been three weeks since we'd last been on the mountain. A long three weeks during which I refused to give up my newfound hope and peace.

Good thing, too, because I needed both of those things to get all the way around and back.

But I managed.

And it was worth it. Looking out at a blanket of green, a sea of blue, and a world of possibilities, the whole world opened up. There on top of the world, I promised myself that no matter what happened, I would never settle. I would never stop growing. I would never give up.

And as the sun sank down over the horizon, I was suddenly at the beginning again.

Hope.

Peace.

And something new as well, something that had truly brought us full circle—heart.

All the way around and back . . . Not much in the way of directions, Amy thought. But she was beginning to wonder if maybe her grandma might have meant that they'd taken the Rim Trail all the way around from the north rim to the south rim. It was a good possibility, or at least the best one she had.

"Amy!" Jan yelled. "Another call for you!"

Amy put the journal away. This time when she picked up the kitchen phone and said "hello," there was a pause but not a hang-up. "*Hello?*" she repeated.

The voice was raspy and male. "Tell Riley that she can run, but she can't hide."

Adrenaline kicked in. "Who is this?"

Nothing.

"*Hello?*" Amy said. "Don't hang up—"

Click.

And then a dial tone.

Dammit. Amy served the food waiting for her and waved at Jan. "Taking five."

"The hell you are."

"Okay, two then." Without waiting for approval that she wasn't going to get, Amy grabbed the new backpack that she'd bought at the hardware store half a block down the street, then stepped out the back door on a hunch.

The hunch paid off.

Riley was sitting on the stoop, under the protection of the overhang, watching the rain come down. Amy sat next to her and set the backpack in the teen's lap.

"What's this?" Riley asked.

"Yours is all ripped up."

Riley ran her fingers over the tags still attached to the pack. "So you bought me a new one?"

"Yeah."

Riley started to shake her head and push the backpack away, but Amy put her hand on it, holding it in Riley's lap. "It was on sale, and Anderson—the shop owner—gave me a big discount, so it's no big deal. I want you to have it."

Riley stared down at the backpack and then unzipped it. Inside were the incidentals Amy had put in there: flashlight, water bottle, beef jerky...

Riley swallowed hard and said nothing.

Amy looked at her for a long moment, not sure how to proceed. When she'd been in Riley's situation, showing emotion had been the same as showing weakness, and there'd been no room for weakness and vulnerability in her life. None. Even if a person had meant well, Amy hadn't been able to let her guard down to show any vulnerability.

Riley couldn't either.

Amy got that, but damn, it was hard to watch, wanting so badly to reach out and help, knowing that Riley wouldn't easily let herself be helped. "There's a set of spare batteries in the inside pocket. Being unprepared sucks beans, and trust me, I know it all too well."

"You didn't have to do this."

"I know." Amy looked at her. "And you could have come inside. I've been hoping you'd show up. I've got a fully loaded club sandwich, fries, and a big fat glass of soda with your name on it."

Riley stared at her, clearly at war between her pride and her need for sustenance. "How did you know I'd be out here?"

"Guessed." Amy didn't have the heart to tell Riley that kids like her were creatures of hard-learned habits. Along with Amy's apartment, Riley had been fed here and taken care of here at the diner. Sheer need would drive her back to the same few places over and over until that changed. "Come on." Amy stood and gestured with a jerk of her chin to the back door. "I've got to get back in there before Jan blows a gasket. Believe me, no one wants to see that."

Amy sat Riley at the front counter and served her a big plate of food. Lucille and her cronies were at a table close by, cackling it up over something one of them had on her smartphone. Josh and Matt came in the front door. Both were wearing climbing clothes and looking like extremely fine male specimens. As they walked through the diner, every female in the place watched. Lucille even snapped a picture on her iPhone, which Amy figured would be on Facebook before she could serve their drinks.

Not that she was immune to the men, or their allure. Josh always looked good, and this evening, even dusty and slightly sweaty, he looked like he could walk right onto the cover of *Outside* magazine.

But Amy's eyes were on Matt. Because if Josh looked good, Matt looked amazing, and *way* too sexy.

Why was he still so sexy to her?

He pushed his dark sunglasses to the top of his head and searched her out. There was no other word for it. His eyes roamed over the diner until he found her. He looked her over, making her every nerve ending tingle with awareness, though his gaze was more inquisitive than sexual, as if making sure she was okay, though she had no idea why she wouldn't be.

Then he smiled, and oh, how her misbehaving nipples loved that predatory smile. If his intense, concerned once-over had done things to her, his smile just about undid her from the inside out.

Then she realized Lucille had left her table and was talking to Riley, though the teen was backing away, shaking her head adamantly. Amy moved close enough in time to hear Lucille say "all the newcomers do it, honey. And putting you up on Facebook will help you make friends."

Riley looked horrified and not a little panic-stricken. Amy stepped between Lucille and the escaping Riley. "No Facebook pictures of her."

"She says she's eighteen," Lucille said. "And she looks lonely. I thought I could help—"

"You can help by *not* putting any information about her on Facebook at all," Amy said firmly.

At Amy's serious tone, Lucille went quiet for a moment, studying Riley's sullen face. "I understand," Lucille finally said, quite gently. "If you need anything…"

"I'm fine," Riley said, and turned and fled for the door. Amy headed after her. "Riley—Hey, wait up."

"Thanks for the food, but I've got to go."

"Just a second." She grabbed Riley's wrist. "I wanted to tell you—that guy called here again."

Riley went still for a beat and then turned abruptly toward the door again, moving much faster now.

Amy followed her outside and stood still on the top step for a beat while her eyes adjusted from the bright diner to the dark, moonless night. "Riley?"

Footsteps. Amy ran after them, barely catching up with Riley just as she was leaving the lot. Backpack slung over her shoulder, she was on the street, thumb out.

"No way," Amy said. "No way am I letting you hitchhike."

"This is Lucky Harbor, right? Nothing bad ever happens in Lucky Harbor."

Amy shook her head. "Something bad is happening to you, and if you'd just tell me about it, I could help."

Riley turned away and waggled her thumb at the cars going by.

"Dammit, Riley. Don't do this."

"Sorry, but I can do whatever I want."

"Where are you going?" Amy asked. "Tell me that much, at least."

Riley waggled her thumb at a passing truck, which slowed.

Crap. Jan was going to kill Amy for walking out on a full diner, but Amy couldn't let Riley go, not like this. "Stay at my place again tonight," she said quickly, watching the truck's blinker come on.

Riley shook her head. Some of her color had come back but not much. She was clearly freaked out, and it didn't take a genius to figure out it had been the phone call. "It's time for me to move on."

She was going to leave Lucky Harbor. Afraid Riley would get into the truck and never be seen again, Amy shook her head. "No. Please stay."

The truck had pulled over, and the driver honked. Riley would have jumped right into it, but Amy grabbed her. "You don't have to do this, you know you don't. Stay. You've got a job here if you want it, and people who care."

The truck driver honked again, and Amy flipped him off. The driver rolled down his window and blasted them with a litany of foul oaths before hitting the gas, choking them with dust.

Riley looked impressed. "Wow, you flipped that guy off."

"*Stay.*"

Riley shook her head, baffled. "Why do you even care?"

Because once upon a time Amy had been in trouble, and there'd been *no one* to care. Because she recognized the helplessness in Riley's eyes. "Maybe I need to see something good happen to someone like us. Stay, Riley. Stay and say you'll think about the job."

Riley stared at her for a long beat. "I'll think about the job."

Relief filled Amy, and she relaxed a margin. "Come on. You can come back inside and wait for me to get off work."

The teen paused and then shook her head. "I still can't stay with you."

"Why?"

Riley's mouth tightened. Clearly, she had her reasons, good reasons, and just as clearly she wasn't going to say what those reasons were. Amy had a terrible suspicion that Riley was in some way trying to protect Amy by not staying—which didn't make her feel any better. "Where will you sleep?"

Riley hesitated.

"Riley."

"You have to promise not to tell."

Oh, boy. Nothing good ever started with that sentence. How could she make such a serious promise like that when Matt would want to know what was going on? "Listen—"

"*Promise.*"

Riley's desperation was palpable, and Amy looked into her eyes and saw fear mixed in with a desperate need to believe in *someone*. Damn. That someone was going to be her. "I promise," Amy said softly. "Riley, I promise you."

"Not a single soul."

Oh, how she hated to make such a promise, especially

one she was already regretting, but the look on Riley's face made her do it. "Not a single soul. I promise."

And still Riley hesitated. "I'm going back to the forest."

"Riley." Amy shook her head. "You know Matt asked you not to camp illegally."

"He won't know."

"He'll ask," Amy said.

"Then tell him I'm still with you."

Oh, no. That was a very bad idea. "Riley—"

"You *promised.*"

Behind them, the door to the diner opened, and the man himself stepped out. How did he do that? Did he sense when she was thinking about him? Amy met his gaze and then turned back to Riley to tell her that they really needed another plan. But Riley was gone.

Matt strode across the lot. Amy had no idea what was on his mind, though she knew what was on hers. Worry for Riley. Anxiety that she'd just agreed to lie to the one man who'd made her feel something since... well, ever. And as always, that conflicting sense of free falling and yet being safe, simply because he was near.

"You okay?" he asked.

She nodded.

"And Riley?"

She nodded again and hoped that covered everything he wanted to know. But she should have known better. Matt wasn't the sort of man she could brush off or fool with a smile. He might be laid-back and easygoing, but he was sharp as a tack.

"Problem?" he asked.

She shook her head no while thinking *yes.* Big

problem. Many problems. There was a secret between them, something that wouldn't have bothered her in the past but was bothering her greatly now. She had no idea what she was doing with him, but the anxiety ratcheted up a notch now. "I'm just really bad with morning-after discussions," she said. "Even though technically, this is an afternoon after. Or evening after. Or—"

"Maybe you'd be less bad at them if you didn't run off."

Yeah, maybe. Probably. But running off was what she did.

"Okay," he said with a shake of his head, as if he wasn't sure how they'd gotten on this track. "Let's start this conversation over. You really okay? And I mean that as a general how-are-you question."

"Yes," she said. "I'm really okay. You?"

"Better than okay."

She rolled her eyes, but felt a smile threaten. How he did that, coaxed the fun out of her when she'd been fresh out of fun, was a big mystery.

He nudged his chin toward where Riley had vanished. "Tell me about Riley."

Well if that didn't wipe her smile right off. He thought Riley was staying with her, and he thought that because she'd told him so. By not correcting that assumption and telling him that Riley now would be back in the woods was as good as lying to him.

But she'd promised. She'd promised a teen who desperately needed to be able to trust. "Nothing to tell, really. I was feeding her."

Matt studied her for a long moment, eyes sharp and assessing. She could feel the heat of his body, the easy strength of him, and felt the utterly inexplicable urge to reach for him. It confused her. She'd spent most of her teens and early twenties doing her best to ruin her own life. This had involved some pretty stupid and massively unsafe things, like hitchhiking across the country, accepting rides and places to stay with no concern for her own safety.

Not having family to call had only increased the sense of walking on a tightrope.

She'd gotten good at it.

She'd also gotten good at self-preservation. She'd managed to survive in spite of herself, and yet here she was at the ripe old age of twenty-eight, and all she wanted to do was turn and burrow her face in Matt's chest and let him be the strong one.

He'd do it, too. If she made the first move, he'd absolutely wrap her in his arms and hold her close. He'd murmur something in that low, calming voice, something she might not even catch, but it wouldn't matter. She'd know everything was going to be okay.

He'd given her that, a sense of security, and it terrified her.

Reaching for her hand, he turned her to face him. "Amy."

With a sigh, she let him tug her in against him, and when he kissed her, his mouth was warm and knowing, tasting both familiar and right. It was like coming home. That was her only excuse for letting him deepen the kiss, for wrapping her arms around his neck and kissing him back until she had no air left. Finally she broke it off because this wasn't like last time, when he'd been just getting off work and they could race to his house to get naked like two horny idiots. She had a long shift ahead of her. "I have to get back inside before Jan kills me," she whispered against his mouth.

He let her unravel from him, but when she would have walked away, he tightened his grip on her hand. "Amy."

"Yeah?"

His gaze held hers, and she did her best to keep her thoughts to herself.

"You'd tell me if there was trouble," he said.

Some of her glow diminished. "What kind of trouble?" she asked cautiously.

"*Any* kind of trouble."

Maybe she wasn't quite as good at lying as she thought. "I can take care of myself. You know that, right?"

"That's the thing, Amy. You don't have to. You have connections here. Friends. People who care. *I* care."

Hadn't she just had this conversation in reverse with Riley? And now Matt was the one trying to be there, for Amy. Hell if that didn't put a lump in her throat, which she ruthlessly swallowed. "There's no trouble." *Please don't ask me to promise.*

He didn't. Without another word, he nodded and let go of her hand, and without much of a choice, she went back inside the diner.

Chapter 12

♥

God gave the angels wings and the
humans chocolate.

Two days later, Matt found Amy at the ranger station, studying the big board of trails. She was wearing her hip-hugging skinny jeans tucked into her kick-ass boots and a snug, thin tee with some Chinese symbols on it that he figured he didn't want to know the meaning of. She was concentrating on the board, brow furrowed, lips moving as she read the names of the trails. Just the sight of her made him both smile and ache.

"Where to?" he asked.

She didn't take her attention off the board. "I'm thinking of walking from the north rim to the south rim."

"For... your heart?"

"For my *grandma's* heart."

He nodded agreeably. "You're going to want to take the eastern trail to the top," he said, nursing the Dr. Pepper he'd picked up at the convenience store on his way in. "It's the longest, but it's the only easy-to-moderate way to the top. There's a loop but don't take it. Come back the same way."

She turned her head and looked at him, and he felt the same punch to the gut that he always felt when they were this close. He wanted to think she felt it too but it was hard to tell. She was damn good at keeping her thoughts inside. "You planning on overnighting again?"

Her mouth curved slightly. "No. I don't think over-nighting in the wilds is for me."

He begged to disagree. He could remember, vividly, how she'd looked in his sweatshirt, in his sleeping bag, in his tent. *Hot.* "Then you want to make sure you turn around by three or four to get back before dark."

She saluted him, the smart-ass, and made him smile. "We could meet up after," he said.

Again, her brow furrowed. "For?"

"To go out."

"Out," she repeated, like the word didn't compute.

"On a date," he clarified.

"A *date*?"

"Yeah," he said, laughing ruefully at himself. At her. "Unless you're allergic to dates. Then we could call it something else."

She opened her mouth, then hesitated.

He cocked his head. "You're afraid to see what happens next."

"There aren't plans for what happens next, remember? *No* getting attached."

"Plans change."

She stared at him as if he wasn't speaking her language. "Why? Why would you want to go out with me? I'm grumpy, and irritable, and frankly, not all that nice a person."

"I'll give you the grumpy," he said. "But you're off on the nice thing. You're a better person than you give yourself credit for, Amy."

She was staring at him suspiciously, like maybe he had an ulterior motive for buttering her up. "Not reason enough to want to go out," she said. "Why, Matt?"

The easy answer was because he wanted her again. That was also the hard answer. "Because I feel good when I'm with you," he said simply.

She let out a breath. "Matt, I—"

"No. Don't say you can't, because I know you're not working tonight. And don't say you don't want to, because there were two of us in my bed the other night. I know what you felt, Amy. I saw it."

She just kept looking at him like he'd lost his mind. And hell, maybe he had.

"You're a hard guy to say no to," she finally said.

"So don't say it. Say yes."

She shook her head, clearly thinking this was a bad idea, but then gave him the word he'd wanted. "Yes."

For Amy, the Rim Trail was much more "moderate" than "easy." But at least it was clearly marked and easy to follow, even if it was a straight-up climb of 2,500 vertical feet.

She'd gotten lucky finding the first two legs of her grandma's journey. She was worried about this last leg.

In the end, she'd gone full circle. That's what the journal had said.

Amy sighed. She could only hope that when it came to the end, she'd figure it out.

Halfway, she took a break at a natural plateau, behind a sheer rock face that was staggering. In front of her was

a narrow creek running from pure snow melt. And far
below, she could see the Pacific Ocean churning under a
sky dotted with white puffy clouds. It looked so perfect
and beautiful that it could have been a painting.

Needing to catch her breath, she sat with the creek at
her feet and pulled out her sketch pad, wanting to draw
this place, wondering, hoping, her grandma and Jonathon had sat somewhere nearby enjoying the view, three
decades earlier.

It took an hour to sketch in the basics enough that
she could finish it up later. As she'd been doing for some
time now, she thought about Riley, and hoped the girl was
okay. Amy wasn't used to worrying about others, but she
worried about Riley, big time.

Hungry, she grabbed the lunch she'd packed and ate
the brownie first. Heaven, but even soft, gooey chocolate
couldn't keep her brain from going back to her shocking
problem.

She was going out with Matt tonight.

A date.

She went for her sandwich next and pulled out her
phone to call Mallory, who didn't pick up. Probably
working a shift at the ER or the health services clinic.
She tried Grace next and got lucky. "I have a problem."

"Oh, thank God," Grace said with feeling. "I've filled
out fifty job apps, and no one's hiring. No one wants me
except you. I need to feel useful. Tell me your problem.
Tell me *all* your problems. Need a good girl lesson? What
number are we up to now, seven? *Always be available
when your friend is feeling like a loser.*"

"I'm available," Amy promised. "And I've told you,
if you're desperate enough, we need a bus person at the

diner. I offered the job to Riley but I don't think she's going to take it."

"Nothing personal, but I'd rather take a shift running the Ferris Wheel at the pier than work for Jan. If I worked for Jan, I might have to do something drastic."

"Like kill yourself?"

"Like kill *Jan*," Grace said. "Now talk to me."

"I'm going out tonight."

"Out?"

Amy sighed. "On a date."

There was a complete beat of silence. "Hang on," Grace said, and there was a click.

Two minutes later, Grace was back. "Okay," she said. "I've got Mallory on the line too. I wasn't qualified to handle this problem alone."

"Hey," Mallory said, sounding breathless. "You just caught me. I'm on break. It's going to be a full moon tonight, and we've already had two women in premature labor and a fight victim from the arcade. Better make this quick. What's the emergency?"

"No emergency," Amy said. "I just—"

"It's a *complete* emergency," Grace interrupted. "Amy has a date with Ranger Hot Buns."

Mallory squealed with delight so loudly that Amy had to pull the phone away from her ear. "Jeez!" Amy said. "Warn a girl. And how did you know it would be with Matt?" she asked Grace. "I hadn't said."

Grace laughed. So did Mallory.

"What?"

"Well who else could it be?" Mallory asked. "Matt's the only guy you've ever looked at twice. And good Lord, the way he looks at you is contributing to global warming."

Amy flashed to the look on Matt's face when he'd been buried deep inside her and felt herself go damp. Yeah, the way he looked at her was pretty boggling. The way he did *everything* was boggling, especially the naked stuff. He was *exceptional* at the naked stuff, knowing when to be sweet and coaxing, knowing when to *not* be either of those things. And the things he'd whispered in her ear…He'd given her everything he had, until he'd been taut and quivering with his own need.

Damn. She wanted him again.

"So where's he taking you on this date?" Mallory asked.

"And what are you wearing on this date?" Grace wanted to know.

"Okay, why do we have to keep saying *date*?" Amy asked. "I mean you eat, you talk, you get naked…we don't have to *label* it."

"It's supposed to be labeled," Mallory said calmly, the voice of reason. "It's supposed to be a lovely time."

Amy rolled her eyes.

"I heard that," Mallory said. "Now tell me what's the problem with a gorgeous guy, a really *good* gorgeous guy, taking you out and calling it a date? He's got a job, a home, and the best abs I've ever seen. Besides, he's already charmed you out of your pants, right?"

"Okay," Amy said to Grace's unladylike snort. "First of all, the *only* reason I took off my pants was because I had a cut on my thigh."

"That wouldn't be my first guess," Grace said.

"And second of all," Amy went on as if Grace hadn't spoken, "it wasn't a big deal! I was on a hike, and I got lost and—"

"—And he rescued you," Mallory pointed out. "Another check in the pro column. The man is hot *and* he rescues fair maidens in distress."

"I wasn't in distress! I called *you* first, and you—"

"—Wouldn't have charmed you out of your pants," Mallory said.

Grace burst out laughing.

Amy thunked her head against her knees. "You aren't listening."

"Then say it again in English this time," Mallory said.

"Fine," Amy blew out a breath. "I've never been on a real date."

Utter silence. Amy checked the phone screen to see if she still had reception. "Hello? You guys still there?"

"How old are you?" Grace asked, sounding confused.

"Twenty-eight."

"And you're still a virgin?"

"I didn't say *that*," Amy said with a laugh. "And no, I'm not." She was just about as far from a virgin as one could get. "Look, it's not a big deal. I left home when I was sixteen, and after that, it was more about survival than dating." She'd done what she'd had to, and sometimes that had involved being with a guy because he had a place to stay or food—neither of which meant a "date" in any sense of the word.

"And then somehow I just never got to a place where dating was really an option," she said, staring at the creek at her feet. A butterfly had landed on the water and was floundering, trying not to drown. Amy knew the feeling. Leaning forward, she tried to rescue the thing but it was swept away in the current. She knew that feeling, too. "Listen, I've got to go so I don't get stuck up here again."

"No, wait," Mallory said. "Please wait. I'm sorry we laughed at you. I think it's lovely that Matt asked you out."

Amy sighed. Mallory was sounding like maybe she was feeling very emotional—which didn't really count because lots of things made Mallory emotional. Like the sun rising and setting. Last time they'd watched TV together, Mallory had sobbed openly at one of those save the puppy SPCA commercials.

"You should go with him, Amy," Mallory said. "Do the eat and talk thing. But not the naked thing, not yet."

Amy winced, keeping to herself the fact that she'd already done the naked thing.

"Just enjoy your first date," Mallory said. "And FYI, I have a good girl lesson for you. This one is serious, Amy. *Really* serious."

"I don't need—"

"You deserve good things," Mallory said anyway. "You deserve good people in your life, and Matt is both good *and* good people."

Dammit. Amy's throat felt tight, and there was no SPCA commercial in sight. "How can a man be both an adjective and a noun?"

"Trust me," Mallory said. "Ty's both. And so is Matt."

"I agree with Mallory," Grace said. "You should definitely go tonight with Matt. But I say *do* the naked thing."

"*Grace*," Mallory admonished.

"Hello," Grace said. "This is Matt Bowers we're talking about. You've seen him. Gorgeous, built, sexy-eyed Matt. And he wears a uniform. With a gun…" She sighed dreamily. "I'm sorry, but Amy has a duty to get naked with a guy like that and report back. With details."

Amy disconnected and resumed her hike. Grace was right, Matt *was* gorgeous and built, in just about every way a man could be, but she'd gotten him out of her system. There'd be no more getting naked.

At three o'clock, she stood at the top of a cliff looking down on the four small lakes she'd been at the other day. *Way* down. She could see a few otters playing along the shore of the first lake, and as she stood there in awe, a fish leapt out of the water, executing a perfect gainer before flopping back.

Her legs were wobbling from the climb. Or maybe it was from looking down from the dizzying height, but in either case, she could hear her grandma's voice in her head.

It felt like a promise. I had my hope, but now I had something else, too, peace. Four Lakes gave me peace.

Amy closed her eyes and inhaled deeply, then opened them again, feeling them burn with emotion. Jesus, what was with her today? But there was no denying the truth. She'd been feeling flickers of hope ever since Sierra Meadows. It was new and tenuous, but it was there. As for peace, she hadn't been quite sure. When she thought about her life, she knew she'd always lived it to survive. But she was beginning to see that there was more to life than mere survival, so much more. And maybe that was peace right there, just learning that.

Which left heart, something she'd never believed in for herself and had, in fact, openly mocked.

But she didn't feel like mocking it now, and she had no idea if maybe that was thanks to Lucky Harbor, to the friends she'd made here, or...a certain forest ranger that was filling up something deep inside her that she hadn't even known was empty.

• • •

Matt knocked at Amy's door. He was early for their date because...well, he didn't really have a reason, other than he wanted to see her. He had no idea what the night would bring, but if it went anything at all like their other encounters, it wouldn't be boring.

Her car was in her parking spot but she didn't answer. He knocked again, and then when she still didn't answer, he tried the door. It opened, which didn't make him feel better—Amy wasn't a woman to leave her door unlocked. "Amy?"

Nothing, so he stepped inside. "Hello?"

Still nothing.

Her place was small enough that he could see from one end to the next. Her bedroom door was open, and he stepped closer. It looked like a bomb had gone off. A female bomb. Clothes spilled out of the dresser drawers and closet and were scattered across the bed, but no one was actually *in* any of the clothes.

The bathroom was damp and misty, as if she'd recently showered. There were girlie things on the counter, tubes and bottles, and the place smelled like sexy woman. A pair of black lace panties and matching bra lay on the floor. Nice. He turned back to the living room.

There was a small slider leading to a tiny deck area, and it was cracked open. He pushed it further. The thing squeaked like hell and was all but impossible to move, and yet the woman sitting with her back to him didn't budge.

This was because she had in earphones that led to the phone or iPod in her pocket and she was singing.

Off-key.

She was drawing, too, sketching something from

memory, as she hunched over her pad, a pencil in hand moving furiously over the paper, a bundle of additional colored pencils in her other hand.

He listened to her sing for a second and felt the grin split his face. Guns N' Roses, "Welcome to the Jungle." He cleared his throat, but she kept singing. *"Welcome to the jungle, feel my, my, serpentine, I, I wanna hear you scream..."*

Still grinning, Matt reached out and set a hand on her shoulder. Amy nearly came out of her skin. Her pad and pencils went flying, and whipping out the ear buds, she whirled around, leading with a roundhouse kick that would have leveled him flat if he hadn't ducked.

"Are you crazy?" she asked when he straightened. "I nearly took off your head."

"You had your music up and didn't hear me." He bent to pick up her pad and pencils, which she snatched out of his hands and hugged to her chest. She was staring at him, breathing fast. Too fast. She wore a strapless sundress with a colorful print that was sexy as hell. She wasn't in her usual kick-ass boots, but the heels in their place were still pretty damn kick-ass. If she'd connected with his head, he'd still be down for the count. "You're not wearing black."

She shifted, then shrugged. "It's Mallory's."

"You look beautiful," he said.

She wasn't impressed by the compliment. "You just let yourself into my place?"

"You didn't answer my knock. I thought something was wrong."

"Well it's not," she said. "And I don't like surprises."

"I'm sorry." He rubbed his jaw and considered her. "I scared you."

"I told you. I told you I don't like it when someone sneaks up on me."

She *had* told him that, last week on the trail, and his gut clenched hard over how she might have learned she didn't like to be surprised. Slowly he stepped closer, taking her iPod, setting it down on the chair she'd just vacated. Then he took her pad and pencils and did the same. "Breathe," he said softly, gently running his hands up her arms and then down.

She exhaled a shuddery breath.

He inhaled slowly and deeply, and she did the same, and this time when she exhaled, she relaxed marginally. "Sorry," she said. "Didn't mean to take your head off. I left my door unlocked for Riley and forgot."

"No apologies necessary."

She tipped her head up and looked at him. "You're being sweet."

"I'm not feeling sweet." Not even close. His hands dropped to her hips. The material of her skirt was silky smooth and thin. He could feel the warmth of her right through it. She smelled so good he couldn't stop himself from lowering his head and pressing his face to her neck.

She slapped a hand to his chest and leaned back. "Are you smelling me?"

"Yeah." He did it again, an exaggerated inhale that made her laugh. "You smell amazing," he said. "Reminds me of how amazing you taste."

She sucked in a breath and moved against him, just a little rock of her hot bod that finished off the job that the panties on the bathroom floor had started. His lips were at her throat. He sucked on her skin, and the sound she made, the soft, feminine sound of arousal, nearly did him in.

The next sound that she made came from her stomach as it rumbled. Laughing softly, he pulled back. "Time to go."

"Where?"

"Food. Wine. Maybe music." Taking her hand, he pulled her through her place. "Whatever you want."

"We were already doing what I wanted."

He stopped and glanced back at her with a smile. "Yeah?"

"Yeah."

His body revved. *Down, boy.* "I like that idea," he told her. "I like it a lot. *After* I take you out."

"You don't have to."

Okay, he was missing something here, and he stopped, dipping down a little to look into her eyes. "Did you change your mind?"

"No." She shifted and looked away. "I'm just saying, I don't need the pomp and circumstance before we…"

"Duly noted," he said slowly. Yeah, definitely missing something. Which meant they were in trouble because she clearly wasn't going to spell out the problem and he was clueless. "Maybe *I* need the pomp and circumstance."

She eyed him with a narrowed gaze. "*You* need to be romanced?"

"You think that's stupid?"

"No." But contradicting that, she laughed, then slapped her hand over her mouth and shook her head, eyes sparkling. "Really, I don't."

"Look at you, lying through your teeth…" Tugging her in, he kissed her, then let their gazes hold. "Such a beautiful liar."

Something flickered in her gaze, and he wondered. Guilt? Regret? But not wanting to ruin the night ahead, he shrugged it off and took her hand, leading her outside.

Chapter 13

The calories in chocolate don't count because chocolate comes from the cocoa bean, and everyone knows that beans are good for you.

Amy had no idea where they were going, but when they passed the pier and got onto the highway, she knew they weren't going to the diner, or anywhere in Lucky Harbor. "So," she said, pretending she wasn't nervous, "where to?"

"Thought we'd try a night out without worrying about showing up on Facebook. I was thinking Seattle."

That sounded good to her. There for a moment, back at her place, she'd thought maybe they'd be getting straight to the naked part of the date, but he'd said he wanted this first. She'd decided to take that in the sweet spirit he'd intended. But who'd have thought that the big, bad ranger truly had a sweet side?

You did...You knew it from that day on the mountain when he'd stayed with you all night.

They were halfway to Seattle when his phone buzzed.

He glanced at the ID and let out a breath and a softly uttered "damn." He shook his head. "Sorry, but it's Sawyer. I have to take it."

Amy listened to him as he spoke to the sheriff. She could tell by Matt's quick, short replies that it was about work, and it wasn't good.

"I have to go to Crescent Canyon," he said when he'd clicked off. "Sawyer arrested a guy this morning, someone that law enforcement here has been looking for, in conjunction with a drug bust we made a while back. He's squealing something about his partners and some more stash in an old abandoned ranger station out at Crescent Canyon, in the north district—my territory. I need to meet Sawyer out there to check it out. I'm going to have to take you back."

"Aren't we closer to Crescent Canyon now than my place? Don't waste time, I'll just go with you."

"No. Hell, no."

This was not the first time that Amy had seen Matt's protective nature. After taking care of herself for so long, watching her own back, she still didn't know how she felt about him doing it for her. But she couldn't deny that it certainly wasn't a bad feeling. "You're not in your work vehicle," she said reasonably. "So it's not against the rules, right? I'll stay in your truck."

He slid her a look, and she held up her hand in a solemn vow, making him smile. "Were you a Girl Scout?" he asked.

"Not even a little bit," she said. "But I rarely make promises." She thought of the last one she'd made, to Riley, the one she was *still* conflicted about. "And I never make one I can't keep."

Or so she hoped...

His eyes held hers. "Never?"

She drew a deep breath. "Not yet anyway."

"Good to know." He left the highway and drove them up toward Crescent Canyon. The road turned into a dirt fire road that forked off a dozen times or more. Amy was completely lost in three minutes, but Matt seemed to know exactly where he was going. The road narrowed, and the going got so rough she ended up clinging to the sissy handle.

Matt glanced over at her. "You okay?"

"You tell me."

He flashed a grin. "No worries, I hardly ever drive off the edge by accident."

She steeled herself and took a peek over the "edge." A three-hundred-foot drop. "Good to know," she said dryly, repeating his earlier words back to him, making him laugh.

Twenty minutes later, they pulled into a clearing in front of a small building, just as Sawyer did the same from the other direction in a black-and-white official Bronco.

There was a car already parked, an older Ford truck of indeterminate color and rust. "Stay here," Matt said to Amy, eyes on the building, reaching into the back for a utility belt, gun, and cuffs. "Under no circumstances are you to get out of my truck. If it all goes to shit, I want you to slide over behind the wheel and drive out of here, do you understand?"

"What? No, I'm not going to leave you here," she said.

He spared her a quick look, mouth and eyes grim. "I can take care of myself. Promise me, Amy."

Goddammit. Thanks to her own big mouth, he now knew that she took her promises very seriously. "I promise."

He and Sawyer got out of their vehicles and drew their guns. Amy watched the two of them as they looked at each other, seeming to communicate without a word. Sawyer gave a quick hand gesture, then went toward the front of the building while Matt vanished around back.

Just as Sawyer reached the front door, it crashed open. Three huge guys flew out, tackling Sawyer to the ground. The dirt pack was dry, and dust flew up, making it impossible for Amy to see anything but a tangle of limbs. From inside the car, she gasped, horrified, sitting up straighter, desperately trying to keep her eyes on Sawyer at the bottom of the pile. Her first instinct was to do something to help, and she whirled around, looking for something, a weapon, *anything*. A baseball bat would have been her first choice but there was nothing. She carried a knife in her backpack, but all she had tonight was a small purse with a little cash and her phone. She hadn't planned on needing anything else except maybe a condom.

And then there was her promise to stay in the truck.

It was the worst feeling, the most helpless thing imaginable, sitting there watching Sawyer go down, unable to help.

From inside the building, another guy came stumbling out. His hands were cuffed behind him, and he was being pushed along by Matt. Matt caught sight of the scuffle and shoved his guy down to the ground. "*Stay*," he barked and broke into a run toward the mêlée.

One of the men broke away from the fight and staggered for his truck. Matt dove after him, taking him to the ground.

Amy gasped again and covered her mouth, as if by making any sound she might distract Matt and get him hurt. The two men rolled twice, and then Matt was on top, flipping the other man over, holding him there with a knee in the small of the guy's back. Matt reached behind himself for a set of flexi-cuffs from his utility belt and cuffed the guy. Without looking at him again, he turned back to Sawyer's fight and waded right in. He grabbed one of the two remaining guys by the back of the shirt and hauled him to his feet. No easy thing considering that the guy appeared to be six and a half feet tall and close to three hundred pounds. "Down," Matt said, and pointed to the ground, both his voice and actions cool and calm and utterly in control.

The big guy dropped to the ground.

Sawyer had the other one facedown in the dirt now and was cuffing him. Sawyer had a cut lip and torn clothes but otherwise appeared unharmed. The cuffed men were all moaning and groaning about their injuries, which both Sawyer and Matt ignored. There was a short conversation between Sawyer and Matt, then they both made calls.

Twenty minutes later, three more black-and-white SUVs appeared. Matt spoke to the officers, then to Sawyer. Then the cuffed men were loaded up and driven away.

Matt turned toward his truck and Amy. He was head-to-toe filthy. He had a tear in one knee and another on his elbow. He was sweaty.

And he looked like the best thing she'd ever seen.

He ambled back over and slid behind the wheel, pulling out of the clearing and back onto the fire road as if nothing had just happened. Like it was an everyday thing to drag bad guys off his mountain and engage in hand-to-hand combat.

And hell, maybe it was.

Clearly, he knew what he was doing. Protecting himself and Sawyer, and by extension her as well, had been as second nature as breathing. Not for the first time, she wondered about all he'd seen and done and how it'd molded him into the man he was, so laid-back and quick to smile and yet ready for battle at all times.

She also wondered why the hell she felt so on edge right now, like she was going to die if he didn't grab her and kiss her. Strip her. Take her.

"You okay?" he asked, making her jump. He swiveled his head to look over at her, and their eyes held. Suddenly there wasn't enough air in the vehicle, not even close, as the tension rose. It was a good kind of tension, the kind that had her squeezing her thighs together. Was she okay? She had no idea, but her insides were quivering, her hands itching with the need to lay them on him. "That was actually my question for you," she managed.

His gaze never left hers. "You're shaking."

Yeah, she was. Every part of her. "I was scared for you." She hugged herself. "Which is ridiculous, since like you said, you're good at taking care of yourself." Something they had in common.

They were on a deserted road, hidden from all sides by trees so thick she couldn't see beyond them. Still trembling, and greatly annoyed, she stared out the window, gasping in surprise when Matt pulled off the road. Turning to her, he slid a hand along the back of her seat, palming her neck. "It's okay, Amy. Everything's okay."

Feeling stupid for her shocked reaction, she nodded and drew in a shaky breath, but his touch had only accelerated her heart rate. She didn't know what to feel, or do. She wanted to jump over the console and personally search every inch of him for injury. She also wanted to rip off his clothes and climb on top of him. "Matt."

"Yeah?"

"I need—" Breaking off, she closed her eyes.

"What do you need, Amy?"

"*You.*"

A low sound escaped him, and then his other hand joined the fray, cupping her face, gliding down her arms, pulling her toward him.

She wasn't exactly sure what happened next, whether she'd done as she'd thought about and climbed over the console, or if he actually lifted her, but then she was straddling him, and nothing else mattered.

He was holding her above himself, trying to keep her from touching him. "Wait—I'm all dirty and sweaty."

"I don't care."

With a groan, he hauled her in close, kissing her long and deep.

He was right; he was hot and dirty. And he was real, more so than anyone she knew, and in turn he made *her* feel real. She forgot that they were stuffed together in his driver's seat, that the steering wheel was pressing into her back, or that anyone could come upon them. She only knew a need for this man so close against her, his scent, his taste, and she rocked into him.

Beeeeeep, went the horn when she knocked against it, startling her into jerking upright, where she banged her head on the visor.

Laughing softly, Matt cupped her head in one big palm, rubbing it. Then he sighed against her neck and dumped her back onto her side of the vehicle.

"Hey," she said.

"Not here."

"Why not? We're on a date."

With a rueful smile, he adjusted himself. "Is that what you think a date is about? Sex?"

"Well...yeah."

He shook his head. "Even if that was true, there's not enough room in this truck for what I want to do to you."

Her nipples tightened even more. "Now you're just teasing me."

"Sweetheart, when I start teasing you, you'll know it."

She shuddered in anticipation. She knew him now, knew the magic of his touch. She knew he could back up that cocky statement with shocking ease.

"I need to go change," Matt said.

"Are you going to tell me what happened back there?"

He looked at her, assessing, and she held his gaze, seeing the concern in it. Was he worried she was too fragile to hear about his work? Had his ex been that way? Because Amy was as far from fragile as she could get. "I *want* to hear about it," she said. "I'd really like to know."

"Not too long ago, we made that big drug bust I told you about," he said. "We found some of the principals and what we thought was all the drugs. Wrong on both accounts."

So casual. But what she'd seen had been anything but casual. It'd been like something right out of a movie. "You and Sawyer took on four guys," she said. "Four *huge* guys."

"We've faced worse."

That thought gave her a shiver as he pulled up to his cabin.

"I'm sorry I screwed up our date," he said.

She shook her head. "You didn't."

"I'll shower and change real quick," he promised, and left her in his living room while he vanished into his bedroom.

Through the open door, Amy heard the thunk of his shoes being kicked off one by one, and then the shower came on. She tried not to think about him stripping down to skin and failed. To distract herself, she looked around. The first time she'd been here, she hadn't had time to take it all in, what with the jumping of each other's bones and all.

He had running shoes half under the couch, a newspaper scattered on the coffee table. Next to the front door was a baseball bat and mitt. A laptop sat on the couch.

This wasn't just a place where Matt hung his hat at night. He *lived* here.

Had he loved here?

She was surprised at the yearning to know. His shower turned off. Next came the sound of a drawer opening and then some rustling.

"We missed our reservations," he called out to her. "But maybe they'll still take us anyway."

It would be at least a forty-five minute drive, and undoubtedly a wait, and while she imagined the food would be worth it, she didn't want the fancy dinner, the crowd, the candles and dancing thing. "We could just eat here," she said.

A beat of silence, and then he appeared in the doorway wearing low-slung Levi's.

And nothing else.

He held a shirt in his hands as his eyes met hers. "You want to stay here?"

His hair was wet and had been barely finger-combed, leaving it standing up and spiky. He smelled like soap and shampoo and himself. And he hadn't been all that efficient with a towel either because his chest was damp.

And so was she. "I'll cook," she said, thinking she was *already* cooking, from the inside out.

He followed her into his kitchen. "You don't like to cook."

Actually, she liked to cook just fine. She just wasn't all that good at it. But she did have one specialty. "If you have bread and cheese and a pan, we're in business."

He shrugged into his shirt, and she wished he hadn't. Eating grilled cheese with the spectacular view of his chest and abs would've been better than any dessert she could have whipped up.

He stepped close, his eyes dark and heated. "I like where your thoughts just went."

"Did I say them out loud?" she asked, startled.

"No, but you were thinking them clearly enough." He backed her to the kitchen counter and caged her in with a hand on either side of her hips. Ducking a little, he looked into her eyes. "You want me."

She blew out a breath. Seemed silly to try and deny it now, especially since she'd said so in his truck. His eyes were deep and dark and beautiful and filled with affection and a devastating heat. He looked so...alive, him and that megawatt smile as he wrapped his arms around her and lifted her to the counter.

"Um..."

With a polite cock of his head to let her know he was listening, he pushed between her legs, spreading them wide so that he was flush up against her. When she didn't finish her sentence—couldn't even remember what she'd wanted to say—he kissed her. He kissed her until she couldn't remember her own name and then backed away and went to his refrigerator.

She stared at his back and tried to access some brain cells. "So what made you decide to be a ranger? SWAT not exciting enough for you? You decided you'd rather rescue fair maidens and wrangle drug runners?"

He pulled butter and cheese from the fridge. He grabbed a loaf of thick sourdough bread from the counter and grabbed a knife. "It's complicated."

"Yeah?"

He set a pan on the stovetop and turned on a burner. He began to butter the bread slices, but she took the knife from him and took over the task.

"I promised to cook for you," she said. "You talk."

He met her gaze. "I didn't think talking was one of your favorite things to do."

He was throwing the ball back at her. She recognized the technique well. And he was right, she wasn't much of a talker. She'd never been all that curious about a man either. There were a whole bunch of firsts going on here tonight. "I want to know," she said simply. "I want to know more about you."

Chapter 14

*There are two food groups: chocolate and fruit.
And if it is fruit, it should be dipped in chocolate.*

Matt turned to Amy, surprised. "You want to know more about me? Why?"

Looking both embarrassed and resigned, she bit her lower lip. "I know, I made a whole big deal about not getting involved..."

He laughed softly at the both of them. Because he knew that *neither* of them wanted to get involved—or attached—but it was happening anyway. "What do you want to know?"

"I suppose you learned to handle bad guys like that in SWAT and probably the military, too. Army?"

"Navy," he said. "Ty and I went through basic together and then spent some quality time in the Gulf."

"Ty...Mallory's boyfriend?"

He nodded.

"That's where your readiness comes from. The cool calm. The ability to take down four huge potheads single-handedly."

"It wasn't single-handedly tonight," he reminded her. "I had Sawyer."

"Still pretty impressive." She paused. "You've seen and done a lot in your life."

He held her gaze. "I have." More than she knew.

"So what made you come here and be a forest ranger?"

Turning in his partner for being on the take. Having his marriage fall apart after failing to keep Shelly safe from his job. Basically, his entire life had detonated in the span of a few months, and he'd needed out. But he wasn't about to spell out his failures to a woman he hoped to have naked and under him by the end of the evening. "I like the uncomplicated life here."

"So you wanted peace and quiet?"

He hadn't yet found the peace, but he *had* found the quiet, and he'd settled for that. "Yeah."

Studying him, she tilted her head to the side a little. "Do you ever miss it? The big city, the people? Your family?"

"I see my family. And no, I don't miss it."

"And your wife?" she asked softly. "Do you miss her?"

"*Ex*-wife," he reminded her. "And no."

"But…"

He really didn't want to have this conversation. He wasn't about to spill his guts and have her look at him differently. So instead of letting her lead him back to a past he didn't like to remember, he leaned in and kissed her. Lightly at first. Warm. Then not so lightly. He kissed her until she let out a low hum of arousal and slid her hands up his chest and into his hair to hold him to her.

Not that he was going to let go. Hell, no. And just like that, what had started out as a distraction technique quickly escalated into something else entirely, into that same unquenchable hunger he always felt for her, the one he'd had since she'd first shown up in Lucky Harbor.

It might have taken him six months to get here with her, but he was done wasting time. Luckily, she appeared to feel the same way because she turned off the stovetop burner, took his hand, and led him to his big sofa in the living room.

The last time they'd been here, right here, she'd commandeered the reins. He had no idea if he'd earned her trust enough yet for it to be his turn, but he hoped so. Either way, he was perfectly willing to give her whatever she needed, just as long as she was with him all the way.

Amy looked into his face, her expression one of reluctant affection and enough heat to steal his breath. He cupped her face for a kiss and she let him do it, even making a soft hum of pleasure before suddenly pushing him down to the couch.

Okay, so she still didn't trust him enough to let him lead. He allowed himself to fall but he made sure to take her with him, tugging so that she landed on his lap. Her short skirt slid up her gorgeous thighs to dangerous heights.

He'd been dying to get a peek beneath all night, but before he could, she nipped his bottom lip, hard, and then soothed the sting with one very sexy, slow swipe of her tongue. He went instantly hard even as he got the answer to the big question.

No, she wasn't ready to make love. This was still going to be sex. Sex was good, but he forced himself to slow down, to slow them *both* down. Stroking back her hair, he murmured her name as he kissed his way to her

ear, because if nothing else, he was going to make damn
sure that there'd at least be some tenderness to go with it.

Amy loved having Matt beneath her, warm, strong,
and hard. She couldn't get enough of him. It was quite
shocking.

He'd called one thing right—she wanted him. Bad.

She turned in his lap, straddling him now. His hands
immediately slid beneath her skirt and palmed her butt.
Gripping his biceps, she kissed him. Letting out a low
growl of pleasure, he kissed her back, plundering her
mouth without trying to break free of her hold or rush
her. He didn't tear off her clothes or roll her beneath him
either. He just took what she gave, all relaxed and at ease,
willing to let her do as she wanted with him.

And there *was* something she desperately wanted. She
ground herself against his erection and heard his breath
hitch, making her realize that he needed her as badly as
she needed him. Releasing his arms, she slid hers around
his neck.

He broke the kiss and gave her a searching look before
kissing her again, his hands shifting on the move. Clever
fingers unhooked her bra so that he could cup her breasts,
his thumbs brushing over her nipples.

Then it was *her* breath that hitched.

God, she really needed him inside her. She needed
the big bang, the relief, and only he could give it to her.
"Condom," she gasped against his mouth.

"Back pants pocket." They broke apart to undress in a
frenzy, and then she was sliding onto him.

"Oh, fuck," he said reverently as he filled her.

It gave her such a rush, reducing this smart, sharp

man to nothing more than single syllables. And she knew exactly how he felt because she could hardly think; he felt so good inside her. She moved on him, slowly at first. When she was ready for more, she tried to pick up their pace but he wrapped a hand in her hair, his other hand going to her hip to hold her still.

"No." His voice was serrated, thick, his grip preventing her from racing them both to the finish line. "Don't move. Not a single muscle—Oh, Christ," he grated out when she clenched on him. "Christ, you feel good." His fingers tightened, and she knew she'd have bruises.

She didn't care. His tongue was back in her mouth, moving in tune to the way his body moved within hers, and it was more than she could take. She broke loose and undulated her hips as she climbed higher, then higher still when he reached a hand between them to stroke his thumb over the current center of her entire universe.

Crying out, she clutched at him, out of control and unable to care. When she came, it was hard and fast. She heard Matt swear reverently as he rocked her through it, and then he was flying with her.

Finally, they stilled against each other. Sated, she laid her head against his shoulder as he pulled her in tight. When her breathing calmed, she sighed. "You make me lose myself."

"Good."

She met his gaze. "Yeah?"

"Everyone should lose themselves just like that, as often as possible." And then he flashed her a smile before dumping her off his lap. He smacked her lightly on the ass, rose to his feet, and then strode naked into the kitchen. "Starving," he said over his shoulder.

She gaped after him. "You going to eat like that?"

"Yeah. And so are you."

She hated being told what to do. Always. It made her run away.

But she didn't run. Instead, she followed him like a love-lorn puppy into the kitchen, where they consumed grilled cheese sandwiches while leaning against the counter. Naked.

He told her about his day, making her laugh at how he'd been followed around by a group of camping biologists who'd wanted him to discuss the bodily functions of the otters in the cold water streams that fed into the water supply. He spoke fondly about his family, about his warm but nosy mom, his take-no-shit dad, his brother who had three little girls of his own now—karma's idea of a joke since his brother had been crazy wild. He told her how he and Ty had beaten the shit out of each other just that morning in the gym, with Josh standing over them on the sidelines like a worried den mother...

And all she could do the whole time was soak up every word and marvel that he trusted her, that he enjoyed her company, and that he wanted to be with her. It softened her in a way she hadn't expected, and she found herself just staring at him.

"What?" he asked, with a small smile.

She shook her head, unable to explain how she felt when she was with him. Like she was on a tightrope without a net. An overdose of adrenaline, terror-filled, excited, and overwhelmed all at once.

"Tell me," he said.

It was that voice of his, the low, calm, utterly commanding voice that made her do just that. "This has been a really great first first date."

"First *first* date? As in your first date *ever*?"

She grimaced. "Yeah, sort of."

He looked at her for a long moment. "Explain."

She opened her mouth and then closed it again. She shrugged, embarrassed, and spent a moment getting a glass of water. It was hard to believe talking about herself made her feel more naked than actually being naked, but there it was.

"Were you a nun until recently?" he asked.

She laughed. "No."

"Sheltered?"

She laughed again, this time a little bitterly. "No. It's no big thing. I've obviously been with men. I've just never done this, the dressing up and going out thing."

"Which we never got to," he said with deep regret.

"It's okay. It was still really great."

He took the drink from her hand and drew her out of the kitchen. They dressed, and he drove them to Seattle after all, to a small intimate bar downtown that had a really great band. They danced, talked, and laughed, and then danced some more.

Amy had never once had a guy set an entire evening around her and her needs. It made her feel things, and for once she didn't mind. She felt special. Cherished. And hours later, when they pulled back up to his cabin, she turned to him and smiled. "Heck of a first date, Ranger Hot Buns." Leaning in, she kissed him softly. "Thank you," she whispered against his mouth, which curved gently.

"You're welcome." He tucked a loose strand of hair behind her ear. "But it's not over yet."

"No?"

He led her inside and to his kitchen, where they shared a three a.m. plate of cookies and mugs of milk, dressed this time. She sat on his counter, and he stood at her side, smiling at her.

"What?" she asked.

"You have a crumb..." He licked the corner of her mouth, then used the excuse to kiss the daylights out of her.

"That was a ploy," she said when they broke apart for air.

"Uh huh." He started removing her clothes, until she sat bare assed on his counter, trying not to squeal at the feel of the cold tile beneath her cheeks. "Okay, this can't be sanitary."

He smiled and stripped, making her heart stutter in her chest because he was so beautiful. "Nice," she said.

He pushed her legs open and stepped between them, and she forgot all about being cold or sanitary.

Wrapping his hand in her hair, he gently tugged her head to the side and kissed her neck.

"Again?" she breathed, melting when he opened his mouth and sucked a little patch of skin.

"Oh, yeah, again," he said. "And then again."

"We won't be able to walk."

He nipped her collarbone and headed south toward her breast. "I'm going to be so good to you, you won't care."

Chapter 15

♥

*Researchers have discovered that chocolate produces
some of the same reactions in the brain as marijuana.
The researchers also discovered other similarities
between the two but can't remember what they are.*

That next morning, Matt's alarm went off. He was
alone. Nothing unusual about that, he told himself, and
rose.

Half an hour later, he and Josh were hanging off a
cliff together. It was barely dawn, and Josh was tense
and bitchy because he'd only gotten three hours of sleep
thanks to a long ER shift.

Matt hadn't gotten even three hours of sleep but he
wasn't tense and bitchy. Maybe a little freaked out. He
had no idea what he was doing with Amy. At least not
other than making her cry out his name whenever she was
naked. *That*, he'd discovered, he was very good at.

"Shut up," Josh said.

"I didn't say anything."

"You didn't have to. Your just-got-laid smile is saying

it all for you. Loudly. Have some sympathy on those of us not getting any."

Matt slid his longtime friend a look. "You could be getting some. What happened to what's-her-name? That hot red-headed nurse you were talking about?"

"She told me how she'd been dreaming about marrying a doctor since she was eight."

Matt winced. "That'll do it. What about that cute brunette you met when you operated on her brother's mysterious head injury?"

"Turns out she's the one who gave him that injury."

"Ah. Okay, how about that new chick...Grace? The one who's friends with Amy and Mallory?"

"Hell, no."

"Why not? She's pretty."

"Yeah, but she's Mallory's and Amy's friend," Josh said.

"So?"

"*So*," Josh said in the tone that suggested Matt was a complete moron. "Ty fell for Mallory. It might be contagious."

Matt laughed. "You're a doctor. Whatever you catch, just give yourself a shot and get over it."

"Is that what you're going to do? After you finish falling for Amy, you're just going to get over it?"

This shut Matt up because he had no clue.

Josh shook his head. "I've given up dating for now. It's just too damn hard anyway, with Toby and Anna."

"Your son and sister wouldn't want you to give up your life for them."

Josh lifted a shoulder. "I'm working seventy-five hours a week. I don't have time to date."

"Man, that's just sad."

"Says the guy who works the same crazy hours I do. How are you fitting your relationship with Amy into that schedule? You prepared for the pissy girlfriend act when she finds out how you're always on the job?"

"She's not my girlfriend."

Josh snorted. "You haven't seen Facebook yet today, I take it."

"You don't have time for women, but you have time for Facebook?"

"My office manager has it as my homepage," Josh said. "Thinks she's amusing. But it was very amusing today. You went out with Amy, a date that ended with you being a fucking action hero."

Matt stared at him. "How the hell did *that* get out?"

"Lucille was at the station when Sawyer brought the guys in. She'd just bailed out Mrs. Burland for running over her neighbor's foot—twice." Josh raised a brow. "Nice start to a date, playing Superman. How did that work out for you?"

Pretty good. He could still remember every breathy pant, every soft moan, every hungry "oh, please, Matt" that Amy had whispered in his ear. Not wanting to go there with Josh, Matt ignored the question and kept moving.

"Wow, evading," Josh said. "Subtle."

"Why don't I climb with Ty?" Matt wondered out loud. "He doesn't ask stupid questions."

"Because he's too pussy to climb."

Matt laughed. Ty wasn't "pussy" about much. Except heights.

They were halfway down when something caught

Matt's attention across the long, broad chasm at Widow's Peak, the cliff three hundred feet across the way. Climbers. They were at the midpoint plateau of Widow Peak's face, which he knew they'd had to have gotten to by way of a closed-off trail. He knew this because he'd closed off the trail himself.

The climbers were whooping and hollering it up, and Matt shook his head. "Shit."

"Kids?" Josh asked.

"Can't tell."

"Isn't that entire area closed off?"

"Yeah," Matt said grimly, scrambling down. "I closed it because of rock slide problems. It's not safe."

Josh hit the ground only three beats behind him, squinting through the sun, shading his eyes with a hand. "Looks like a total of four idiots. Nope, five."

Matt pulled binoculars from his pack and took in the sight of the climbers passing something between them. Tension gathered in a ball at the base of his spine. "They're getting high first," he said, shoving the binoculars at Josh, then gathering his gear.

"We going to go scare them off?"

"Hell, yeah."

They moved to Matt's truck, where he replaced his climbing gear with a utility belt, including weapons.

"Do I get one of those?" Josh asked.

"No."

"But I get to look all scary and intimidating, right?"

Matt looked Josh over. Out of his scrubs, Josh didn't look much like a doctor. He looked like a six-foot-four NFL linebacker. "I don't know," Matt said, baiting him. "Can you do scary and intimidating?"

Josh narrowed his eyes. "If I hadn't taken an oath to *save* lives, not take them, I'd show *you* scary and intimidating right now."

"Save it for the idiots."

Fifteen minutes later, Matt parked at the trailhead to Widow's Peak. "Hell."

"What?" Josh asked.

"The gate's open." And he'd locked it personally. "The CLOSED sign is missing."

"That's not good."

"Nope." Matt drove through the gate, taking the fire road that would bring them to the same midpoint plateau that the climbers were on. They had to park about a quarter of a mile from the area, where they found another truck—the climbers' vehicle, no doubt. Matt and Josh hiked the rest of the way in, startling the guys just as they were getting ready to take a go at the peak.

"This area is closed," Matt told them.

The climbers were in their late teens. Three of the four of them took one look at Josh and Matt and just about shit their pants. Not their ringleader, whom Matt recognized as Trevor Wright, the teenage son of Allen Wright, a very successful builder who thought he was God's gift to the entire county. With a cocky grin, Trevor held his ground. "Who're you, the climbing police?"

"Yeah, I'm the climbing police." Matt badged him. "And you're not supposed to be here."

"Public property, dude."

Matt shook his head. This was the problem with the Wrights in general. They thought they owned Lucky Harbor, and everything around it. They also thought the laws didn't apply to them. All four boys smelled like weed.

Hell, there was practically a cloud of it around Trevor's head. "The gate was shut and locked," Matt said mildly. "And there was a CLOSED sign."

"Sorry, man. That gate was wide open, and I didn't see no sign. And you're hassling us for no reason. We haven't done nothing wrong."

Trevor's friends weren't looking so comfortable anymore and had started to back up. "Come on, Trev," one of them said. "Let's hit it."

Trevor widened his tough-guy stance. "They can't do anything to us," he said, smiling right at Matt. "They're only rangers. They know the names of the flowers and how to start a fire."

"Luckily I know how to do a little more than that," Matt said. "And if you're carrying drugs, I'll arrest you."

Trevor shrugged out of his backpack and tossed it over the cliff, where it promptly vanished into thin air, careening off the rocks as it fell to the valley floor hundreds of feet below. "I'm not carrying anything."

"Jesus, Trevor," one of his friends said. "You're crazy."

"Yeah," another said. "We're outta here." He and the others took off.

Trevor stood there posturing for a long beat and then started after his friends, shoulder checking Matt hard as he did. "You see that?" the little dickwad said to Josh. "Your partner *pushed* me." He pointed at Matt. "Not cool, man."

Josh waited until Trevor vanished down the trail after the others. "Okay, so why didn't we crack some heads, specifically his?"

Matt slid him a look. "You have a contact high. You *save* lives, remember?"

"Yes, but the occasional head cracking would be fun."

Matt shook his head. "My job's to chase them out of here. They're chased. Let's go."

They closed the gate, and Matt radioed dispatch that he needed a new lock and sign brought out. Then he and Josh drove all the way around the canyon and hit the meadow floor, looking for that backpack.

They didn't find it.

An hour later, Josh, who'd called in to the hospital that he was going to be late so that he could help Matt search, rubbed his stomach. "I'm starving. You're buying."

"Why me?" Matt asked. "Your paycheck's a *lot* bigger than mine."

"You got laid last night."

"What does that have to do with who's buying breakfast?"

"Everything."

"How much farther?" Grace asked breathlessly.

"We've only gone a quarter of a mile," Amy said.

"But I'm ready for a chocolate break." This was from Mallory, who swiped an arm over her damp brow.

"You both walk farther for your morning coffee," Amy said. She'd been worrying about Riley, and was tired of waiting for the girl to come to her. Amy was going proactive. So they were heading toward the Squaw Flats campgrounds, though Amy had told the Chocoholics only that it was a great day for a hike and had lured them up the mountain with the promise of brownies as a prize.

"Here's another good girl lesson," Mallory said. "Never refer to your friends' lack of fitness."

Grace looked around at the lush, thick growth and inhaled deeply. "It smells like Christmas out here."

"Tell me again why we're hiking instead of sitting in a nice booth at the diner?" Mallory asked.

"We're calorie burning," Amy said. "It means guilt-free brownies. Just another quarter of a mile or so."

"Seriously," Grace said, huffing and puffing as they moved along. "This taking the Chocoholics on the road experiment might be a bust. Are we almost there yet?"

Amy shook her head. "And I thought *I* was a city girl."

"I have to pee," Grace said.

"There's a bunch of trees," Amy said. "Pick one."

"Like I trust *your* judgment on pee spots."

"Maybe you should," Mallory said. "It caught her Ranger Hot Buns."

"True," Grace mused. "Do you ever call him that?" she asked Amy.

Amy laughed. "Not if I want to live."

They came across a small clearing. The sun was strong here, and it was beautiful. But they weren't the only ones enjoying it. Leaning with their backs to a fallen log sat Lance and Tucker. The two brothers were eating sandwiches and sucking down bottled water. Covered in dust from head to toe, their grins appeared all the whiter when they flashed them.

"Hey, ladies," Lance said in his low and husky voice, roughened from years of the lung-taxing coughing the CF caused him. "Looking good."

Tucker held up a baggie of brownies. "Anyone want to join us?"

"Oh my God, *yes*," Grace said with great feeling. "Amy's being a brownie Nazi."

Mallory put out a hand and halted her, serving the

brothers a careful, narrow-eyed gaze. "Are those brownies *home*-made?"

Tucker grinned, slow, lazy and unabashed, and Amy burst out laughing. She hadn't thought about the *quality* of their brownies, but she should have when it came to Tucker.

Mallory shook her head at the guys. "What did I tell you about your brownies?"

"Uh..." Tucker said, trying to think. "That they kill brain cells?"

"Chocolate doesn't kill brain cells," Grace said, oblivious to what they were talking about. "Chocolate is God's gift."

"Not the way these two make it," Amy told her as Mallory gave them the bum's rush back onto the trail.

A few minutes later, they neared Squaw Flats. "You two rest here for a few," Amy said, and pulled out the lunch she'd packed from the diner, handing out sandwiches. "I'm going to just go up the road another half a mile to check out a vista I want to draw later. Wait here."

"Where're the brownies?" Grace asked.

Amy pulled out the stash. "Not as good as what Tucker had," she said dryly. "But they'll do. I'll be right back."

"Don't fall down any ravines," Mallory said, and took a big bite out of her brownie. Apparently she liked dessert first, too. "I've got the same first aid skills as Matt, but I doubt I've got the same bedside manner."

Grace snickered, and Amy rolled her eyes. But it was true. Matt had some seriously good bedside manner.

Amy found Riley about a third of a mile away, sunning on a rock, staring pensively out at a colorful meadow. The rains had been steady last season, leaving the meadow alive with head-high grass and wildflowers. All around them, the air pulsed with buzzing insects and butterflies.

Riley looked over, caught sight of Amy, and sighed.

Amy pulled a bag from her backpack and dropped it at Riley's feet.

"What's this?"

"Look inside," Amy said.

Riley paused for a long beat, making it clear that she would do only whatever she wanted to do and on her own schedule. But clearly her curiosity finally got the best of her and she opened the pack. Inside was more bottled water, a lunch like the one she'd packed the Chocoholics, and soap and shampoo.

"Thought you might be low on supplies," Amy said.

Riley nodded. "Thanks." While she looked over the goods, Amy looked *her* over. Riley had shadows in her eyes and dark circles under them. She wasn't getting enough sleep, that much was clear.

"There's a key to my place in the side pocket. It's yours." Amy paused. "Come back with me."

"I'm good here."

"You're not supposed to be here."

"You said you wouldn't tell."

Amy sighed and sat next to her. "I haven't. I won't. But it's not safe for you."

"Trust me," Riley said, pulling out a sandwich. "It's safer than anywhere else."

Amy's heart squeezed. God, she'd so been there. "I realize you think you have no one to trust, but it's not true."

Riley slowed down the inhaling of her sandwich. She didn't respond, but Amy knew she was listening.

"I ran away from home when I was sixteen," Amy said softly. "I never looked back. My goal was to get as far away as possible. I hitchhiked with strangers and slept in alleys. I trusted no one, and as a result, no one trusted me."

Riley hugged her knees to her chest. "How did you do it?"

"I lied about my age and took whatever jobs I could get. Except for hooking, I managed to avoid that one."

"I never hooked either," Riley said quickly.

"Good. Because you're worth far more than that. You know that, right?"

Riley hunched her shoulders. "I know I don't want any guy's hands on me."

Amy let out a shaky breath as her own memories hit her hard. This was as she suspected, and as she feared. "Who put his hands on you?"

Riley laid her head down on her knees, her face turned away from Amy.

"Someone at home?"

Still as a statue, Riley didn't respond.

"Your dad?"

"Don't have one. And I got taken away from my mom. She wasn't fit."

"So you were in foster care," Amy said.

A pause. Then a quiet, "yeah."

Where she'd probably been mistreated, possibly sexually abused, and had decided that the entire male species sucked golf balls.

Couldn't blame her, though Amy herself had gone the opposite route. Sex had become power, and for a long time, she'd really liked holding the power.

"I just want to be free to do what I want," Riley said. "Without anyone trying to force me to do something I don't want to do."

"Well, of course. *Everyone* wants that," Amy said. "Everyone deserves that. Riley, you aren't alone."

Riley turned her head and looked at Amy, seeming heartbreakingly young.

"You have me," Amy said. "And together we're a 'we.'"

"But you're already a 'we.' With the ranger."

Amy had never been a "we" with a man. At least not for more than a few hours, and that Riley thought Amy was with Matt startled her. But she sure as hell didn't want to explain to Riley that all she and Matt had was a mutual enjoyment of rubbing their favorite body parts together.

"Not exactly," she said. "Did you think about the job?" It would keep her in sight, and Amy could watch over her, make sure she was safe and eating. She waited for Riley to once again ask why Amy cared but she didn't.

Progress.

"I've thought about it," Riley said. "I'll do it."

Baby steps, but that was okay. Amy had discovered life was all about baby steps.

Chapter 16

One of life's little mysteries is how a two-pound box of chocolate can make a person gain five pounds.

Matt had a hell of a long day, which included noncompliant picnickers, a search-and-rescue mission for a beginning biker on an advanced trail, a small wildfire in the fourth quadrant, which had nearly gotten away from them, and the arrest of an idiot for illegal poaching. When he finally left his post, he went to the diner for a late meal.

Okay, he went to the diner to catch sight of Amy. He deserved it after the day he'd had. Amy happened to be on a break when he walked in, sitting at a small table in the far corner, bent over something.

Drawing, he realized when he got closer. She was sketching on her pad, oblivious to the room. Or at least she was until he got about halfway across the diner, then suddenly she went still, lifted her head, and met his gaze.

Lots of things flickered across her face, with heat leading the way. But what grabbed him by the throat and held on was the reluctant affection.

She wanted him. He'd proven that. Hell, he wanted her right back. But she also liked him. She didn't want to, but she did. Inexplicably buoyed by that, he slid into her side of the booth, pressing his thigh to hers. "Hey."

"Hey." As always, she closed her sketch book and slid it away from him. "I was just taking a break."

"You ever going to let me see your drawings?"

"I don't know. They're sort of personal."

He leaned in close. "You've shared your body with me. And that felt pretty personal."

She gave him a little shove and a laugh. "*Not* the same thing."

Enjoying the sound of her amusement and the fact that she looked so pretty smiling, he let one of his own escape. "One of these days, you're going to *want* to share with me."

"My drawings?"

"Those too."

She nudged him again, less of a shove this time. "Move. I'll get up and get your order going."

He didn't move, but he did enjoy her hands on him, one on his arm, the other on his chest, especially since they lingered as if she couldn't help herself. "I'm a patient man, Amy. I can wait."

"It's late, and you've got to be hungry," she said, purposely misinterpreting that sentence. "At least let me put your order in. The usual, right? Or a double-double?"

They'd shared a double-double just last night, and it hadn't been food. And actually, she'd gotten more than two orgasms. Maybe even a quadruple. He smiled at the memory, and she pointed at him.

"Stop that," she said.

"Stop what?"

"You know what. You're thinking *things*."

He laughed. "Okay, you caught me. I'm definitely thinking...*things*."

She looked around to see if anyone was paying them any attention. No one was. He'd come late enough tonight that the place was nearly emptied out. Only two customers were at the counter and one at a table on the far side of the diner. Leaning in, Matt put his mouth to the sweet spot just beneath Amy's ear. "Why don't you tell me what things you think I'm thinking?"

She actually blushed beet red, which was so adorably revealing that he laughed. She shoved him again, which made him laugh more.

"You're crazy," she said.

Yes. It was entirely possible that he was crazy. Crazy for her.

Riley walked by. She was wearing ratty jeans, battered sneakers, a sweatshirt he recognized as Amy's, and a bright pink Eat Me apron. She was carrying a tray of dirty glasses and dishes and a very large chip on her shoulder. Matt looked at Amy.

"I got her a job," she said, and when he smiled at her, she lifted a shoulder. "It was no big deal."

But it was. "You're helping her."

"Anyone would."

"That's the thing," he said. "They wouldn't. They don't."

She stared at him. "You seem to have this blind faith in me, like I'm a good person and some sort of decent influence."

"You are." He reached out and pushed a strand of hair

back off her face, stroking it behind her ear. "You don't give yourself enough credit."

She was already shaking her head. "You don't know me."

"I know enough. It's all there in your eyes."

Those eyes met his now, filled with a warmth he didn't know if he'd ever get used to.

"Your life has been very different from mine," she said.

"Does it matter?"

"Depends."

"On what?"

She looked around the diner, then back at him. And then she put her hand on her sketchbook and pushed it across the table toward him.

Not one to squander an opportunity, Matt put his hand over hers on the book. "Yeah?"

She paused and then pulled her hand free. "Yeah."

He held her gaze, smiled at her, then opened the book and found himself completely speechless at the sheer mind-blowing talent leaping off the page. Each drawing was a rendering of the Pacific Northwest in some fashion or another. Squaw Flats, Eagle Rock, Four Lakes, Sierra Meadows, and Widow's Peak, she'd done them all, rendering them in colored pencil, so perfectly that he could almost smell the pines and feel the breeze. "Amy, Jesus. You're amazing."

"Thanks." Her cheeks were a little pink with the praise, making him wonder if she'd ever shown anyone her drawings before.

He flipped back to Sierra Meadows. "This is close to where I found you that night, when you were . . . not lost."

That earned him a small smile. "The night I fell down the ravine. The night you shared your tent."

"Which has been in heavy rotation in my fantasies ever since."

"You have some sort of a rescue fetish, Ranger Hot Buns?"

"No, I have a pale blue panty fetish."

She let out a low laugh. "It was dark."

"I have panty x-ray vision. God-given talent."

She laughed again, and the sound warmed him, but he couldn't take his eyes off her work. "You're so talented," he said, truly awed. "You should show these more often. You know Lucille runs an art gallery, right? She'd love these."

"They've always been just for me."

He met her gaze. "So what changed? Why show me now?"

She paused. "Well, I guess it's because you let me in. You told me about your childhood, your family. Your past. You've counted on me to help Riley." She shrugged. "You shared yourself with me, so I guess that somehow makes it okay for me to share with you."

At this, Matt felt his smile slowly fade, and guilt twisted in his gut. She thought he'd opened up, when in fact he'd purposely told her only the good things. What was even worse was that he'd let her think she could trust him, count on him. He liked the idea of her trusting him, a lot, but the last time he'd been down this road, he'd fucked up. Royally. His ex could attest to that. He'd promised not to get attached, but he was.

Deeply.

And suddenly, he wasn't in the least bit hungry.

Suddenly his stomach was burning and churning. Suddenly, he had to go. Be alone. Now. Gently, he pushed her sketch pad back to her.

She cocked her head to the side, eyes on his, clearly sensing a change in him, but just as clearly not understanding what.

As he couldn't understand it either, there was no way to explain it to her. "Jan's trying to get your attention," he said.

She held his gaze a moment longer, eyes sharp. He hadn't fooled her. But in classic Amy fashion, she took the easy way out and let him distract her. She glanced up at Jan, who was indeed pointing to her watch.

Matt stood up and let her out of the booth. She brushed against him as she did and sucked in a breath at the contact.

He did, too, but he managed to keep his hands to himself, shoving them into his pockets to ensure it. *She's not for you...*

Amy hesitated for a moment, and Matt held his breath, though he shouldn't have bothered. She didn't press for answers. She wouldn't, because as he'd counted on, that's not how she operated. And then there was the bottom line—she didn't want this any more than he did.

That night Amy went home, running through the light rain to her apartment, hoping the damp had brought Riley back.

It hadn't.

She grabbed her mail and dropped it all on the kitchen table. Mostly junk, but there was a manila envelope from New York, and she recognized her mother's handwriting.

She spent a moment staring at the package as if it were a striking cobra before she opened it.

Inside was a short note and a small notebook. The note said:

I've had this all these years, but it occurred to me after you called that maybe it's your turn to hold onto it. Mom

The notebook was identical to her grandma's journal. She opened it and then realized it wasn't identical at all. The paper in this notebook wasn't lined. And someone had filled the pages with sketches. Not in colored pencil, like Amy did, just black charcoal, but the sketches were so eerily similar to her own that Amy sank to a chair, weak-kneed. Lucky Harbor, Sierra Meadows, Four Lakes, Squaw Flats... the images wavered as Amy found herself choked up.

She hadn't known her grandma could draw.

She flipped through, marveling, swiping her eyes on her sleeve. There was only one picture she didn't recognize, the very last one—a vista of rough-edged, craggy mountain peaks that was so wonderfully depicted she could almost smell the trees.

This drawing was different than the others. This drawing had a figure sketched in, a woman. Drawn in shadow, she stood in profile on the plateau, the wind blowing her hair and scarf out behind her as she held something above her head. A container. From it came a cloud of dust—

Oh, no. Amy's heart sank. Not dust. She thought back to the journal entry before, where her grandma had switched from the "we" to "I."

She'd not been with Jonathon on this journey, at least not a living, breathing Jonathon.

Amy turned to the journal and reread the last entry again.

> *... standing at the very tippy top, looking out at a blanket of green, a sea of blue ...*

Amy eyed the drawing. It certainly looked like the tippy top. She opened her map. The highest peak was Widow's Peak. Her grandma hadn't left her initials on that mountain.

She'd left Jonathon's ashes.

> *I would never settle. I would never stop growing. I would never give up ...*

Coming here had given her grandma the hope and peace she needed to go on with her life after losing Jonathon. She'd gotten the hope to go on. And the peace to live without him. Amy understood that. She'd followed her grandma's journey to make a change in her life, too, to learn about herself. To grow.

Baby steps, and like Riley, she was taking them.

She ran her fingers over her drawing of Widow's Peak. Her grandma had never settled, and she wouldn't either. She'd never give up. She went through the pictures one last time, and when she finally closed the book, her resolve to finish this journey was renewed. She definitely had hope and peace now, and she wanted the rest. She wanted to find her heart.

• • •

Two days later, Amy had a day off and was mountain-bound, equipped with her grandma's drawings. She'd studied the map and had found a trail called Heart-Stopper. Was it possible that grandma's "heart" moment had been a play on words? The problem was that the Heart-Stopper Trail ran perpendicular along the Rim Trail, except higher up, along the top of the peaks, from the north rim all along to the south rim in a huge semi-circle, connecting the two. The loop that Matt had insinuated was too hard for her. She'd have to break it up into a few separate trips.

Or she could show Matt the drawing and see if he could help.

And she would have—except she kept playing that night in the diner over and over in her head. He'd backed off, and she didn't know why.

But it was okay. She could figure this out, just like she'd figured all her other shit out.

She cheated by taking the fire roads up past Squaw Flats and Sierra Meadows, straight to the trailhead of Heart-Stopper. It was beautiful, but she felt...off.

That's because you miss Matt...

How ironic was that? She'd told him not to get attached, and then she'd done it. She'd gotten damn attached.

Not that it mattered, not that it would slow her down. Matt wasn't her journey. *This* was her journey.

But though she managed to hike half the Heart-Stopper Trail before she had to turn back, she never found anything specific. Unlike at Sierra Meadows or Four Lakes, there was nothing obvious, nothing in her notes to point out a direct item. And of course, there were a million trees. It was like looking for a needle in a haystack, and she'd had to admit defeat for the day. She got back to the North District Ranger Station just before dark. Matt's truck was in the lot, and seeing it put butterflies in her belly. She *never* got butterflies. Damn man. So they hadn't spoken in a few days, so what? It wasn't a big deal, and certainly not the reason why she entered the building. Nope, she just needed a new map is all.

And maybe, if she saw him, she'd tell him about her grandma's drawings. Not that she wanted to see him…

But she did. He was on the phone behind the reception area, his broad back to her. Amy picked out the new map and paid the young ranger-in-training behind the desk while simultaneously trying not to notice that Matt really earned the moniker of Ranger Hot Buns.

He turned and caught her staring. Still on the phone, he arched a single brow.

She waved her map at him and ran out. "You," she said to her reflection in the rearview mirror when she was in her car and on the road, "are an idiot."

At home, she showered then joined Mallory and Grace for a night out. They went to the Love Shack, Lucky Harbor's one and only bar and grill. The place was done up like an old Wild West saloon, complete with walls of deep bordello red, lined with old mining tools. Lanterns hung over the scarred bench-style tables. The bar itself was a series of old wood doors attached end to end. Run by former world sailing champion Ford Walker and Lucky Harbor's mayor Jax Cullen, the place was never wanting for customers.

The three women got a table and ordered a pitcher of margaritas, which was served by Jax himself. Tall, dark, and handsome, Jax poured them each an iced, salted glass with a smile that could charm the panties right off a nun. "Enjoy, ladies."

"He's hot," Grace said, watching his ass as he walked off.

"Yes," Mallory agreed. "And very taken by one sweet Maddie Moore, who runs the B&B down the road." She lifted her glass. "To leaving Chocolate-ville for Margarita-ville."

Grace lifted her glass. "To new chapters."

Amy clicked her glass to theirs. "To *no* good girls tonight."

They all drank to that, until Grace suddenly choked.

"What's the matter?" Amy asked, pounding her on the back.

Grace coughed and sputtered some more, then recovered, as in unison Amy and Mallory swiveled their heads to see what she'd been looking at.

Two tables over sat three guys. Three gorgeous guys. Ty Garrison, Dr. Josh Scott, and Forest Ranger Hot Buns, all focused in on the Chocoholics' table, smiling as if they saw something they liked.

Ty set down his drink and ambled over. He pulled a grinning Mallory from her chair and into his arms, and without a word, planted a long, hot, deep kiss on her. Finally, when surely they had to be out of air, he pulled back. "See you later," he said with a naughty smile, then guided Mallory carefully back to her chair as if she were a precious commodity.

He was back at his table with the guys before Mallory recovered. "He's mine," she said, sounding shell shocked. "Can you believe it?"

Grace was fanning herself. "Does he always kiss you like that?"

"That?" Mallory asked, still looking dazed. "That was just the appetizer on the Ty menu of kisses."

"You are one lucky woman," Grace said.

Mallory grinned. "I am, aren't I?"

Amy's gaze was still locked in on Matt. He was as fixated on her.

The music was loud, the sounds in the bar joyous and rambunctious. There was dancing, and after a few minutes, Ty came back and stole Mallory away. Several other guys lined up to ask Grace to dance, and someone asked Amy as well.

But she didn't want to dance with a stranger.

She didn't want to dance at all.

What she wanted felt complicated and scary, but hell, baby steps, right? *Right.* So she got up and walked to where Matt and Josh were sitting. Both men smiled at her, but she had eyes only for Matt. He was still in his uniform, hair mussed, eyes shadowed and brooding. He'd gotten some sun today, but he looked weary to the bone.

Clearly it'd been a long day.

But there was something about this quiet, brooding Matt that got to her. He was so...real. Everything he was, everything down to the bone, was genuine.

And he'd come here instead of to the diner. To avoid her? Something settled in her gut. Disappointment. Regret. Worry. She tried to gauge his thoughts but couldn't. He wasn't drinking; the only thing in front of him was a soda, no doubt his beloved Dr. Pepper.

Maybe he was still working...

Josh stood up and took her hand. "You owe me a dance."

She laughed. "I do not."

"Okay, I owe you a dance. For all that great service you always give me at the diner, complete with such sweet smiles."

She gave him a long look. She wasn't known for her sweet smiles. They all knew that she wasn't known for her sweet *anything*.

But he flashed her a grin and smoothly pulled her onto the dance floor before she could protest. "Look at you," she said, surprised. "You can move."

"You know it," he said, dancing with the kind of abandon only a big white guy with absolutely no sense of shame could pull off.

She had to laugh, and then again when he moved in close and purposely bumped his very nice body up against hers, his hands on her hips. "Josh," she said, smiling up at him, "why are you flirting with me?"

He grinned. "Because it's pissing off Matt."

She glanced over at Matt, still at the table, still nursing his soda, staring at them with an unreadable look on his face. "Nothing pisses Matt off," she said. "He doesn't let anything get to him."

Josh chuckled and leaned in closer. "Don't let his cool exterior fool you. He lets plenty eat at him. He's just good at hiding it."

"Well, then you're mistaken about his feelings for me," Amy said. "He won't care that we're dancing."

"Hmm," Josh said, noncommittally. The music slowed, and he pulled her close so that she felt his chest rumble with his own amusement. "What's he doing now?" he asked.

Amy took a peek, and her heart skipped a beat at the sight of Matt, still slouched in his chair. "Just watching."

"Watching, and getting more and more irritated with me, I'd bet." Josh sounded quite pleased at the thought. "He cares, Amy, big time."

"And you're doing this why?"

"Because I'm banking on the fact that you care, too."

The song ended, and Josh gave her a hug, and then ambled off toward the bar. When she walked past Matt's table to get to her, he stood up.

"Hey," she said, her heart taking a good hard leap just before she realized he wasn't looking at her. He was on his cell phone. "Sorry," she mouthed.

He shook his head, silently telling her it wasn't her fault, but he didn't stop. Instead, he headed straight for the door.

She stared after him. There was no denying it. She'd hoped to see him tonight, maybe talk. And if he hadn't looked so...well, distant, she might have also thought about stealing a kiss.

Or two.

Yeah, that's what she really wanted. She could admit it to herself. She wanted his arms around her. She wanted his warm eyes looking into hers, making her feel like the only woman on earth, like only he could do.

She wanted to taste him, have him taste her. She'd wanted to slide her fingers into his silky hair and feel his warm strength surround her, making her feel safe.

And instead, he'd walked away from her without looking back. And though she'd done just that too many times in her life to count, she hadn't realized how bad it sucked to be on the receiving end until now.

Chapter 17

Chocolate. It isn't just for breakfast anymore.

Matt moved out of The Love Shack and into the night. As he got behind the wheel of his truck, Josh opened the passenger door and took the shotgun position without a word.

"Hell no," Matt said. "You're walking."

Josh chuckled but locked his door and buckled in. "Man, you are so gone over her. You ran out of there like a scared little girl and nearly forgot your wing man."

"You suck as a wing man. And I was heading out because I got a call. Climber down."

Josh's smile faded. "Injuries?"

"Bad. That's all I know."

"Hit it."

"You had a beer," Matt said.

"Never got a chance to even take a sip, so I'm good."

Matt nodded and hit the gas, heading toward Widow's Peak while Josh pulled up a GPS of the area.

"I know exactly where we're going," Matt said grimly.

"The guys we chased off of the face last week went back tonight for a moonlight hike."

"Shit."

Matt turned off the highway and spared Josh a glance. "And since when are you Fred Astaire?"

Josh shrugged. "Pretty girl in my arms. What's not to like?"

Matt ground his teeth. Amy *was* a pretty girl. She was *his* pretty girl.

Except she wasn't.

He'd caught the look she'd given him tonight as he'd left. In spite of the fact that he'd been an asshole, she was concerned. Worried.

About him.

When she looked at him like that, all sweet eyed and tenderhearted, it did something to him. She'd looked at him like she wanted to take care of him, like she wanted to make it all better for him, and for a beat, he'd wanted her to do just that.

Which was not going to happen. He didn't need anyone to take care of him.

"And you told me to find a woman," Josh said. "Remember? You said—"

"Not *that* woman."

"Well you should have been more specific," Josh said in such a reasonable tone that Matt wanted to wipe the floor with his face.

Knowing it, Josh laughed softly, which Matt ignored because his phone was going crazy. First dispatch checking his ETA, then his boss wondering what the fuck a group of climbers were doing on Widow's Peak at ten o'clock at night, in an area supposedly closed off to the public.

Matt would like to know the same thing.

"Did you get an injury update?" Josh asked when he'd hung up.

"No one's on scene yet. S&R are en route, too." Matt took the fire road that would bring them to the same midpoint where they'd found the climbers before. Once again, they had to hike the last quarter mile in, this time in the dark.

At the cliff's edge, two guys were huddled, glancing anxiously down. A third had attempted to climb over to rescue the fourth and had gotten stuck, terrified, about ten feet down.

Much farther down, thirty feet or so, was the fourth, lying still on a ledge.

Trevor Wright.

Search and rescue arrived just as Matt and Josh did. Everyone mobilized quickly, and in ten minutes, they had the first climber up. He had no injuries. Ten minutes more and they had the still-unconscious Trevor on a stretcher belaying him up with ropes, where he was then immediately airlifted out with Josh on board, looking grim.

Matt headed back to his truck alone and drove to the station, where he wrote up his report before heading to the hospital. He was furious, at himself. He'd known those kids would be trouble and should have found a way to keep them off the mountain.

Unfortunately, the update on Trevor wasn't good. He was in critical care, and his very connected father was already making noises about suing the state, the county, the forest service, and Matt as well. Everyone and anyone over his son's injuries.

The North District station was going to have a battle

on its hands, and for Matt, it felt like Chicago all over again.

He grabbed an hour of sleep and by dawn was heading out with Sawyer to talk to the three uninjured climbers. Each of them vehemently denied that drugs or booze had been involved in the previous night's climb.

Matt could only hope that the tests run on Trevor proved otherwise. He and Sawyer had just pulled away from the last climber's house when Matt's boss called, reaming him for the entire fiasco from start to finish.

"What?" Sawyer asked when Matt hung up and swore. "The kid take a turn for the worse?"

"No," Matt said. "In fact, he woke up long enough to claim that none of them touched the gate, that they honestly believed the trail was open."

"Bullshit."

"Gets worse," Matt said. "He also says that I put my hands on him that day I chased him off the peak. That I pushed him."

"Little dick syndrome," Sawyer said. "Fucking punks."

"Yes but he's also a punk with a lawyer, who's already all over it."

"Fine," Sawyer said. "You have Josh as a witness that you didn't touch any of them."

"There's still going to be a formal inquiry. I'm going to have to go in front of the board to explain how this happened on a closed trail, a trail I shut down myself."

Sawyer shook his head and spoke grimly. "They're going to blame you for minors vandalizing the gate locks and sign, then trespassing on a closed trail while possibly under the influence. Fuckers."

"They're going to do what they have to in order to

resolve this without a lawsuit." Matt punched Josh's number into his cell. "Talk to me."

"He's lawyered up."

"Tell me something I *don't* know," Matt said. "There's going to be an inquiry. This is a great time to spill about Wright being under the influence of something."

"Shit, Matt." Josh let out a long breath. "You know I can't tell you that. He's a minor. He's got all sorts of rights." He paused. "But per protocol, tests have been sent to the labs."

Okay, Matt could read between the lines on that one. There was the hope that in case of a lawsuit, the results could be subpoenaed. But hope wasn't good enough. Hope wasn't going to save his ass. He disconnected and swore again.

Sawyer took a look at Matt's face and whipped his SUV around.

"What are you doing?"

"You're taking me to the site," Sawyer said. "We're going on a little evidence scavenger hunt."

For the second time in twenty-four hours, Matt climbed up to Widow's Peak and scoured the area. He and Sawyer also searched the meadow floor just beneath the cliffs, where they found five empty bottles of beer and a roach clip. Sawyer bagged them up for DNA evidence.

"Christ," Matt said, the situation hitting him. "This could actually go to trial."

"I don't think it'll get that far," Sawyer said. "These guys are all about the bragging. Trust me, someone will open his mouth about attempting Widow's Peak, and then we'll nail them for trespassing, underage drinking, and whatever else we can get them for."

Matt hoped he was right.

•   •   •

The next night, after a long shift, Amy drove toward home, then made an unexpected detour.

A big one.

She headed toward the mountain and parked in front of Matt's cabin. His truck wasn't there, and she didn't know if that was a good or bad thing. For the third night in a row, he hadn't come to the diner for food, and this time she knew why. All day long she'd heard the gossip about the fallen climber and Matt's supposed negligence. She glanced at the bag she'd packed up, the one sitting on the passenger seat, and called herself all kinds of a fool.

Matt didn't need her to look after him. He was a big boy. But she got out of the car and then found herself standing on his porch, trying to figure out if she should leave the food for him or if that would attract bears, when a truck drove up.

Matt, of course.

Their eyes met as he got out of his vehicle, and her tummy quivered. He was still in uniform, looking dusty, hot, exhausted, and like maybe he could use a good fight.

"Hey," she said softly when he hit the porch.

"Hey." He unlocked his door then turned to her. "I'm not much company tonight."

"You've had a bad day."

He let out a sound that didn't hold any mirth. "Yeah. A bad day." He stepped inside, leaving the front door open.

Not exactly an invite, and she paused, knowing damn well that he clearly wanted to be alone. She recognized the need, since it was how she felt most often.

Sometimes being alone isn't all it's cracked up to be...

He'd said that to her, all those nights ago on the mountain at Sierra Meadows. And he'd been right.

So she stepped inside and shut the door behind her.

He glanced over. Obviously he'd expected to find her gone because he raised a brow at the sight of her.

"Want to tell me about it?" she asked.

"What, the gossip train didn't come through the diner today?"

"Yeah, and I'm the type to get on that train," she said dryly. "How's the guy who fell?"

"In ICU, but it looks like he's going to make it." He shoved his fingers through his hair. "He shouldn't have been on the peak. I had the trail closed off. I chased him and his friends out of there less than a week ago, but they came back."

There was something in his tone that caught her attention. Self blame. "Matt, it's not your fault."

"Yeah, it is." He let out a long, jagged breath. "My district. My problem."

She'd never known anyone like him, so willing to be in charge, and just as willing to take the responsibility that went with that. "Come on, give yourself a break here. You couldn't have known those guys would go back on that climb."

"I knew."

She moved closer. "Well then you also know that you couldn't have stopped them. You're just one man. How are you supposed to keep the entire area patrolled?"

"It's my job to figure out a way."

She ran a hand down his tense back. "God complex much?" she teased.

He moved away from her touch, and while she tried

to be okay with that, he spoke again. "I fucked up, Amy. And it's not the first time." He strode into the kitchen and opened the refrigerator. Yanking out a beer, he stared at it, then set it back in the fridge and grabbed a soda. He opened it and handed it to her, then took another for himself. "You asked why I came here from Chicago."

"Yes." She took a long drink because her throat felt suddenly dry.

"I came after everything went to shit. My job, my marriage...*Both* my fault, by the way."

"Matt," she said, setting down her soda, shaking her head. "You—"

"No, it's true. My partner was on the take. I knew it, and I was told to look the other way. I didn't. He tried to implicate me. He couldn't quite pull that off, but he caused enough doubt about me on the job that it hurt my career, and I—*Hell.*" Again he shoved his fingers in his hair and turned away from her, staring out the window.

"You what?" she asked softly.

"People didn't like what I'd done, turning Ryan in. He maintained his innocence throughout his trial, and he was well liked. No one wanted to believe it of him."

So he'd taken the heat for turning on him. "You did the right thing," she said, aching for him. He always did the right thing, even when it wasn't the easy thing. "My God, would they have rather he continued?"

He shrugged. "People believe what they want to believe. And it was damn hard for them to believe that of Ryan, even after he went to jail. It was easier to..."

"Blame you?" She shook her head. "You did what you had to. You couldn't have lived with yourself if you'd done nothing."

"I ruined his life. And I ruined Shelly's, too."

"Your ex?"

"Yes. Our marriage failed because she hated being a cop's wife, hated the privacy restrictions my job imposed and the extra security it took to keep her safe when there were bad guys gunning for me. She never believed there was really a threat until she was stalked by someone I'd once put away."

"Oh my God. What happened?"

"He got out of jail and came after her and found her an easy mark. He jumped her in a grocery store parking lot. Pulled a gun on her, but she was able to get away without injury." He shook his head. "The marriage, not so much."

"She blamed you," Amy said quietly.

"She did."

"She knew who she was marrying, Matt," she said carefully. "She knew what she was getting. Telling you that you ruined her life doesn't seem anywhere in the vicinity of fair—"

"It had nothing to do with fair." His voice was grim. He'd obviously blamed himself for it, all of it.

"Oh, Matt." She had no idea how to console him, but he clearly had no desire to be consoled. "I'm sorry."

"You wanted to know," he said. "You wanted the story, and you've got it. You should stay as far from me as you can get, before I screw up your life, too."

"Okay, that's a little—" She broke off because he snatched his keys off the counter and headed out the door. "Matt—"

He turned back to her. "You told me not to get attached, that this was just sex. That still true?"

Shocked, she stared at him, unable to think.

He took in her expression and nodded as if she'd answered the question. "I have to go." He shut the front door behind himself, leaving her alone.

In his house.

She heard his truck start and take off, and she shook her head. *What had just happened?* Did she really let him go, thinking that what they had was just sex? And did he honestly believe that he didn't deserve happiness? He was the best man she'd ever known. If anything, *she* was the one *he* should run from. *She* was the one who'd been stupid and hurtful to the people in her life, not Matt. With every fiber of her being she wanted to help him, but she had no idea how or what to do. Nothing in her life had given her the experience required for this. Good girl lessons certainly hadn't covered this. She was way out of her depth and out of her league.

She drove back to town, still reeling. She glanced at the time. Riley was due to get off work from the diner. The other day, Amy had caught her hitchhiking back to the forest.

Hitchhiking was a good way to get around. Amy had done it herself for years. But it was also a good way to get dead.

She pulled into the diner's parking lot with the intention of driving Riley herself. Jan was closing up, locking the front door. "Girl's out back," Jan called through the glass. "Dumping the trash."

Amy walked around and found Riley standing on the back step tying up a trash bag. "Hey, I'll give you a ride."

Riley looked up. She actually almost smiled before she caught a good look at Amy's face. "What's wrong?"

"Nothing." Since when were her feelings that visible?

How had that happened? Once upon a time, she'd been so good at hiding them that no one had ever been able to gauge her moods.

Riley wasn't fooled. "Something's wrong."

"Long day," Amy said. "Come on, I'm parked out front."

Riley shrugged and tossed the trash into the Dumpster, and a minute later, they'd walked around and gotten in Amy's car.

"You going to tell me now?" Riley asked.

"Tell you what?"

"Why you're pissed at me."

Amy blew out a breath and studied the pier ahead of them, shame filling her that she'd let Riley think she could be mad at her, even for a second. "It's not you. I'm sorry if I made you think that." It was late, and everything was quiet and dark. Even the Ferris wheel was still, as still as her heart. "I had a fight with someone."

"Yeah? You kick their ass?"

"Not that kind of fight."

"Oh." Riley sounded disappointed. "Was it with Matt?"

Without warning, Amy's throat tightened. Not wanting to speak, she simply nodded.

Riley sucked in a breath. "He hurt you?"

"No." She turned to Riley and saw the worry in her expression. "No, he'd never hurt me."

Riley relaxed slightly. "But he made you sad."

"Well... a little, yeah. Forget it. It's not your problem."

Riley rustled around in her ratty backpack and came up with two lollipops, clearly pilfered from the small can at the hostess station from the diner. She very sweetly offered out the stolen loot.

Reminded of just how young Riley was, Amy took one. Under normal circumstances, Riley would probably be having her first relationship with a boy about now, writing his name on her notebook, dreaming of proms and football games instead of figuring out where to find her next meal or who was going to try to hurt her next.

"You'll make up," Riley said. "Because he's totally into you. I can tell by the way he's always looking at you. Not like pervy looking," she said quickly, "but like ... like he loves you."

Amy doubted that very much. She knew Matt loved being in bed with her, and as it turned out, she loved that, too. And maybe deep, *deep* down, she'd told herself she might have eventually let it turn into more, but she'd been fooling herself. He didn't know her well enough to even think about loving her.

And if he had, he'd have run from her even sooner. "Where's the sweatshirt I gave you?" she asked Riley. "It's cold tonight."

"Crap," Riley said, smacking her own forehead. "I forgot it in the kitchen. Wait here, I'll try to catch Jan before she locks the back." She dashed out of the car and vanished around the corner of the diner.

Amy sighed and set her head down on her steering wheel. Her mind was going too fast.

Or not fast enough.

She didn't understand how it had gone so badly with Matt. And if she was admitting not understanding that, she also didn't understand something else.

He'd walked away from her. Actually, not walked. *Run.*

If it had truly been just physical chemistry between

them, then why? There'd been no reason for him to go, though she understood the concept well enough. After all, she'd spent her life making sure she was always the one to go. Now it was second nature.

And yet somehow, this time, this one time with Matt, she'd felt different. Like maybe she'd thought that this time there'd be no walking away.

She'd been wrong.

She lifted her head, wondering what was taking Riley so long. *Too* long. She got out of the car and retraced her steps to the back door of the diner.

Riley was there, pinned up against the alley wall by a guy in a hoodie and homeboy jeans. "You owe me, you greedy little bitch," he was saying, hand at Riley's throat, the other one on her breast. "You know you do."

"*Hey!*" Amy yelled, white-hot fury taking over. And something else just as white-hot: Fear. And a terrible sense of déjà vu. "Let her go!"

Mistake number one. Because the guy dropped Riley and turned toward Amy.

Swamped with the memories of another time and place, of a different man who'd wanted Amy to pay what she'd owed, she took a step backward. She tripped over her own feet and went down. Mistake number two.

Because then the guy was on her.

Chapter 18

♥

*Man cannot live by chocolate alone, but it sure
is fun trying.*

Panicked and driven by horror, Amy scooted back on
her butt, but the guy was fast and already towering over
her. She reacted with instinct, swinging out with her foot.
He hit his knees on the cement steps, and she flung her
keys as hard as she could into his face.

"Bitch," he snarled, and slapped a hand over his eyes.
"Goddammit, bitch."

"No, Troy, *you're* the bitch," Riley yelled from behind
him and clobbered him over the head with what looked
like an empty beer bottle.

It shattered.

The guy's eyes went blank, then rolled up in his head,
and he slowly fell over.

"Oh my God." Amy lunged over him and grabbed
Riley's arms. "Are you okay?"

"F-fine," Riley said, clearly not fine, shaking like a
leaf. Amy knew the feeling since she was shaking, too.

She pulled Riley over the crumpled body, and they both tumbled inside the kitchen.

Jan, sitting alone at the island, counting receipts, looked up in surprise. "What—"

"Police," Amy managed, slamming and locking the door. "We need to call—"

"No," Riley gasped. "Please don't. I'm fine. He'll go."

Amy looked through the back door window, mouth gaping in surprise. The back stoop was empty. "You're right, he's gone."

"Told you," Riley whispered.

"Who's gone?" Jan asked.

Amy ripped open the back door and stared in shock at the spot where there'd been a body only a moment before. She whipped around and looked at Riley.

Riley lifted a shoulder.

"You knew him," Amy said, once again shutting and locking the door.

"He was just some guy."

"No, you *knew* him. You called him Troy. He said you owed him."

"Just a misunderstanding," Riley said, staring out the window into the night. She'd gathered her wits quickly.

Amy supposed she'd learned how to do that the hard way. "Riley—"

"Don't sweat it."

"Don't *sweat* it? He was attacking you."

"It's nothing I can't handle," Riley insisted, then paused. "He's my stepbrother."

"*What?*"

"Yeah, um, thanks for the help back there but I've gotta go."

"No. Riley—"

But Riley had unlocked and unbolted the door and hightailed it into the night. Amy swore and helped herself to Jan's purse hanging on a hook.

"Hey," Jan said.

Amy pulled out the pepper spray she'd known that Jan carried, waving it. "Borrowing this!" she said, then went outside after Riley, pepper spray at the ready in her hand in case Troy showed up again. She had a pounding headache and a nagging side ache to boot, which made no sense, but there was no Troy.

And no Riley either. She was gone.

Completely gone.

Hoping she'd show up at home, Amy went there first.

No Riley. Teeth gritted, she grabbed her flashlight and went back out into the night, heading to the forest.

No Riley there either.

Tired, hurting, terrified for Riley, Amy finally gave up and went back to her apartment, hoping against hope the girl had miraculously shown up.

But it wasn't Riley she found on her doorstep. When the unexpected shadow rose, tall and built, moving toward her, she gasped in terror.

"Just me," Matt said, stepping under the light. His gaze was steady and his expression solemn, not so much as a glimmer of a smile on his usually good-humored, affable face.

Amy drew a deep breath to deal, but suddenly her vision swam, then shrank to a pinpoint. From what seemed like a great distance, she heard Matt call her name. She opened her mouth to answer, but couldn't.

Odd.

Odder still was that her bones seemed to dissolve. Matt grabbed her just as she would have fallen. She blinked and then pushed at him, but he completely ignored her struggles and held on.

"I'm okay," she said.

"You just about passed out."

"I'm fine now." She shook her head to clear it. "It was nothing. Why are you here?"

"Because I'm an ass," he said. "And bullshit, it was nothing. Something scared you nearly into a faint."

"I don't faint. But you almost got a face full of pepper spray." She tugged free, and this time he let her go, reluctantly.

"Why are you wet?" he asked, looking at his hand before going utterly still. "Amy, you're bleeding."

"What? No, I'm—" She stared down at her sweater, which had a growing dark patch, making it cling to her side. "Huh." She gulped in a panicked breath and nearly passed out again, but Matt's hands were back on her, utter steel.

Her anchor.

"I've got you," he said, nudging her down to the step, lifting her sweater. They both looked at the two-inch-long gash on her side.

"Look at that," she said weakly. "He got me."

Matt yanked his own shirt over his head and turned it inside out before gently pressing it against her side. "He who?"

"Actually, I think it was the bottle," she said. "It broke, and I must have rolled on it."

"What bottle? Amy, stay with me."

She struggled to do just that, but the pain of the cut was

hitting her now, stealing her breath. "Riley used a bottle to hit her stepbrother over the head. It broke, and I rolled away from him but..." More old memories surfaced. Her stepfather's footsteps coming down the hallway toward her bedroom. *You owe me, Amy. You owe me big*... Yeah. She knew *exactly* what Troy had wanted from Riley. Amy had escaped her own nightmare before it'd come to fruition by being strong and mean. She hoped Riley had escaped as well, but she was having her doubts.

"Amy." Cupping her face, Matt made her look at him. "Keep your eyes open." He spoke evenly, his voice remarkably matter-of-fact, as if he might be inquiring about the weather. She found the simple tone incredibly steadying.

"Riley's brother," he said. "That's who attacked you?"

"No, he attacked Riley. I attacked him."

He drew a breath and squeezed her hand very gently. "Are you hurt anywhere else?"

"I don't think so."

He nodded, then ran his hands over her body himself, checking to make sure before lifting her in his arms and carrying her toward his truck.

"Where are we going?"

"The ER. You need a few stitches."

"What?" Adrenaline surged. So did panic. She hated doctors. Hated hospitals. "No. I want to try to find Riley."

He didn't slow down.

"Matt, no. No hospital."

"No would normally work on me," he said. "But not this time."

"I—"

"Nonnegotiable, Amy."

• • •

Matt carefully buckled Amy into his truck and jogged around to the driver's seat, simultaneously calling Josh. By luck, Josh was at the ER and promised to be waiting for them.

Matt had been on an untold number of search-and-rescue calls and highway patrol assists, not to mention all he'd seen and done as a SWAT cop in Chicago.

But Amy bleeding undid him.

She undid him. Completely. He hadn't wanted to get involved in a relationship with her, but given his current accelerated heart rate, he'd done exactly that. For so long he'd blamed himself for his failed marriage, which had allowed him to easily keep his distance from other women.

And then Amy had walked right past all his brick walls. What was it about her?

"I don't need stitches," she said for the tenth time.

He turned to glance at her as he pulled out of her parking lot, but the interior of the truck was too dark.

"I don't," she said firmly, but her voice trembled, giving her away.

"Did you know that Riley had a brother?" he asked, hoping to distract her because they *were* going to the ER.

"Stepbrother," she said. "And no, I didn't know."

"What did he want?"

"Riley," she said grimly. "He had her pinned to the wall. I yelled at him, trying to get his attention off of her and onto me instead."

Jesus. "And that's when he cut you."

"No. I was backing away from him and tripped. He was on me before I could blink, and that's when Riley came after him with a bottle. Knocked him out." She shook her head. "I dragged us into the diner to call the police, but then Troy vanished. And so did Riley. I ended up at home, and you were there. Why were you there again?"

Good question. He'd felt like such a complete dickwad about how he'd acted earlier. He had no excuse, none, and he'd come to her place to apologize. "Did he touch you? Did he—"

"I'm fine. I just want to go home."

"Soon." He pulled into the ER. Josh met them as promised. Mallory was there as well, in her scrubs, ready with a warm hug and a calm, steady smile as she got Amy settled into a cubicle and prepped for stitches.

Josh examined the wound. "Nicely done, Champ. What happened?"

Amy was shaking. The pain and shock had hit her. "Had a fight with a broken bottle," she said.

Josh *tsk*ed. "Hate that." He nudged Matt out of his way, then sat on the stool at Amy's side. "I have a few questions. Want me to kick out the brooding ranger first?"

Amy's eyes slid to Matt, who did his best to look like a piece of equipment. A very necessary piece of equipment. Amy shook her head. "No. He can stay."

Which was good, since he wasn't going anywhere.

Josh shooed him around to the opposite side of Amy's bed, where he could take her hand and be the moral support team. Mallory stayed next to Josh, behind the instrument tray, ready to assist.

"So who was wielding the bottle?" Josh asked.

"Riley," Amy said, and rubbed her temples. "But it wasn't her fault. She was fighting off her stepbrother."

"He touch you? You hurt anywhere else?"

"No."

Josh ran a gentle finger over her cheek, where a small bruise was forming. "What's this from?"

"I don't know. Maybe from when I fell. I'm not sure."

Josh nodded, not taking his eyes off hers. "Sometimes a victim doesn't like to talk about what happened to them, but—"

"*Nothing* happened." Amy met first Mallory's concerned gaze, and then Matt's, before looking back at Josh. "Really. Riley knocked him out, and he vanished before I could call the police. The end."

"Did you call the police afterward?" Josh asked.

"I never got a chance to make the call. Troy vanished, and then I was with Riley..."

"That's okay," Josh said. "You've got a law enforcement officer right here." He gestured to Matt.

Amy turned her head and looked up at him. He nodded, stroking the hair back from her face. "We'll make a report," he said. "Then find Riley. Okay?"

She hesitated, her gaze searching his, then slowly, she nodded.

"Stitches first," Josh said.

"I'm not good at stitches," Amy said.

Josh smiled. "That's okay. I am."

"This is true," Mallory assured her. "He's the best."

Josh was examining the wound closely. Looks like maybe five to six stitches total. Won't leave much of a scar."

"Can't you just glue it or something?" Amy asked.

"Not this time," Josh said. "But I'll be quick, and you'll be nice and numbed up, no worries." From out of Amy's range of sight, he reached for a fat needle and nodded to Matt.

Matt bent low and brushed his lips over Amy's temple, palming her jaw to keep her face turned to him and not at what Josh was doing. "Hey, Tough Girl."

"Hey back. This sucks," she said, wincing when Josh began to numb her. "This sucks golf balls."

"It'll be over before you know it," Josh promised. "That's how good I am."

Amy grimaced again but said nothing as he continued to work.

Matt did his part to keep her attention off the needle, stroking a finger over a small scar bisecting her eyebrow. "This one looks interesting. How did you get it?"

Amy let out a shaky breath. "When I was seventeen, I stole my boyfriend's brand-new bike to get to work, then crashed it."

Josh chuckled, his big fingers working quickly, efficiently. "If I'd been around back then, you wouldn't still have the scar."

"Cocky."

"Just very good," he said. "Keep looking at pretty boy there."

Matt slid Josh a look, which Josh ignored with a smirk.

"Check out his chin," Josh said to Amy. "Two years ago, Matt fell at the South Rim. It was a pussy climb, too. Luckily for him, I was right there. He dislocated his shoulder and cut up his face. I fixed him up so that he can still be a cover model any time he wants."

Amy laughed softly. "Cover model?"

Matt opened his mouth but Josh beat him to it. "He

made the cover of *Northwest Forestry* last year. You probably missed that issue, but the nurses here have it hanging in their break room." Josh was smiling as he told this story, and if he hadn't been wielding the needle with smooth dexterity while he was at it, Matt might have been tempted to shut his mouth for him.

"You're doing great, Amy," Josh said. "Three stitches in, only a couple more to go."

When he'd finished, he helped her upright, gave her some prescriptions, and then was paged away.

"You okay?" Matt asked her.

She nodded. "I'm good to go."

Impressed with her toughness, he slid an arm around her. "I'll take you home. I want to talk to Riley."

Amy went still for a beat, then did a forced relax thing that had Matt taking a second look at her. "What's the matter?" he asked.

"Nothing."

He shouldn't care that she didn't trust him. It shouldn't matter. He hadn't wanted her to trust him, hadn't needed her to trust him, because this wasn't going to be a relationship. But apparently he'd finally gotten over himself and could face the fact that he was ready to move on from the past. Because for the first time in recent memory, he *wanted* to be trusted. By her.

Amy was definitely not on her A-game, which was the only explanation she had for walking right into a trap of her own making. Riley wasn't staying with her. Riley wasn't going to show up to sleep at her apartment tonight. Which Matt didn't know because Amy had lied to him. She'd known this would happen, that it would come back and bite her in the ass. She needed to think, but the problem with that was her brain wasn't in gear.

"Amy." Right there in the hospital hallway, Matt sat her in a chair, then crouched in front of her, weight balanced easily on the balls of his feet. "Where's Riley?"

Conflicting emotions battered her, but she let anger lead the pack. He'd walked away from her so he didn't get to look at her like he was right now, all warm, genuine concern. It hurt. It hurt more than her side did, which was really saying something.

"Amy."

Damn. Damn him. Because she wasn't angry at all. She was sad. She ached to tell him the truth—that Riley wasn't staying with her. But how could she? The terrified teen was going through hell, and she'd *trusted* Amy.

Trust that hadn't been easily given.

If Amy told Matt the truth, he'd be forced by his job to act, and Riley would think she couldn't trust anyone.

But it was more than that. No one had ever really trusted Amy, not like Riley had. Not even Matt trusted her like that. There was no way in hell that Amy would betray her.

"Amy." Matt's voice was low and calm, and also laced with steel.

He wanted answers.

"I don't know where she is exactly." She didn't owe him more, she reminded herself. "How can I? I'm here."

Matt didn't say anything to this, though he registered her defensive tone with an arched brow.

"I'd like to go home now," she said. "I'm tired." Tired of the both of them.

Matt rose to his feet, wrapped his jacket around her,

then led her outside to his truck. They went to the pharmacy first for her antibiotics and pain killers, then Matt drove her home in silence, for which Amy was eternally grateful. She was hurting, both physically and mentally. She was also confused. Historically, she'd made her most craptastic decisions while hurt and confused, which meant that the best thing for her right now was to be alone.

Matt parked, and she made her move before he'd even turned off the engine. She opened the door to hop out, but was snagged by the back of the jacket he'd loaned her.

"I want to go with you and check things out," he said.

No. If he came inside, she'd forget to be upset with him. She'd also have to face her lie about Riley. "Not necessary."

"Maybe not, but I'm doing it anyway."

"No," she said.

He went still. "Excuse me?"

He probably wasn't told *no* very often. He looked as if the word didn't even compute. "I'm fine," she said.

His expression was carefully blank. She suspected that he thought she was being an unfathomable pain in his ass. "Look," she said. "You don't owe me anything. I can get inside my own place without help."

"Goddammit, Amy. I was wrong to walk out on you like that."

"No," she said flatly. "You weren't."

"I was. I had a shitastic day and took it out on you, and I'm sorry for that. So goddamn sorry."

Not used to apologies or people taking responsibility for their own mistakes, this set her back. "It's okay."

"No, it's not," he said.

Diversion, she thought desperately. "Is that kid, the climber, still going to be okay?"

A muscle in his jaw twitched, and for a moment she thought maybe he was going to call her out on the quick subject change, but he didn't. "Yeah," he finally answered. "But his family is gearing up to sue everyone, claiming negligence on the forestry's part."

He'd spoken calmly enough, but she sensed that the situation was causing him some heavy stress. She could see it in the fine lines around his eyes and the tightness to his mouth.

Or maybe that was *her* making him so unhappy. "It seems more like vandalism," she said. "If they took down the signs and broke the lock on the gate."

"We're working on it."

She nodded and slipped out of his truck, but almost before her feet touched the ground, he'd come around to help her.

"Don't brush it off," he said, and she instantly knew he wasn't talking about his work, but about how he'd left her before, at his place. "Don't give me a free pass." Gently he pressed her back to the truck and cupped her face, stroking her bruised cheek. He moved his head next to hers, and his lips traced over the line of her jaw. "I'm sorry," he said again, softly.

Her knees wobbled, and she locked them because he was right. She shouldn't give him a free pass. She never gave anyone a free pass. "I'm going in now."

He looked up at her place. Dark. "Riley say where she was going?"

"I'm not her keeper."

He said nothing to this, and short of telling him the entire truth, there was nothing more she could add.

"Wait here," Matt said at the top of the stairs and left her on the doorstep while he pulled his gun and entered her place.

He came back a moment later, gun holstered.

"Overkill much?" she asked.

"You were attacked tonight, and he could have tailed you home."

She let out a breath as the truth of that hit her. "I don't think I was followed."

He nodded and gestured her in. All the lights were on inside. Matt followed her through the living room, silently regarding her when she sank to her couch, leaned carefully back, and stared at the ceiling.

"Can I get you anything?" he asked.

"No, thank you."

He grimaced at her polite tone. "Amy—" He broke off when his phone buzzed, looking down to read his screen. "Fuck."

"You have to go," she guessed.

"Dispatch." His expression was grim when he came close and crouched at her side. "Someone shot and killed a bear tonight. I don't want to leave you alone but I have to get out there and—"

"I'm fine, Matt."

He looked at her for a long moment. "You'll call me if you have any problems."

"I won't have any problems."

"Amy." His voice was serious. His eyes were serious. Everything about him was terrifyingly serious.

"Okay," she said on a sigh and closed her eyes. "Okay. I'll call you if there are any problems."

She felt his weight shift, then the brush of his mouth

against her temple. "Lock up behind me," he said, and then she heard the front door closing, leaving her just as she'd told him she'd wanted—alone.

It was three in the morning before Matt got done, and he made a drive-by past Amy's place.

It was dark.

He stared up at her window, hoping Riley was there now, and that both she and Amy were sleeping.

At home, he fell into bed exhausted and got two hours of sleep before his alarm went off. On his way to the station, he made another drive-by, this one at the hospital. He still hadn't gotten to talk to Trevor. Unfortunately, the kid was sleeping and not to be disturbed until visiting hours, when of course his attorney would be present.

Matt made his way to Josh's office and found him pacing in the hallway, looking down at his phone. Josh's five o'clock shadow had its own five o'clock shadow. His eyes were dark with exhaustion. He was either hungover as shit or hadn't slept either. Matt shook his head. "Let me guess. You fucked up at work, and a stupid kid got himself hurt, and now his rich daddy is trying to ruin your life."

Josh huffed out a mirthless laugh and dropped his head, rubbing a hand over the back of his neck. He was in scrubs and a white doctor's coat with a stethoscope hanging around his neck. "No. There was a gas leak in my house, had to evacuate Anna and Toby."

"Where are they?"

Josh grimaced. "In there," he said, gesturing to his office. "I gave Anna money to go to the cafeteria and get them breakfast, thinking they could sit quietly in my office and watch videos on my computer while I made morning rounds. Anna got donuts."

"Any left?" Matt asked hopefully.

"I don't know, but there's a sugar high going on in there that rivals Looney Tunes. They're both bouncing off the walls." Josh stared at his closed office door like it was a hissing cobra. "Toby's nanny is sick. I've called everyone in my contact list for a temp babysitter, but no one answered my calls."

Matt laughed softly. "That's because Thing One and Thing Two have worn out everyone in town."

Josh blew out a breath. "Mallory called Lucille for me. Lucille said she'd give me a couple of hours if I promised to pose for her Facebook photo album."

Matt found a laugh in what was proving to be a shit day. "With clothes, or without?"

"Fuck you."

"Not my type." Matt pulled open Josh's office door.

Anna was spinning in her wheelchair. Toby was in her lap, the both of them howling with laughter. At the sight of Matt, Anna grinned wide but didn't stop spinning. "Matty!" she yelled, knocking a stack of files off Josh's desk.

Matt caught and righted the stack, then stuck his foot into the spokes of one of the wheels of her chair, stopping her on a dime. Leaning down, he hugged them both, then smiled at Toby. Josh's mini-me was holding a donut in one hand and a lightsaber in the other, chocolate all over his face.

"What's with the lightsaber?" Matt asked, snagging a donut.

Toby slashed the lightsaber through the air. It lit up and made a *swoosh* sound.

Matt rumpled the kid's hair. "So you're a Jedi."

Toby nodded.

Matt looked at Anna. "You guys are driving your brother nuts. You know that, right?"

Anna grinned. "It's a short drive."

Matt laughed softly. "Try to take it easy on him."

"Why?" Anna asked.

Good question. Matt took a second donut because it was a second-donut kind of day and left to face it. Double fisting his breakfast jackpot, he went back into the hall just as Josh was shoving his cell phone in his pocket.

"Your climber's awake," Josh told him. "His lawyer's on his way. You might want to get a better breakfast than that," he said, nodding to the double donuts. "You look like you haven't slept in days."

Matt finished donut number one. "It's the job."

"Yeah?" Josh asked. "Thought maybe it was the sexy waitress."

"Bite me."

Josh grinned for the first time all morning. "Ah, man. You're so going down. Just like Ty. Give me half that donut."

"Hell no."

"I need it more than you."

Matt shoved it into his own mouth.

"You're an asshole," Josh said.

"Maybe." He chewed and swallowed. "But I don't have two people swinging from the chandeliers in my office."

Chapter 19

*Sure, chocolate has more calories than love,
but it's way more satisfying.*

Amy woke up at dawn, groggy from the pain pill. Josh had put a waterproof bandage on her wound, so she was able to shower. After, she dressed and then walked out of her bedroom to start the coffee, stopping short on her way to the kitchen.

Riley was asleep on her couch.

"Hey," Amy said in surprise.

Snapping to immediate alertness, Riley jerked upright, her hand coming up with something glinting in her fist.

A knife.

"Whoa," Amy said, bending a little at the waist to ease the tightening on her stitches. "Just me."

Riley's hand vanished behind her. "Sorry. You startled me." Her eyes narrowed in on the way Amy was favoring her side. "What's wrong?"

"Nothing. I got cut on the broken glass last night, needed a few stitches."

Riley paled. "Oh, my God. *Oh, my God.*" She rushed off the couch and came toward Amy. "I'm so sorry. Are you all right?"

"Yes. Are you?"

"I'm fine—Forget me. How many stitches? *How did I not know this?*"

"Maybe because you vanished on me. Are you really okay?"

Riley blew out a breath and nodded shakily. "This shouldn't have happened to you."

Amy pushed a pale, shaky Riley back to the couch. She sat next to her and reached for her hand. "I'm okay, honest. And I'm glad I was there. If I hadn't shown up when I did..."

Riley closed her eyes. "I know." She opened her eyes, her expression fierce. "I didn't do anything wrong."

"I know."

"I mean, I've changed. I'm changing."

Amy leaned in and hugged her tight. "It wasn't your fault."

"But it was! He was after me, not you." Riley pulled free and stood. She picked up her backpack.

"Riley," she said softly. "Can't you tell me about it? I can help. I can—"

"No." Riley shook her head violently. "I've screwed everything up." Riley closed her eyes for a beat, then headed to the door.

"I know more than you think," Amy told her. "I was the queen of screwup when I was a kid, and I only got worse as a teen. I screwed up over and over again, and then, by the time I was in real trouble, no one cared. I'd made sure of it."

Riley turned to face her but said nothing, breaking Amy's heart with her doubt.

"You can tell me anything," Amy said. "*Anything.*"

Riley hesitated, then shook her head and reached for the door. "Sorry. I'm so sorry, but I gotta go."

And then there was nothing but the sound of the front door shutting hard.

Amy was still sitting on the couch when her cell rang.

"I'm giving you today off," Jan said.

"Not necessary."

"You were stabbed on my premises last night," Jan said. "I don't want Lucille getting the story or pics. The negative press will kill me. Take a damn day off."

"I wasn't stabbed!"

"Good. Go with that."

"But—"

But Jan was already gone.

Fine. Amy loaded her sketchpad and a few snacks into her backpack. If she couldn't work, she'd clear her head and draw. In fact, now that she thought about it, she needed that more than anything she could think of.

Well...other than the need to be near Matt, the guy she'd promised herself she wouldn't fall for. Except she'd broken that promise. How else could she explain parking at the North District Ranger Station? She could have gone out on her own patio to sketch, but she'd come here.

Fine. Maybe she wasn't up for a hike or figuring out her grandma's cryptic journey right now, but the grounds here were beautiful and peaceful, and she spent an hour sitting on a rock in front of a creek with her sketchpad, trying to clear her mind.

It refused to be cleared. Instead, it kept wandering to

Matt. This distance between them was her own doing. Not a surprise, as she'd been sabotaging her own happiness for a long time. She'd known this thing with him would eventually fall apart, but she'd been secretly hoping it wouldn't.

And if that wasn't a terrifying thought. For the first time in her life, she wanted to ride the train to the end of the line instead jumping off before it even stopped.

You lied to him...

Worse, she'd lied to herself. All her life she'd lived with something hanging over her head. But being in Lucky Harbor this year, staying in one place, making a life for herself...she'd lost her vigilant edge.

She didn't regret that.

She liked having a decent place to live, a job that paid the bills and allowed her the freedom to draw when she wanted. She liked making the kind of keeper friends she'd always dreamed of having.

That's what Mallory and Grace were to her, keepers.

Matt, too, if she was being honest. Yeah, she liked him, *way* too much. She was going to have to face that sooner or later. The truth was, she'd long ago given up believing or trusting in others.

And then she'd come here to Lucky Harbor.

Inhaling the damp forest air, she looked up and locked eyes on Matt. He stood a football field away, on the porch of the ranger station building, his back to her as he talked to two other uniformed officers. He looked big and tough as hell, with his shirt stretched taut over his broad shoulders, the gun on his hip gleaming in the sun.

Flustered to find herself aroused just looking at him, she glanced down at her sketch and then up again, insistently drawn to him.

244 Jill Shalvis

He was gone.

She forced herself to sit there another few moments. He hadn't seen her, she told herself. Because if he had, he'd have come over. He wasn't a coward like her. She inhaled a deep breath, found her backbone, packed up her things, and headed to the building. "Is Matt Bowers busy?" she asked the ranger at the front desk.

The guy laughed. "Always. But his office is the last on the right, go on back."

She found him standing before his desk, hands on hips, jaw dark with stubble, looking down at a mountain of paperwork like he was facing a firing squad. He seemed impossibly imposing, and a little pissed off. His eyes tracked directly to her and though nothing in his tough-guy stance changed, his eyes warmed.

In response, *everything* within her warmed. She didn't really understand that, how it could still be this way, how it felt stronger each and every time she saw him. He'd hurt her. She'd hurt him—though he didn't even know it yet. And still, she wanted him. She wanted his hands on her, his mouth on her, *him* on her, making her forget everything in the way only he could. "Am I interrupting?" she asked.

"Not even a little bit."

Given the stacks on his desk, this was an obvious lie. His gaze roamed over her. "How are you?"

"Fine."

"Truth, Amy."

Truth... The truth was that his shoulders were so wide they practically blocked out the light, plenty wide enough for her to set her head down and lose herself in him for a few. Only a few.

Not that she would. "I'm managing."

"I drove by your place last night. Everything looked dark and quiet. You sleep okay?"

"Yeah."

"I came by again about an hour ago to talk to Riley. She wasn't there."

"She had things to do."

Their eyes met and held for a long beat.

"You're not okay," he finally said. "You're flushed."

"Sunburn. I forgot sunscreen."

He didn't say anything to that, and the silence just about did her in. "It's not just sex," she said. "Not to me."

He still didn't speak, but she knew by his absolute stillness that she had his undivided attention.

"I'm sorry I let you think it," she said. "And okay, maybe some of it *is* about the sex, but that's because it's the best sex that I've ever had. But it's not *all* about the sex."

Matt might be laid-back and easygoing but he wasn't slow. In three steps he closed the distance between them and pulled her in, right up against him. He felt so good she actually moaned, a sound he silenced with a kiss.

She had no idea how a man could be so terrifyingly gentle in the way he held her and yet at the same time plunder her mouth so roughly. But that's exactly what he was, both gentle and rough.

It was exactly what she needed.

"Don't let me hurt you," he said, lips on her jaw, making their way to her ear.

Too late, far too late. To share the pain, she turned her head and nipped his lower lip. Sucking in a breath, he laughed softly. "Tough girl," he murmured, and cupping her face, kissed her again. There was nothing controlled about him now as his tongue tangled with hers, his hands wandering madly from her face to her hips, ending up back in her hair to hold her head still. She pressed even closer, needing him in a way she couldn't even fathom. She wanted him, wanted him to pull off her clothes, wanted to pull off his, *now*. She glanced at his overloaded desk.

Matt followed her gaze, his own darkening. "I like the way you think," he said, and shoved all the stacks of paperwork to the floor. "Lock the door."

Her nipples tightened into two ball bearings. "Will anyone hear us?" she whispered.

His smile was lethal and filled with nefarious, bad boy intent. "Us?"

She flushed, and he laughed softly. "You're going to have to be quiet. *Very* quiet," he said.

She quivered and went damp. "I can do quiet."

"The door, Amy."

She turned to do just that, but it opened before she could and Ty strode in. He had a bag from Eat Me in one hand and two long-necked soda bottles dangling from the other. He wore dark, reflective sunglasses and the navy blue coverall of a paramedic with FLIGHT CARE across his back in white letters.

He dipped his head and eyeballed them over the top of his glasses, taking in Matt's hair standing up on end from Amy's fingers and then her disheveled appearance as well. His lips quirked. "I take it you forgot I was bringing lunch," he said. "Since it looks like you're already in the middle of yours."

•   •   •

"It's not what you think," Amy said.

"No?" Ty asked, amused. "What do I think?"

Amy opened her mouth, then sighed. It was *exactly* what he thought.

Matt came forward, grabbed the bag and both drinks from Ty, then pushed his friend backward over the threshold and shut the door in his face. "I'm going to pay for that in the gym in the morning," Matt said, handing Amy the sodas and food. "So we should probably enjoy this."

"What if he's hungry?"

"He's always hungry. And on second thought, so am I." Matt took the stuff back out of her hands and set them on a chair, then hauled her up against him. "Where were we?"

Amy slid her fingers back into his hair. "You had your tongue down my throat. And your hands up my shirt."

He nodded and slid his hands up her shirt again, fingertips resting just beneath her breasts, which were tingling from his touch.

"And you?" he asked, voice husky. His bedroom voice. "Where were you?"

She bit her lower lip. They both knew exactly where she'd been. Her fingers had been heading for his zipper.

He laughed softly at her, kissed her long and deep, then tore his mouth from hers. Grabbing her hand, he tugged her to the door. "Change of plans. I've got fifty-five minutes left on my lunch break."

"That's enough for lunch *and* dessert."

He smiled. "Yeah, and we're going to have dessert first. But not here. It's not nearly private enough for what I want to do to you."

Her knees wobbled as she followed him out, having

no idea where they were going and not caring. She'd probably follow him anywhere.

And if that wasn't unsettling, he walked them down the hallway past several coworkers, moving with unconscious confidence that spoke of a man on a mission. And he *was* on a mission—to do her. At the thought, she cracked up, and he looked back questioningly.

"Nothing," she said.

As if he could read her naughty thoughts, he gave her a heated look. "We're doing this."

"Yes, please."

He smiled. "I like the 'please.' More of that."

And she laughed again. It wasn't often that she wanted to laugh and jump someone's bones in the space of a few seconds. But then again, it wasn't often that she wanted to both run like hell from someone and hold on tight to him either.

Normally Matt could make the drive from work to home in eleven minutes, allowing for the occasional deer crossing or traffic if he got behind someone not used to the narrow, two-lane, curvy highway.

Today, with Amy next to him practically vibrating with sexual tension, he made it in seven. He pulled up to his cabin with a screech of tires, then turned to her with some half-baked, Neanderthal idea of dragging her into his house. But she beat him to it, crawling over the console to straddle him before covering his mouth with hers.

His first response was a resounding *oh, hell yeah*. This was what he'd needed. Amy in his arms like a tempting, forbidden treat, her dark eyes full of wanting.

And then there was her mouth. God, that mouth, it

could give a full-grown man a wet dream. He staggered out of his truck, pulling her out with him, careful to protect her injury.

At his front porch, they stopped to kiss. "Matt," she whispered, and God, how he loved the sound of his name on her lips. He pressed her against his door. *Take*, his body demanded. Instead, forcing himself to be gentle, he leaned in and nibbled at her throat.

With a moan, her head thunked back to give him access. Trusting... that was new, and tenderness swamped him as he kissed her softly now, a sweet brush of his lips over her skin.

She moaned again, and damn if all his good intentions didn't go up in smoke, the kiss quickly deepening into a hot, hungry intense tangle of tongues.

Tearing her mouth free, she rained kisses down his jaw, her small hands very busy at the buttons of his shirt, her expression one of such fierce intent that he groaned. "Amy—"

She gave up on his buttons and went for his belt and zipper, having some trouble working around his gun and utility belt. And then he was in her hands. Literally.

"Not here," he heard himself say roughly, though he was gentle as he lifted her up, still aware enough to be careful of her stitches. She wrapped her legs around him, and he cupped her ass in one palm, supporting her as he unlocked the door with his free hand. Kicking it closed, he strode with her through his house, ignoring the couch, the fireplace rug, everything except his big bed. By the time she'd begun working off her clothes, he'd stripped naked and was reaching for her.

She'd toed off her kick-ass boots but was still

struggling out of her jeans. He tugged them off and the rest of her clothes as well. His arms glided up hers, taking her hands in his above her head. Palm to palm, chest to chest, thigh to thigh, he looked into her beautiful face and lost his breath. But as he knew she would, she tugged to free her hands. "Amy." He nuzzled at her throat but then made eye contact. "Let's try it my way this time."

She went still. In fact, she appeared to stop breathing. "What way is that?"

"The way where you trust me."

Her eyes met his, heartbreakingly wild. He steeled himself against the surge of unexpected emotion and held her gaze, willing her to look deep and see what he was finally starting to get about himself. He *could* be trusted. She could trust him.

"Matt—"

"I would never hurt you," he breathed, lowering his head to kiss her softly. "Trust me."

She closed her eyes, then opened them again, relaxing her body into his. "I do. I do trust you."

Chapter 20

Nine out of ten people love chocolate.
The tenth person lies.

Hunger and desire pounded through Amy's veins, but there was unease now. And fear. Not that she believed Matt would ask anything of her that she wouldn't be willing to give, but that she'd give him everything. Willingly.

He lowered his head and whispered her name against her lips before kissing her slow and deep. He took his sweet-ass time about it, too, and her entire world came to a stop on its axis. "Matt—"

"Still right here," he murmured, spreading hot, wet kisses down her jaw, along her collarbone. Her breast. "Mmm, you smell like heaven, Amy."

"You have to hurry," she reminded him, rocking into him, trying to get him to pick up the pace. "You don't have much time left."

"I don't like to hurry."

No kidding! His tongue curled around her nipple, and he growled in approval when it beaded for him.

She bucked, and he did it again, reaching for the bedside drawer, grabbing a condom. *Thank God.* He'd come to his senses. They were going to get this show on the road. He protected them both, and then palmed her thighs, opening them. This wrenched a groan from his throat, and he took his time eyeing her all spread out for him. "Missed this," she heard him say, the softly uttered words making her heart kick crazily in her ribcage as he lowered his head and kissed her. Lapped at her. Sucked, until she climaxed with shocking ease.

She was still shuddering when he brushed a kiss over her bandaged side and looked up at her. "You okay?"

Her entire body was humming, and she couldn't feel her toes. Or access her brain cells. "I'll get back to you on that one."

"You do that," he said huskily, and slid into her.

She cried out and arched up. *Hard and fast,* her body demanded, every muscle straining with the need to feel him possess and take her.

But Matt didn't get the hard and fast memo. As if he had all the time in the world, he cupped her face, kissing her as he slowly began to move, grinding against her body in fluid, rhythmic motions, like the ebb and flow of the waves against the shore. Each movement sent a current through her body, making her arch into him, molding herself to him. "More, Matt. Please, more."

"Everything," he promised, then dipped his head to her breasts, taking his time with each before pressing a kiss between them, right against her heart.

Which leapt against his mouth. Never in her life had she felt more open, more... vulnerable. It shocked her. It overwhelmed her.

Because this *wasn't* just sex. He was making love to her, so thoroughly and completely that he'd sneaked in past her defenses, leaving her feeling cherished.

Loved.

He slid his hands to her hips and stilled them, making her realize that she'd been bucking against him. He moved against her, slowly, surely, even deeper now. Thinking became all but impossible as her fingers roamed, touching every part of him she could reach, his shoulders, his back. His face. Her heartbeat was different, faster yes, but beating just for him, it seemed.

Only for him, and she panicked at the barrage of emotions, freezing up.

"I've got you," he murmured, stroking her, holding her. It wasn't the first time he'd made this promise, but it was the first time she really heard him, believed him. He thrust into her, again and again, and her senses took over. The sight of his face, drawn in fierce concentration as he gave her pleasure, the delicious scent of him, the sound of her own heart thundering in her ears, and her panting echoing off the walls as she fought for air. Toes curling, her gaze locked on his, and she was hit with the one-two punch of his eyes. Her heart tightened along with the rest of her as she barreled toward the mother of all orgasms. When it hit, she called out his name in shock, in surprise, in sheer overwhelming passion. He stayed with her right into the waves of ecstasy, and then followed her there, coming with a rough, ragged groan as he pressed his hips to hers in one final, hard thrust. Seeing stars, she clutched at him, her only anchor in a spinning world.

She was still trembling from the aftermath when she

felt him push the damp hair from her face. She kept her eyes closed because *oh, God.*

God, she'd really done it now.

She'd fallen for him.

She had no idea how he felt as he held her snug up against himself, stroking her slowly cooling skin, and that was for the best. Knowing she was desperately close to making a complete fool of herself, she turned over to crawl out of the bed, but found herself pinned flat.

"What?" she asked, not liking how her breath hitched, how her body wanted to rock into his, unable to get enough of him.

Matt flipped her over and looked into her face. He searched for something, probably for a hint that she was still on board with the whole trusting him thing. Whatever he found made him smile. "That's more like it," he said, all male smug and satisfied, the big, sexy jerk.

"Move," she said, trying to buck him off.

"Why? Going somewhere?"

"Yeah, and so are you. Back to the station."

"Not yet." He rolled to his side and pulled her in, kissing her slowly and leisurely until she curled right into him like she belonged there. "Your side hurt?" he asked.

"No."

"Good."

She waited for him to make a move for round two but though he pressed his mouth to her temple and ran a hand down her back, he just held her. "Last night shook you," he finally said quietly.

Her gut tightened. "Well, yeah."

"You were scared."

"I was terrified. For Riley."

"I know. But it was something else, too."

Her heart took another hard leap—into her throat.

"You don't scare easily," he said. "You waded right in to protect her. You were brave as hell."

She didn't like where this was going and tried to push him away. "You really have to get back to work."

"Soon." His grip was gentle but inexorable. "What got you, Amy? Something triggered some bad memories. What was it? That it was Riley's brother hurting her?"

"*Stepbrother.*"

He nodded. "You've told me about your grandma, about how after she died you went back to your mom's. You didn't last there long, leaving when you were sixteen, right?"

"Yeah. So?"

"So what happened to send you running from your only family?" His gaze was steady, calm, his body warm and strong around hers as he delivered his final, devastating question. "And what happened last night that reminded you of it?"

She opened her mouth to deny it but her breathing hitched, audibly. She closed her eyes, pressing her face into his throat, finding comfort in the scent of him. He smelled like the woods, like his soap, like Matt the man, and it had the most amazing calming effect on her.

But Matt pulled her face back and met her gaze before lowering his head, brushing his lips sweetly over hers, letting her know he was there, right there. She was safe with him, safer than she'd ever been. She could tell him.

But in his eyes, she was strong and fierce and could handle anything. She liked that he saw her like that and not as a victim. If she told him about her past, about who she'd once been, that would change, and it would break her.

Matt slid a hand up Amy's slim spine. So deceptively fragile. But in truth, she was a rock. And she was holding back. He slid a hand into her hair and tilted her face up to his.

She met his gaze. "I...I was a horrible teenager."

"Horrible *is* the definition of teenager."

"No, I mean *really* horrible. And it got worse after my grandma died."

"You were grieving."

"Yes, but I was awful about it," she said. "I acted like my grandma had left me on purpose. My mom had this new husband, and he was rich. I never realized how poor we'd been until I moved in with my mom. Suddenly we had things, and I was in a very different environment, with no experience on how to handle it. I really stuck out like a sore thumb. I think I did it on purpose."

"Probably for attention."

"Yeah." She lifted a shoulder, not meeting his gaze, and he knew there was more, a lot more, and that it was bad.

"My mom," she said. "She's not good at picking men. But this guy, he seemed different than her usual. He was on the board of some exclusive school, so they sent me there. I didn't fit in any more than I'd fit in anywhere else." She paused. "I stole stuff. I ditched. And if I wasn't ditching, I was cheating. I got in a lot of trouble, and every single time I had a ready lie about how it was never my fault."

"Seems about right for the age," he said.

"No." She shook her head, and her hair spilled silkily over his arm. "I was really rotten, Matt. To the core. The girls hated me and with good reason. The boys... they didn't hate me. I made sure of it. I led them around by their egos, which at that age is between their legs." She squeezed her eyes shut. "I was constantly looking for trouble and then weaseling and scrambling my way out of it and blaming someone else." She paused. "Until I couldn't."

It was her grim tone, more than the words themselves, that sent a chill up his spine. "What happened?"

"I finally ran up against someone bigger, older, and smarter than me, someone I couldn't control or manipulate. He wanted—He wanted something I didn't want to give him."

His gut clenched. "And what was that?"

"Me." Her heart kicked as she said it. He could feel it beat against his own.

"He—" She broke off and shook her head.

"Ah, Amy. No." He pulled her in a little closer, hugging her tight, wishing like hell he could fight this years-old battle for her. "Did he rape you?"

"No." She swallowed hard again, and he thought maybe she wasn't going to say anything more, but she forced the words out. "I was able to stop him."

"Good," he said fiercely.

"It wasn't out of the blue, what he wanted. I mean I'd been promiscuous at best and totally indiscriminate. Everyone knew that."

"I don't care if you were *selling* yourself," Matt said tightly. "No is no. And you were just a kid. Tell me you turned him in. That you told someone."

"I did. I told my mom."

Something in her voice told him he really wasn't going to like what came next.

"She thought it was another of my stupid lies."

Yeah, he'd been dead right on that one. He didn't like it, not one fucking bit. He opened his mouth, but she put her fingers over his lips. "I was the girl who'd cried wolf," she said quietly. "I'd lied for so long, *no one* would have believed me."

"Who was it?" he asked, knowing by what she'd said and everything that she *hadn't* said, that she'd known the fucker. "Who did this to you?"

She hesitated. "My stepfather."

He tensed, and Amy ran a hand down his arm. She was trying to soothe *him*. Jesus. Still holding her tight, he cupped the back of her head in his palm and pressed her face into the crook of his neck. He needed a moment, maybe two.

"It was a long time ago," she murmured.

"I know." Just as he knew it didn't matter how long, not if it still came back to her in an instant when she'd seen Riley with her stepbrother. "I'm glad you told me, Amy. I'm so sorry it happened to you."

"It's okay. I've got some perspective now. I was hardly blameless."

"You were fucking sixteen. You *were* blameless."

"I wasn't sixteen when I spent the next five years using sex to manipulate anyone in my orbit."

"You did what you had to."

"I was at least smart enough to always use protection," she said softly.

"You did good, Amy."

"No. I used sex as a weapon. As power, as a tool." She pressed her face into his throat. "At least at first. I stopped when I realized I was becoming immune to emotions, especially during..."

"Sex?"

"Yeah," she said softly, face still hidden.

"Until me."

She didn't say anything, and he pulled back to see her. "Until me," he repeated softly.

"Until you." She paused. "But maybe that's because it'd been so long."

"Bullshit." He'd been there, experienced just how explosive it'd been every time. How before, during, and after he'd been so into her he couldn't breathe, and hell if she hadn't been right there with him. He knew she had been. He'd lay everything on the line with that bet. The way she'd wrapped herself around him when he'd been buried so deep that there'd been no telling where he ended and she began. How she'd kissed him like she was going under for the count and he was the only thing that could save her. The look in her eyes as she clung to him, those unbelievably sexy little whimpers in her throat when he'd taken her where she'd needed to go.

Everything he'd ever dreamed of he'd found there in her arms with her mouth hot on his, her body moving against him, all warm, soft, desperate hunger and need, and she'd felt it back.

So fuck no, it hadn't been just because it'd been a long time for her. He met her gaze and shook his head. "You know it was more than that. Much more."

Chapter 21

Coffee, chocolate, men... some things are just better rich.

Amy didn't know how to respond to Matt, but her body didn't seem to have the same problem. It was responding to just his voice. It always had. She kept figuring it would stop, any minute now, but that hadn't happened yet. "It's nothing personal," she said, not wanting him to be angry. "I've just never been one to feel much."

He stared at her. "No," he said, to what exactly, she had no idea. He rolled her beneath himself, taking care to keep his weight off of her side by bracing himself up on his forearms. "*No*," he repeated. "You felt something different with me."

Her hands slid up his arms, his taut, ripped, gorgeous arms, because she couldn't help herself. She had to touch him. "You can't tell me how I feel, Matt. Nor can you make me tell you what you want to hear."

"Maybe not." But apparently she'd issued some sort of challenge to his manhood because he stripped the covers from them and looked down at her naked body with more than a little wicked, purposeful intent. "But I can make you show me," he said.

Her good parts rippled with anticipation. "Don't be silly. You have to get back to work."

"After."

"After what?"

"After I prove that you feel a whole hell of a lot when I touch you."

Which he did with slow, purposeful, shocking ease.

Much later, after Matt had brought Amy to her car, she headed back to town. Halfway there, she got a cryptic call from Jan to "get here, *fast*."

Having no clue what she could possibly want after she'd told Amy not to come in today, she drove straight to Eat Me.

"Good Lord, girl," Jan said at the sight of her.

"What?"

"What? You just got yourself some, that's what. You're glowing. That should be illegal, flaunting your good fortune around like that."

Henry was at the stove. He stopped stirring and stared at Amy, then let out a slow grin.

Amy clapped her hands to her cheeks. "You can't tell just by looking at me."

"Okay, and I suppose you still believe in Santa Claus," Jan said. "I'd ask if it was any good, but that's all over your face, too. You'd best get yourself together, Sawyer's gonna be here any second. We have a problem."

It had to be a big one if the sheriff was involved. Most problems Jan took care of herself—with sheer orneriness. "What's up?"

"Mallory's money jar went missing, that's what's up," Jan said. "She's on her way, too."

Amy's stomach hit her toes. "Her HSC money jar? The one for the teen center?"

"Yep. Luckily you emptied it out a few nights back. Still, I reckon we lost about a hundred bucks, and it pisses me off. That girl's ass is grass."

Amy had thought her stomach couldn't get any lower than her toes, but she was wrong. "What are you talking about? What girl?"

Jan looked at her like she was a dim bulb. "Riley."

"Wait—You can't think that Riley did this."

"Hell yeah, I can," Jan said. "She stole the money, sure as day."

"Did you catch her at it?" Amy asked.

"Well, no. But she was in earlier, and it's her day off. She was slinking around, and then she was gone. And so was the jar."

Amy's gaze slid to Henry, who gave her a slow nod. "Sorry, babe," he said. "But she was in here, just like Jan says, and she was looking guilty as hell."

"But you know how she is," Amy protested, feeling sick. How many times had she herself done something so stupid, something so desperate? But Riley wouldn't. She had no such need anymore, Amy assured herself. She'd been feeding and clothing her, not to mention the girl had been working at the diner, so there was no reason for this. "She's just sullen and defensive naturally. She *always* looks guilty."

"She's a loose cannon," Jan said. "An unknown."

"*All* teenagers are loose cannons," Amy said. "It doesn't mean she did it. How many customers have you had in here today? How many people at the counter?

Hell, how many helped themselves behind the counter to pour their own coffee because you were too busy watching the cooking channel to be bothered?"

Jan shrugged, unwilling to be repentant about her own serving deficiencies. "She's an *unknown*," she stubbornly repeated.

"*I* was an unknown," Amy said. "And you took a chance on me."

Jan shrugged, again signaling that Amy might not quite have 100 percent proven herself yet either. Nice. "Look," Amy said, not nearly as calmly as she'd have liked, "it wasn't Riley, okay? She wouldn't do that. She's trying to get her life together."

Jan was shaking her head. "That girl is feral. She'd do whatever she needed to in order to survive, and you know it."

Yeah. She knew it all too well. Just as she also knew how shitty a person's life had to get in order to live that way. "Well, I refuse to believe it of her. And I can't believe *you* believe it. My God, Jan, just last night there was some guy out back attacking her. You saw that, both of you," she said, encompassing Henry. "You both saw us come in here right after the fight. She's *in* trouble. She's not *the* trouble."

"I saw you both afterward," Jan allowed. "But I didn't see anyone attack her."

"So I made it up?" Amy asked in disbelief. "Because *I* saw, Jan. I saw him." She lifted up her shirt to reveal the covered stitches. "I was there."

Jan sighed. "Look, I get that, and I'll be sure to tell Sawyer what I know. But the person who stole this jar was someone *inside* the diner. *Today*. Not the guy in the alley outside. This was someone who walked through here, familiar enough with our comings and goings, someone we recognize, someone we serve or talk to on a regular basis. Someone we know."

"Yes," Amy agreed. "So let's start talking to the customers."

"Oh, hell no." Jan was already shaking her head. "It was the girl. I know it."

Sawyer walked in the back door, immediately followed by Mallory.

And then Matt.

The sight of him both stopped Amy's heart and filled her with dread, because she knew right then and there that the promise she'd made to Riley was about to blow up in her face. She whipped back to face Jan, who met her gaze evenly and without apology.

Thirty minutes ago, Matt had sent her skittering over the edge into an orgasm with just the heat in his eyes. Now those eyes were filled with concern.

For her.

She shook her head as the dread doubled, heavy in her gut.

Jan pushed everyone out of the kitchen and into the dining room, where they all sat at one of the big corner booths. Jan gave the gist of what happened, including last night's alley fight.

All eyes turned to Amy, who then spent the next few minutes repeating the story from her point of view. When she was done, Jan jumped back in with her theory on Riley, making a damn tight case.

"Okay, so it looks bad," Amy agreed. "But it wasn't Riley. I really think we should question the customers—"

"No," Jan said, standing up. "No way. I can't have this getting out. I don't want people to think I don't trust them, or worse, that I hire thieves. I don't want anyone to be worried about coming here."

Amy opened her mouth, but Matt put a hand on her arm. She met his calm, quiet gaze, and got his silent message. He wanted her to know that this would be okay.

But she had no idea how.

"No one can know," Jan insisted to Sawyer. "No one!"

"Then you should stop yelling about it," Sawyer told her. "Sit down, Jan."

Jan's lips tightened, but she sat. "I'm not yelling."

"Yeah, you are." This from Lucille, who'd been eating two tables over with her entire blue-haired, bingo-loving, trouble-seeking posse. "And I couldn't help but overhear..."

Jan rolled her eyes.

"You hired the girl," Lucille reminded her, coming over. "Scoot," she said to Sawyer, who scooted. Lucille sat. "You knew Riley was trouble. So raising your voice at everyone else isn't doing you any good."

"Riley's *not* trouble," Amy said, and when Matt's hand tightened on her arm, she yanked it free. Screw being calm. "None of you know what you're talking about. There's no proof it was her. It could have been anyone."

"Honey," Mallory started.

Amy shook her head. "No. Riley's doing her damn best to make a life for herself. She's working hard at changing—" Horrifying herself, her breath hitched. She sucked in some air and met Matt's warm gaze.

They both knew she was talking about herself.

Dammit. "Move," she said, shoving at him, needing the hell out of the booth.

He slid out in his usual unhurried manner, and she barely resisted shoving him again to make him move faster. When his big, stupid, *perfect* body was out of the way, she jerked to her feet and went to pull out her ordering pad because she needed something to do. She planned on insisting that everyone order a damn meal just to keep herself busy, except she pulled out her pocket sketchpad instead.

Before she could replace it, Lucille gasped in delight and yanked it from her hands, flipping through the small sketches, making little noises of approval as she went through. Finally, she looked up at Amy, eyes sharp. "You're not a waitress."

"Actually, I am."

"Girl, you're an artist."

"Well, I . . ."

"A damn *artist*," she repeated, almost accusingly. "And you've been right under my nose this whole time?" She looked around the group, thrusting the book at them of each in turn. "Seriously? I keep track of every single one of you and your needs, and no one bothers to tell me that I have the next hottest thing serving me coffee?" She snatched the book close and hugged it as she turned back to Amy. "I want to see all of it."

"Excuse me?"

"Your portfolio. Your drawings. Your pads. All of them. Bring them to me."

"I don't—"

"Whatever you have," Lucille said, waving a bony finger in her face. Then she sent Jan a calculating, shrewd look. "She won't be a waitress for long. You should know that right now. Look at this." She opened the pad to a colored-pencil sketch of Lucky Harbor at night, drawn from the end of the pier looking back at the town, with the brightly lit Ferris wheel in the foreground. "This one should be on all the town's marketing efforts and on the website, at the very least. It's a work of art and a pot of gold waiting to happen."

Amy stared down at it. "Is it?"

Lucille smacked Matt upside the back of the head. "How could you not have told her this already? How could you have kept such a secret?"

"Jesus, Lucille." Matt rubbed the back of his head. "And I *did* tell her they were amazing. But her head is even harder than mine."

Lucille turned back to Amy. "You listen to me. People *love* local art. Especially Pacific Northwest art." She waved a dramatic hand in the air. "I'm seeing a series of hand-drawn postcards, detailing all the popular trails." She smiled. "You're going to hit it out of the ballpark, honey. Out of the ballpark, I tell you."

Amy shook her head, her brain too full to deal with this right now. Sawyer stood up and gestured to Matt.

"Where are you going?" Jan asked. "I'm a crime victim here."

"We're going to talk to Riley." Sawyer looked at Amy. "She's at your place, right?"

"Uh…" Unexpectedly cornered, Amy went still. "Actually, no."

"No?" Matt asked.

"No." Suddenly uncomfortably aware of everyone's attention on her, she met Matt's gaze pleadingly, not even sure what she wanted from him. Here she'd thought her biggest problem today would be keeping her mind out of the gutter after what she and Matt had done back at his place. No such luck. "She's not staying with me."

"Since when?" Matt asked.

She managed to hold his gaze, knowing there was no way to keep this from him now. "Since that first night. Well, she was around this morning, but I think that was only to make sure her stepbrother didn't come after me for saving her."

There was a very heavy beat of silence at this. Sawyer looked at Matt, but Matt didn't take his eyes off Amy. "Where has she been staying?"

This wasn't the guy who'd cuddled her after she'd fallen down a ravine. Or the one who'd slid his body down hers and put his mouth on her until she'd come, crying out his name. This wasn't that easygoing, sexy guy at all. He was the law now, distant and cool.

"In the woods," she said quietly. "Camping."

More weighted silence. And a muscle ticked in Matt's jaw. "Illegally camping, you mean?"

She gave a mental cringe. "Yes."

Oh, he was good, an utter professional, not allowing his shock and anger to show, but Amy felt the blast of it just the same. And something else, too, something far more devastating.

Hurt.

"Riley's innocent," she said. And knowing she had no right, she turned and appealed directly to Matt. "Completely innocent."

His gaze roamed her features but didn't soften like they usually did, and she tried again. "She's been through hell..." Her throat tightened. He knew this, goddammit, he did. "And I know you might not understand it, but you have to believe me. She wouldn't do this. She's just a scared, lost runaway, and she needs us. She needs to be trusted, to believe someone cares."

"Honey." Lucille took her hand and gently squeezed, her rheumy eyes surprisingly shiny. "You know we all love and trust and care about *you*, right?"

Her own past was biting her in the ass, all those times she'd screwed up, lied, pushed people away...until no one had believed her. She'd hated that. She'd felt so helpless. Just like she felt now. "Then believe me about this."

Lucille squeezed her hand again. "Love and trust are earned, Amy."

No one knew this better than she. Unfortunately, she'd just blown any hope of either of those things with Matt, which made her sick to her stomach. She knew that, in his eyes, she'd chosen Riley over him, and that sort of thing couldn't be undone.

Sawyer turned to leave, and Matt was right on his heels. Amy excused herself and ran after them, stopping Matt just outside the diner with a hand on his arm.

Sawyer looked at them both, then met Matt's gaze.

"Two minutes," Matt said to him.

Sawyer nodded and gave Amy what might have been the briefest glance of sympathy. "I'll be in the truck," he said.

When they were alone, Matt just looked at her.

"I'm sorry," she said in a low voice. "I couldn't break my word to Riley."

"But you could break your word to me."

"I never gave you my word."

"No," he said in a voice that sounded terrifyingly final. "You sure as hell were careful not to do that."

She felt like he'd slapped her. "What's that supposed to mean?"

"Nothing." He took a step back. "Nothing at all."

"Look, I said I was sorry, but I had to do this for her. She needed me."

"I understand," he said. "After all, all you and I ever had was sex, right?" And with that, he turned and walked to Sawyer's truck.

Chapter 22

Love's a fad. Chocolate's the real thing.

In the end, Matt drove up to Squaw Flats by himself. Sawyer had gotten an emergency call, leaving Matt alone to search for Riley.

That she'd been camping, alone, vulnerable—not to mention against the law—drove him nuts. And she'd been doing it with Amy's blessing, which really fried his ass. He understood that Amy's loyalty to Riley had a lot to do with Amy's own painful past and lack of adult guidance, but damn.

He parked at the campgrounds and headed into the forest where he'd first found Riley, all too happy to have something concrete to do rather than think about Amy and what had just happened.

She'd lied to him, and he was good and pissed off about that. Except it hadn't been an out-and-out lie, more like an omission. Even as furious as he was, he understood her thought process. He knew how badly she wanted, *needed* to believe in Riley.

Just as he knew that Riley had taken the damn money.

Amy wouldn't thank him for finding out one way or the other, but he made his way to what was most likely going to be the final nail in the coffin of...whatever the hell they had going. Which was fine. His life had been fine before Amy had been in it, and it would be fine without her.

Fucking fine.

As he walked, he couldn't help but remember how he'd found Amy up here not that long ago, and let out a reluctant smile. She'd been so out of her element.

And now he was out of his.

Ten minutes later, he found Riley at her illegal camp spot. She was packing, shoving things into the backpack that Amy had bought her. When he stepped closer, she spun around and jumped up, something glinting in her hand.

A knife.

The minute she registered him, the knife vanished, tossed behind her. She shoved her hands into her ratty pockets, shoulders hunched.

"Expecting someone else?" he asked.

"No."

"Where you going?"

She shrugged and didn't meet his eyes. "Nowhere."

"You're packing."

"Well, you told me I couldn't stay here."

"I told you that two weeks ago," he said. "And you've been staying out here anyway."

Nothing.

He blew out a breath and walked up to her backpack.

"That's mine," Riley said, but before she could snatch it, he pointed at her.

"Stay," he said, and crouched at the bag.

"Hey, you can't just look in there—" She broke off when he reached inside.

And pulled out the charity jar.

"Damn, Riley." She hadn't even tried to hide the thing. The money was still in it. Furious, *sick*, he sat back on his heels and regarded her.

She was studying something fascinating on her battered sneakers.

"You have any idea what this is going to do to her?" he asked.

At that, Riley's head snapped up. She'd paled to a pasty white. "You can't tell her!"

Matt stood. "No?"

"No!" Riley's cry was fierce. She nearly deflated with it, her entire body sagging as if the only thing holding her up had been Amy's belief in her. "*Please don't.*"

"Okay."

Riley sagged in relief.

"I'm not going to tell her," Matt said quietly. "Because *you* are."

She went from pale to flushed in an instant, her eyes shimmering brilliantly. "I can't do that."

"If you can steal it, you sure as hell can give it back."

Riley's lip quivered, but she bucked up and shook her head. "No."

So she was going to be difficult. Shock. "Let's go."

"You going to arrest me?" she asked.

Matt would rather be just about anywhere other than here, facing this. Give him Afghanistan. Give him a crack house to bust. Anything other than this. But that's not how his day was going so far. "Your knife."

"Huh?"

"Give me your goddamn knife."

She bent and picked up the knife she'd tossed behind her and handed it over.

He took it and then held out his hand. "And the other one."

Riley stared at him.

He stared back, steadily.

She let out the sigh of a martyr and bent, pulling a Swiss Army Knife from her sock.

"What else do you have on you?" he asked.

"Nothing."

He picked up the backpack and shouldered it. "Get your other stuff."

She grabbed an ancient looking folded-up tent and sleeping bag. He had no idea where she'd gotten them and didn't want to ask, afraid he'd have to add to the list of things she'd stolen.

"I didn't take them," Riley said. "If that's what you're thinking. Some old guy out here gave them to me."

Great. "You got anything else?" he asked.

"You see anything else?"

He ignored the belligerent tone because he recognized false bravado when he saw it. For the moment, he was willing to let her have that. It beat the shit out of tears any day of the week.

But it killed him that those two things, along with the backpack on his shoulder, were her entire worldly possessions. "My truck's down the road."

"So?"

"So you're going to walk there with me and get in it."

"Why, so you can arrest me?"

"Just get moving, Riley."

"I want to hold my backpack."

"I've got it," he said, patience wearing thin.

"I want—"

"Now, Riley."

She hesitated, just long enough to make him wonder if he was going to have to force her. Finally she started walking—practically dragging her feet—but she was moving.

At his parking spot, she stared at his truck. "There's no backseat for prisoners."

"You're not a prisoner."

They tossed her tent and sleeping bag into the truck bed, and her gaze locked in on her backpack.

"No," he said, and put it behind his seat.

"I didn't ask anything."

"Just making a blanket statement. Get in. Buckle up."

"Where's the handcuffs?"

Jesus. "Just get in the damn truck, Riley."

Matt drove the sullen girl and her evidence back into town. Instead of heading to the sheriff's station, however, he drove to the diner. He parked, pulled out his cell phone, and called Amy.

"You find her?" she asked breathlessly, as if she'd been waiting on tenterhooks for his call.

His gut twisted again. He didn't want to give a shit. Not even a little bit.

But he did.

He was still angry, but he knew damn well how hard this was going to hit her. "Come out to the lot."

There was a very loaded pause. "Are you going to arrest me for something?" she finally asked.

What the hell? Were all the females in his life crazy? "No," he said with a calm he didn't feel. "Why would I arrest you?"

"I don't know. Why would you command me to the parking lot?"

He rubbed the ache between his eyes with a finger. "Just come out to the damn lot." He paused. "*Please.*"

"That still needs work," she said, "but I'll be right there."

Amy walked out to the lot, not at all sure what to expect. It sure as hell wasn't to find Riley in Matt's passenger seat. Amy had been sick with worry, but now a very bad feeling settled inside her to go with it. "You okay?" she asked the teen.

Riley nodded.

Matt had gotten out of the truck and gestured Amy to the back, where presumably he could speak without Riley overhearing. Amy knew whatever it was, she wasn't going to like it.

"Problem," Matt said.

Before Amy could respond, the passenger door opened, and Riley joined them, shoulders hunched, hands shoved in her front pockets. "It's me," she said, staring at her shoes. "I'm the problem."

Amy looked at Matt, then back at Riley, her heart pounding dully in her ears. "Tell me."

"He didn't already do that?" Riley asked. "Text you on the way over here and let you know what happened?"

"No," Amy said carefully. "Why would he do that?"

"Because you two are a thing."

"No, we're not," Amy said, not looking at Matt. "Tell me what's going on, Riley."

Riley blinked. "Wait—What do you mean you're not? You *were*." She divided a confused look between them, and when neither of them responded to her, she seemed to deflate even more. "Because of me?"

"No," Amy said, heart tight and heavy. "Now talk to me."

"I did it," Riley whispered. "I took the money."

Amy felt the words lance right through her. She made a low, involuntary sound of shock and denial, and Riley spoke quickly. "I was going to pay it back, I swear!"

Amy reached out and grabbed the side of the truck. "You took the money."

A big, silent presence at Amy's side, Matt opened the truck bed and gestured for her to sit on the tailgate, which she did, staring at Riley.

Riley sat next to her and focused straight ahead. "I only did it because I had to pay Troy back, or he wasn't ever going to leave me alone."

"Troy," Amy said quietly. "Your stepbrother?"

"Yes. Last year I had to change foster homes again. Troy was there. He said he'd be my brother."

"Being in the same foster home doesn't make him your brother in any sense of the word."

"I know," Riley said. "But he wanted to be related to someone. He called us brother and sister and said he'd take care of me. But then he..." She looked away. "He wanted payment. And not with money or anything."

Amy felt sick. She knew this story and knew the ending. "Oh, Riley." She hugged the girl, looking over her head to Matt.

He had his cop face on. No help there, which she could admit wasn't a surprise. She'd led him to believe she trusted him, and then she'd held back. Riley had held back. He had good reason to be quite over them both.

"What happened next?" Amy asked Riley.

"I turned eighteen and was released from the system." Her voice was muffled since she had her face down, pressed into Amy's shoulder. "I left the house, but I needed money. Troy loaned me some. He said I had to pay it back, but I couldn't get a job. No one was hiring. So I had to borrow some more from him."

"Where was he getting his money?" Matt asked.

Riley lifted her head. "I don't know. Finally I got work at a fast food place, but it didn't pay enough for me to live and pay him back. He kept showing up and..." She closed her eyes. "The manager told him to leave me alone, and they fought. Troy broke the manager's nose, and the next day I got fired."

"Is that when you came to Lucky Harbor?" Matt asked.

She nodded. "I camped out, hoping Troy would forget about me. But he didn't. He found me, and he wanted money."

"So you stole it to give it to him," Matt said. "Instead of coming to me or Amy and telling us the problem."

Riley stared at him as if he'd grown a third eye. "You wouldn't have believed me." A tear slipped down her cheek, and she angrily swiped it away. "You don't even like me."

"Actually, I do like you," Matt said. "I like you a lot. You've got grit and determination. You were picking yourself up, dusting yourself off, and trying to make a go out of the cards you were dealt. I liked that a whole hell of a lot, too. And for the record? I'd have believed you, Riley. Remember that for next time."

"But now...now you don't trust me."

"You've lied. And you're right, like you or not, I don't trust liars."

Amy flinched. Lost in her own misery, Riley crumpled. "I'm sorry," she said in a small, breathlessly rushed voice. "I thought I could do this and be free." She stared down at her shoes, but her words were directed at Amy. "I didn't mean to hurt you. You were the first person to ever believe in me, and if I could have, I'd have stayed forever. I'm really sorry."

"I know," Amy told her. "It's okay. I—"

"No, it's not okay." Riley swiped at her nose with her arm. "Because now I made you and Matt break up. I messed everything up. I always do."

"You are not responsible for me and Matt," Amy said fiercely, throat burning. "You're not taking the blame for that." That was all on her...

"But the money..." Riley whispered.

"That," Matt said, "you are going to take the blame for."

For Amy, it was a terrible, gut-wrenching déjà vu. *She'd* always been the one to mess up. She was supposedly an adult now, but at the moment, watching Riley suffer through her own mistakes was bringing back those awful memories. Hardly able to breathe, she glanced at Matt.

Sympathy was the last thing she expected to see, but that's what was on his face. He let out a breath, the kind a very frustrated man lets out when he's been put in a bad situation by a female he cares about. And Amy's heart hurt even worse.

Riley pulled her knees up and dropped her head to them, hunched into herself on the tailgate next to Amy, her face covered by her hair. "Why couldn't you just let me go? I could have kept running. I could have—"

"No." Matt crouched at her side, waiting until she lifted her tear-stained face and looked at him. "Listen to me," he said. "You can get through this. You can get through anything and still make your life something. You hear me? All you have to do is want it bad enough. I believe in you, Riley. I believe you can do this, make this all okay."

Amy's heart rolled over and exposed its tender underbelly. She'd never seen anything quite so fierce and amazing as Matt telling Riley, a girl who'd done nothing but give him trouble, that he believed in her.

It gave her a terrible ache and miraculous hope at the same time.

Riley stared up at Matt, solemn, red eyed. And slowly nodded.

He gave her a nod right back, then rose to his full height and turned to Amy. "We need to go see Sawyer. It'll be up to Mallory and Jan if they want to press charges. Whatever happens, we'll deal with it."

Amy nodded and again hugged a trembling Riley, then watched her get back into Matt's truck like she was going to the guillotine. She got one last unreadable look from Matt, and then they were gone.

Amy swiped her nose and stood there in the lot and called Mallory. "I'm sorry, Mal. I have no right, but I'm going to ask you for a favor."

"Yes," Mallory said.

"You don't even know what I'm going to ask."

"The answer's still yes."

Amy's throat burned. "That's like a blank check.

Didn't anyone ever tell you to keep your guard up when someone's going to ask something of you?"

"That's the thing," Mallory said. "You're not supposed to have a guard with good friends."

Her heart swelled, feeling too big for her chest. "Dammit, Mallory."

"Part of the pact. Are you learning nothing from those good girl lessons?"

In spite of herself, Amy's eyes filled, and she sniffed. *Shit.*

"Are you crying?" Mallory asked.

"No, I have something in my eye."

Mallory laughed. "You're such a cute sap. Who knew? What's the favor? Like I said, anything. Well, unless you want Ty. I'm afraid I can't share him. Not even for you, babe. He's all mine."

Amy choked out a laugh. "Keep him, you deserve him."

"I do." Mallory let out a dreamy sigh, then got to business. "Okay, so spit it out. I have to get to the clinic. I'm running a thing tonight."

"Riley stole your money," Amy said.

"I know."

"What? How do you know?"

"I might have been born here in Lucky Harbor," Mallory said, "but I wasn't born yesterday. What can I do to help Little Sticky Fingers? I'm thinking she had a damn good reason for that level of desperation."

"She does," Amy said grimly. "Matt has the jar with the cash. He has Riley, too. They're heading to see Sawyer now."

"Oh, boy. Poor kid."

"I know..." Amy knew both Mallory and Jan had the

right to press charges against Riley. Amy wouldn't interfere there, but she could try to soften Riley's way. "Do you think that if charges are pressed, you'd be willing to let her make restitution?"

"Absolutely," Mallory said. "And if you want it to be painful, I just opened a Parents' Night Out at the clinic. Starts tonight, in fact. Parents get to drop off their kids for a free night of babysitting. I'm short babysitters. Can't think of a more fitting punishment for a teenager to face than babysitting little kids, can you?"

Amy found a laugh in the day after all. "You're amazing, you know that?"

"I do know it," Mallory said. "But I'll be sure to put out a press release."

Amy barely made it through the rest of her shift. She played phone tag with both Matt and Sawyer, but didn't connect with either, until just as she was getting off work, Sawyer came by.

"Mallory didn't press charges," he told her. "Jan might have, but Matt managed to convince her that the girl would be paying restitution and making it right. I guess he called Mallory, who suggested Riley be forced to volunteer weekends at the health services clinic for the next three months."

Not for the first time that day, Amy felt swamped with love for Mallory. Restitution, *and* Riley would stay in Lucky Harbor for a while longer. "So where is Riley now?"

"Working her first shift," he said. "I dropped her off with Mallory." He laughed ruefully. "I don't know who I feel more sorry for, Riley or the kids."

When he'd left, Amy looked down at her phone. No message from Matt. She supposed she hadn't expected one.

But she'd wanted one.

She drove to the HSC. Mallory met her in the foyer of the building, holding a Nerf bow-and-arrow set. "I'd hoped you'd show up—" She broke off to whirl around and shoot a soft Nerf at a boy tiptoeing up behind her. He had his own Nerf bow-and-arrow set slung over his shoulder, but Mallory was faster, and her arrow nailed him in the chest.

With a wide grin, he spun in dramatic, action-adventure fashion before throwing himself to the ground. He spasmed once, twice, and then a third time, drawing out his "death scene" by finally plopping back and lying still.

"Nice," Mallory told him. She looked at Amy. "You look like you need a brownie, bad."

"Or a hammer upside the head."

Mallory's eyes filled with sympathy. "Aw, look at you, showing all your feelings. No more good girl lessons for you. You've graduated. I'm so proud."

Grace popped her head out of one of the rooms. "The babies," she declared with exhaustion, "are asleep. They all zonked out like a charm."

"Maybe you should get a job as a nanny," Mallory suggested, loading another arrow as she eyed the hallway with a narrowed eye.

But the boy who'd come around the corner was already locked and loaded and got her in the arm. She sighed. "Hit," she said, and lay down on the floor.

"You're supposed to fall," the boy complained, looking greatly disappointed.

Grace continued the conversation through this chaos as if Mallory weren't prone on the floor. "There's not enough money in the world for me to take a nanny job. Are you kidding? Me and kids do not mix." She grabbed Mallory's bow and arrows and shot a second kid busily sneaking into the foyer. "Hey, Amy," she said as three more boys appeared. "You going to pitch in or what?"

"She came to check on Riley," Mallory said, sitting up.

"Hey," the first boy said. "You're supposed to stay dead."

"If I stay dead, who'll hand out snacks?"

The boy thought about this for a moment and nodded. "Plus, now I can shoot you again."

"Not if I shoot you first," Mallory said, making him laugh and run off. She stood and brushed herself off. "Riley's doing okay," she said to Amy. "She's quiet, reflective I think, but okay."

Relief filled Amy. "I'm so sorry about the money."

"We did this already. *You* didn't take it."

"No, but—"

"Hush," Mallory said, and when she told people to hush, they generally hushed.

Amy tried, she really did, and for about five seconds she managed. But in the end, she wasn't much for remaining quiet when she had something to say. "I brought Riley into the diner. I'm the one who got her the job."

"Yes," Mallory said. "And Matt's the one who brought her to you. Is he here saying he's sorry for that? Is *he* apologizing for what Riley did?"

Matt wasn't doing much talking, period. Amy was painfully aware of her silent phone in her pocket. "It wasn't his fault."

"And...?"

Amy let out a breath. "Fine, I get it. It's not my fault either."

Mallory smiled and hugged her. "I love you, Aimes, but you sure do like to carry that chip on your shoulder, don't ya?"

"I do not." But she did. She so did.

"Riley said she made you and Matt break up," Grace said.

"No," Mallory said. "That wasn't her fault."

"Was it yours?" Grace asked Amy.

Amy sighed. "Very possibly."

"Honey, do you remember when I was so stubborn about falling in love with Ty?"

"You mean do I remember when you wore those five-inch stilettos to get his attention and then ended up giving Mr. Wykowski a heart attack?"

Mallory grimaced. "Heartburn."

"*And* a boner," Grace added with a shudder.

"Hello," Mallory said. "I have a point here. It hurts to love."

"Well that's no newsflash," Grace said.

"It is if you let me finish my damn sentence," Mallory said. "It hurts even more if you love someone and don't let that person know how you feel." She gave Amy a long, meaningful look.

"Okay, wait a minute," Amy said. "I never said I love Matt." Her heart raced just from saying the words out loud. "In fact, that's ridiculous. Totally ridiculous. *One hundred percent* totally ridiculous."

Grace shook her head. "Party foul. *Two* too many uses of ridiculous." She looked at Mallory. "She's in love all right."

"You know what? You've both taken a few too many Nerf arrows to the heart," Amy said, backing to the door. "I just came to check on Riley, that's it. I wanted to make sure she was okay, that *you* were okay," she said, pointing at Mallory. "And that everything was—"

"Okay," Mallory finished for her. "It is." She snagged Amy's hand and tugged her down the hall, cracking open a door.

Riley sat on a rug in the middle of a room, surrounded by toys and four little kids. Two were climbing on her, one was playing with her hair, and the last one was attempting to tie her shoelaces together.

They were all laughing, including Riley.

Amy looked at her and felt a clutch in her heart. She was still so furious at her for taking that money. Furious and sad and... messed up. Why had she so blindly trusted her? Had she so immersed herself in Lucky Harbor that she'd let her guard down? Apparently so. She'd let Riley in. She'd let Matt in.

And gotten her heart stomped but good.

Mallory touched her shoulder to Amy's. "She's going to stay at the new women's shelter until Sawyer finds the guy who's been harassing her and puts an end to it. Just like you wanted."

No, what Amy had wanted was for everything to go back to how it'd been before.

Too late for that.

"And Sawyer *will* find the guy," Mallory said. "You can lay money down on that, you know you can. Matt's helping him. Together they'll handle it."

Amy nodded. Sawyer was a good man. Matt was a good man.

The best.

Riley had support. She could make it through this.

The question was, would Amy?

Chapter 23

Chocolate cures adversity.

Matt spent the next long hours dealing with bureaucratic bullshit. His superiors were taking heat from Trevor Wright's parents, who were filing civil lawsuits all the way to hell and back. Matt's own interdepartmental inquiry was in two days. He had no idea how it would go, but given the meetings he'd had so far, things weren't good.

It was late, but he made yet another stop at the hospital. Trevor was still too doped up to talk. Matt was just leaving the hospital when someone whispered for him.

"*Pssst.* Ranger Hot Buns. Over here."

He turned and found Lucille standing in the doorway to the staff's break room. She was wearing sunshine-yellow sweats that made him wish for his sunglasses. "You did *not* just call me that."

She grinned unrepentantly. "Sorry, you don't like it?"

Before he could strangle her, she laughed again.

"Guess you haven't been checking Facebook, huh? The poll there is two-to-one in favor of making a Ranger Hot Buns calendar. In your honor, of course."

He shook his head, trying to rid his brain of that image. "What are you doing here?"

"I volunteer here." She gestured to her badge. "I bring patients magazines and read to them, that sort of thing."

"In the middle of the night?"

Lucille smiled. "It's bingo night, and it went late on account of Mr. Swanson falling over in the middle of calling out the numbers. He wasn't our first choice—Mr. Murdock was—but he lost his dentures, so Mr. Swanson filled in. Anyway, he was calling out the numbers and then he started clenching his chest, saying he was dying of a heart attack. I followed the ambulance here because I greet all the new patients and also because I was his date. Normally he's quite the live wire."

"Is he okay?" Matt asked.

"Oh, sure. He's made of hardy stuff, that Mr. Swanson. Peasant stock, he always says. Turns out, he ate fettuccini and sausage for dinner and had heartburn but they're keeping him overnight for a few more tests. I was just sitting with him for a while until he fell asleep."

Matt felt dizzy. It was a common condition when he was in Lucille's presence. "I've got to go."

"I know. You're probably still looking for evidence that those punk-asses were doing something you can nail them for, right? Like, say, underage drinking and smoking?"

"I can't discuss the case with you, Lucille."

"Well of course not. But I can discuss it with you." She whipped out her phone. The screen was a picture of her art gallery, which reminded Matt of Amy—as if he needed a reminder. She was a hole in his chest at the moment, and now he felt a headache coming on. He pinched the bridge of his nose. "Lucille, I don't really have time for—"

"You're handsome," Lucille said. "I'll give you that. Probably in the top five here in Lucky Harbor, though Mr. Swanson himself could give you a run for his money. But looks aren't everything. Brains are, and the thing is, I figured you for having some."

He narrowed his eyes at her, then took another look at her screen. Facebook, of course. "Now," she said, "*you* wouldn't be able to see this picture because you're not his friend. But I automatically friend everyone in Lucky Harbor. I do that because I'm nosy as hell, and it keeps me up-to-date on the goings on."

"Lucille." He needed Advil. An entire bottle. "I don't—"

She thumbed to a different page. Caleb Morrison's Facebook page. Caleb was Trevor Wright's best friend and had been one of the uninjured climbers the other night. Caleb's latest Facebook post said: *Check out our latest climb!* This was accompanied by a photo of four guys in climbing gear sitting on a group of rocks with Widow's Peak behind them, *all* of them smoking what appeared to be weed.

Lucille smiled at the look on Matt's face. "Who do you love?" she asked.

"*You*," he said with great feeling.

"Aw." She beamed. "Honey, you're just the sweetest, and very good-looking, as I've mentioned. But I'm trying to land Swanson right now, so you'll have to be satisfied with being just friends."

• • •

Amy lay awake staring at the ceiling. She'd really thought she'd been onto something good, that her life here in Lucky Harbor was going to be the life she'd always secretly wanted.

But she'd been too afraid to really go after it.

After all she'd been through in her life, was she really going to let her own fears of trust and love hold her back?

Her mind wandered to her grandma's journey. Hope. Peace. Heart. Her grandma had found the courage to come out here to find her heart—

Whoa. Wait a minute. Amy sat straight up in bed and opened the journal, skimming to the part she wanted.

It's been three weeks since we'd last been on the mountain. A long three weeks during which I refused to give up my newfound hope and peace.

Good thing, too, because we needed both to get all the way around and back.

Full circle.

It was worth it. Standing at the very tippy top, looking out at a blanket of green, a sea of blue, and a world of possibilities, the whole world opened up. I would never settle. I would never stop growing. I would never give up.

And as the sun sank down over the horizon, we were suddenly at the beginning again.

Hope.

Peace.

And something new as well, something that brought us full circle. Heart.

Full circle. Without thinking, she picked up her cell phone and called her mom.

"Amy?"

Amy winced at the husky tone of her mother's voice. "I woke you, I'm sorry."

"Are you okay?"

Amy couldn't speak for a minute, stunned that her mom would ask.

"Amy? You still there?"

"Yes," she managed. "I'm sorry, I didn't think about the time. I'm fine. I just wanted to thank you for sending grandma's drawings. They're beautiful. I had no idea..."

"Her drawings were personal to her. She kept them hidden. I think they reminded her of Jonathon."

Amy nodded, which was stupid, her mom couldn't see her. "He died before their trip."

"Yes, of course. I thought you knew from the journal."

"No."

"I guess it was too painful to write about. Jonathon lived longer than was expected, and she always said that the trip, taking his ashes to his favorite spots on earth, gave her the tools to go on."

Tools. Hope. Peace. Heart. In her own heart, Amy knew that was it. "I was just wondering if you could remember anything about grandma's journey at all. In the end, she went full circle but—"

"I told you, she never discussed the trip details with me. I'm sorry."

"It's okay." But it wasn't. The disappointment was a bitter pill.

"I don't mean about that. I...I don't know how to

say this, Amy," her mom said. "I made a lot of mistakes
with you."

Amy opened her mouth, shocked to discover that
hearing those words actually meant something to her.
"Well, I made mistakes, too."

"No," her mom said. "Well, yes, but not like mine.
I'm the mom. I'm supposed to believe in you, every
time. Nothing can undo what happened, I know that, but
I wanted you to know, I think about you. I think about
you all the time."

Amy had spent so much of her life mistrusting everyone, especially her mom, but the fact was the woman was
as human as Amy. No, nothing could undo the past, but
if Amy held onto that past, she would turn out like her
mother. Full of regrets. She didn't want that. For either of
them. "I think about you, too."

"Take care, Amy. And maybe you'll call."

"Yes. And maybe you will as well."

When she'd set her phone down, Amy sat there in the
dark, the ache in her chest just a little bit less intense. She
and her mom had come full circle, it seems.

Full circle...

She blinked. Maybe Rose and Jonathon had gone full
circle, back to where she'd started, at Sierra Meadows.
It seemed *exactly* like something her grandma would
do. And Amy would bet that it'd been an *accidental* full
circle, which meant her grandma had come at Sierra
Meadows from another way, possibly stumbling into it
again by sheer luck. There was no way of knowing for
sure, but Amy was willing to give it a shot.

Hell, she needed to give *something* a shot.

Before dawn, she was packed. No mistakes this time,

no more being unprepared or getting lost. She had a journey to finish, and there was nothing to stop her.

Not a runaway.

Not a man.

Not her own hang-ups or history. After all, she'd just lectured Riley on not letting her past rule her life, so it was time to live what she preached.

She sent texts to both Grace and Mallory with her hiking itinerary. Just in case of... well, anything. She started at the North District Ranger Station and purposely didn't allow herself to look for Matt's truck. She'd checked out the map and had planned her route. She managed to move along the trail at a good clip. Apparently she couldn't get her life in order, but she'd accidentally gotten in shape.

Good to know.

She adjusted her backpack and kept going.

And going.

She was going to figure out this last leg of her grandma's journey if it killed her. Which she knew it wouldn't. She'd experienced much worse and was still breathing.

By late afternoon, she was approaching Sierra Meadows from the opposite direction as last time. She was exhausted, but forced herself to keep going, and just when she thought she couldn't take another step, she turned a particularly tight switchback corner and... came out at the top of a ravine that looked down at Sierra Meadows.

But this time, because she was on the opposite side of where she'd fallen down, she was looking down at the diamond rocks. She dropped her pack and sat on a rock, staring at the most incredible, awe-inspiring, 360-degree vista she'd ever seen.

She pulled out a bottle of water and her sketchpad.

She flipped through the drawings, each as familiar as her own face. All her life they'd given her comfort, like a security blanket. That had always vaguely embarrassed her, but Lucille's reaction had given her something new.

Hope.

Peace.

She had her grandma's drawings, too, and she looked at the last one, with the vista of rough-edged, craggy mountain peaks—

It was Widow's Peak.

And even more important, it was the exact same view Amy had from this very spot. Heart pounding, she pulled out her grandma's journal. *Standing at the very tippy top, looking out at a blanket of green, a sea of blue...*

Here. Right here was where her grandma had come full circle, staring at Widow's Peak as she'd sprinkled Jonathon's ashes. The late afternoon sun slanted over the precipices, right into her eyes. Amy shaded them with her hand and looked at the beautiful mountains. It was unbelievable to her that by following her grandma's adventure, she'd somehow stumbled into her own as well.

She loved this place. She loved that she had real friends. She loved the sense of community here. Lucky Harbor had become home in a way that no other place had.

But there was more. She'd found herself here. She'd salvaged a crappy life and carved out a little niche for herself.

She'd also fallen in love. How was that for making changes and facing fears? She'd been looking for her grandma's heart, and she'd lost her own.

The sun set a little lower, and its rays burst through the sharply defined rock and trees in such a way that it lit up Widow's Peak like it was on fire. Quickly she grabbed her pencils, wanting to capture it on paper. It took her less than a minute to stare down at her drawing and realize what she was seeing, and she squinted through the bright sun to look at the view again.

With her eyes squinted in protection, the outline of the peaks took on the shape of two interlocking hearts. And within those hearts, the tree lines seemed to form letters. RS. And there was a J, too. And if she squinted really, *really* hard, she could just make out an S...

Amy stared in disbelief at the mountains, then down at her drawing, and let out a low laugh. Just her imagination? Wishful thinking? Probably. But it was also fate.

I left my heart on the mountain, her grandma had told her. And it was right there for Amy to see. It'd been there all these years, waiting for her.

Eventually she walked across the meadow and climbed up to the site of her first overnight camping trip. The sun began to sink, but Amy had prepared for it this time, planned to sleep out here. Alone. She'd faced so many of her fears lately that she'd wanted to look her last one in the eye and prove she could do this.

Leaning back, she could almost feel her grandma smiling down at her.

In the morning, she would finish her drawing and hike out in time to get to work for her afternoon shift. She texted Mallory and Grace again with her whereabouts for the night so that no one called out search and rescue.

Or Matt. Not that he'd be looking for her.

Don't go there...

She started a fire and pitched the tent that she'd borrowed from Ty. Then she sketched until the light was gone.

Once that happened, it was dark. Very dark. But she'd gotten good at facing her fears: letting people in, loving people, trusting people... *camping*! Yep, she could check off the entire list. She crawled into her borrowed sleeping bag and lay still, listening to the forest noises, wishing she had her sexy forest ranger to warm her up.

Matt pulled up to Amy's place and stared at her dark windows.

She wasn't home.

His formal inquiry was at eight a.m. sharp. He would present his findings and hopefully prove that there'd been no negligence on his part or on the part of the forest service. Thanks to Lucille, he had his ducks in a row—at least all the ducks he had—but that didn't necessarily mean anything in the land of bureaucracy. He knew it could go either way, and at the moment, he didn't give a shit. The only person he gave a shit about wasn't home, and he had no idea where she might be.

Trust.

That's what it was all about for her, being able to trust. Not that she'd extended the courtesy to him. He stared up at her dark windows and had to admit he hadn't given her a whole lot to go on in that regard either.

He was such a fucking idiot.

He called her cell but it went straight to voicemail. He'd already checked the diner, but she wasn't working. So he called Mallory. "Where is she?"

Mallory gave him nothing but an angsty silence.

"Mallory."

"I can't tell you."

"Tell me anyway."

More angsty silence.

"Mallory," he said tightly.

"I pinky-swore, Matt! I'm sorry but us Chocoholics have to stick together. It's the Good Girl Code of Honor."

Jesus. "Since when does a good girl hold out on her boyfriend's best friend?"

"Okay, that's not fair," she said. "Asking me to pick loyalties between Ty's BFF and mine."

"Nothing's fair in love or war."

"And is this love or war?" she asked very seriously.

"I need to see her. Now. Tonight."

She went quiet, and Matt knew he had to get this right if he wanted her help. "Is there an emergency clause in that Good Girl Code?" he asked. "Say, for guys who are a little slow on the uptake and need to prove themselves trustworthy?"

"Maybe," she said slowly. "Maybe if, say, I didn't actually *tell* you where she was because you *guessed.*"

"Give me a hint."

"Okay...Oh! Remember when I called you and said my friend needed a rescue because she'd gotten lost on the trail?"

Jesus Christ. "Tell me she did not go back up the Sierra Meadows Trail by herself."

"Exactly. I'm not telling you." She hesitated. "You're going after her, yes?"

Matt could hear Ty in the background saying, "Of course he's going after her. He's *whipped.*"

Matt ground his back teeth into powder. "Tell him I'm going to wipe that smile off his face the next time we're in the gym together."

"You will not," Mallory said. "I love his smile."

In the background, Ty laughed, and given the sounds that came over the line next, he also thoroughly kissed Mallory, then he came on the line himself. "You're going down, man," Ty said. "Hard."

Matt wasn't sure if Ty meant in the gym or over how Matt felt about Amy. Both, probably. He disconnected and started his truck. Amy had gone to finish her grandma's quest.

Alone.

At night.

He whipped the truck around and headed to the station, telling himself he was wrong. She wouldn't be crazy enough to do this, but sure enough, he found her car was parked in the lot. Engine cold.

Okay, so she'd probably left much earlier in the day, which brought a whole new set of problems. Why wasn't she back? Was she hurt? He thumbed through his contacts and called Candy, the ranger-in-training who'd been running the front desk today.

"Yep," she said cheerfully. "That car was there when I locked up for the night."

Damn. He called Mallory again, but this time Ty picked up.

"Man, you're *really* starting to ruin my sex life."

"Overshare. Ask Mallory when she last heard from Amy."

There was a muffled conversation, and Mallory took the phone. "I got a text from her half an hour ago. She was fine and settled in for the night."

"She's staying the night up there? Alone?"

Silence.

"Cone of silence, Good Girl. We're in the cone of silence. Just tell me."

"Overnight camping without a permit isn't allowed," she said primly.

Shit. He hung up and glanced at the sky. Dark-ass black, which sucked. He pounded out Josh's number next. "Problem."

"Are you bleeding?" Josh asked. "And by bleeding, I mean an aorta nick because I'm in the middle of something here. And by something, I mean sleeping. For the first time in thirty-six hours."

"I'm going to miss my inquiry in the morning."

"Ah," Josh said agreeably. "So not an aortic bleed, but a brain leak. *Have you lost your fucking mind?*"

"Amy went up to Sierra Meadows. Alone. I'm going after her."

"This is your job on the line," Josh reminded him. "Job before chicks, man."

"That's *bros before 'hos.* And irrelevant. I let her think I didn't believe in her, that I didn't trust her. I have to prove her wrong."

"By throwing away your livelihood?"

"If Toby needed you, you'd do the same."

"I love Toby."

Matt blew out a breath. "Yeah."

There was a loaded beat of silence, but it didn't last long. "Jesus," Josh breathed. "You're as bad off as Ty. Go. Go do what you have to. If you lose your job, I'll hire you as my nanny."

Matt hung up, grabbed his emergency pack out of the back of his truck, and hit the trail. Ten minutes later, at midnight, his flashlight died. He pulled out his backup. He was halfway there and had downed his five-hour energy drink stash, and now his eyes were flashing and his heart was pounding from the caffeine. He hadn't slept last night thinking about Amy and Riley. He hadn't slept the night before because he'd spent the hours tearing up the sheets and expending some high-quality passion with Amy. And the night before that, he'd never hit the sheets at all because of the injured hiker.

If anyone else had come out here in the forest in his condition, he'd think they needed a psych eval. Hell, he *did* need a psych eval.

It was twelve thirty a.m. when his backup flashlight died. So much for the Energizer Bunny. He pulled out his iPhone. He had no reception but he did have a flashlight app. Apple was his new best friend.

It was 1 a.m. when he got close. It was 1:05 when his cell phone died.

Apple was relegated to below the Energizer Bunny on his shit list, a fact that was drummed home when he took a step off the trail to take a leak and fell.

And fell.

Amy had fallen asleep by her fire, but at some point she sat straight up, startled, heart pounding. She'd heard something. A loud something, a crash...

Her fire had died down. She tossed more wood in, then grabbed her flashlight, surveying the forest around her.

Nothing.

Had she imagined it? She stood up and walked to the edge of the clearing, shining her light all around her. "Hello?"

No one answered. That was good, she decided. Unless it was a hungry bear...She glanced around nervously at the thicket of trees in front of the ravine and was vividly reminded of what had happened last time she'd been here at night.

A smile curved her mouth in spite of herself, and she moved closer, shining the light down, remembering how she'd fallen and been rescued by Matt, and—

Oh, God. There was rustling down there, *big* rustling, and she immediately thought of that bear. But a bear wouldn't be swearing the air blue.

In Matt's voice.

Chapter 24

Love is like swallowing hot chocolate before it's cooled off. It takes you by surprise at first, but then keeps you warm for a long time.

"Matt?" Amy stared into the dark ravine with utter shock. "Is that you?"

"No, it's fucking Tinker Bell."

This irritated statement was followed by more rustling and more swearing.

"What are you doing down there?" she asked, flicking her light in the direction of his voice, but not seeing much. "You told me not to go down that way, remember?"

"Yes, Amy, I remember, thank you." He paused. "I fell."

"Oh, my God. Are you okay?"

He didn't answer right away, and she panicked. "*Matt?*"

"Yeah. I just jacked up my shoulder a little bit."

Fear joined the panic as she stared down into the inky black abyss. "I'm coming down right now." *Soon as she figured out exactly how to do that in the dark.*

"Don't," he called up to her. "I'm fine."

Ignoring that line, which was her own personal favorite bullshit line, she began to make her careful way down.

"Go back, Amy. I'm coming up right now."

That'd be great, if it were true, but she couldn't hear him moving so she kept going. This proved tricky as it was harder going down than it had been coming up. It was steep, and she needed both hands. She also needed her flashlight, so she stuck it down her top and into her bra. This mostly highlighted her own face but gave her enough of a glow that she could see.

Sort of.

"Amy, *stop*."

"I'm not leaving you here—" She broke off with a startled scream as her feet slid out from beneath her on the damp, slippery slope. She fell the last few feet and hit her butt.

"You okay?" Matt demanded.

"Sure. Lots of padding." She rushed to his side.

"You don't listen," he said. He was sitting up, his back to a stump, jaw tight. "Are you sure you're not hurt?"

"Yes."

"Is that your flashlight down your top?"

"Yes again. Is your shoulder broken?"

"Just dislocated, I think. Lean a little closer."

"Why?"

"So I can see down your top."

Okay, so he wasn't on his deathbed. "I'll flash you when we get you back to my camp," she promised, realizing he was breathing through clenched teeth. Pulling out her flashlight, she used it to take a good long look at him. Despite the chilly night, a drop of sweat ran down his temple, and he seemed a little green. "What can I do, Matt?"

"You could flash me now as incentive."

"I'm serious."

He sighed. "I'm okay, just give me a minute."

Well isn't that just like a man. "You shouldn't have come."

"No shit," he said. "And neither should you."

"I meant because you have your inquiry in the morning. In a few hours! Your job—" It all hit her, and she sank back on her heels to stare at him, waving her hand aimlessly. "God, Matt, you're going to miss it. Why would you do this?"

He took her hand, caressing her wrist with his thumb right over her pulse point. Bringing her hand to his mouth, his lips pressed against her palm. "I wanted to be here with you. Did you find what you were looking for?"

"Well, yes, actually."

"I knew you would. That was your goal, and you're not a quitter. You finish what you start. And I came to finish what *we* started."

Her heart caught. "We already finished. And for the record, I *am* a quitter. I quit everything and everyone. That's who I've always been."

"Don't bring Amy-the-teenager into this," he said. "She quit a bad life and got herself a new one. She—" He shifted and broke off with a grimace of pain.

"Oh, God, Matt. We need to—"

"Here— Hold this," he said, and using his good hand, lifted his arm to a certain angle. "Hold tight and don't let go."

She wrapped her hands around his arm. His muscles were quivering. "But—"

Matt jerked, and she heard a pop, and then he sucked in a harsh breath and sagged away from her.

She followed his movement, practically straddling him to see into his face. He was sweating good now, but his color was coming back, and he offered her a weak smile. "Got it in one," he said, and then closed his eyes.

"Matt!"

"Shh," he said, not moving. "I'm not quite up to chasing off any curious bears at the moment. And I don't think the ones in China heard us yet. Help me out of my shirt."

She leaned over him and unbuttoned his shirt, then spread it open to gingerly pull it away from his bad shoulder.

"I like it when you take off my clothes," he said.

"I thought you liked it when I took off *my* clothes."

"That, too." His voice was soft and silky. "I *really* like that. Tear the shirt in half for me."

She tried but she didn't have enough strength so he took it back from her, and holding it between his good arm and his teeth, easily tore the shirt in half.

This caused her to get a hot flash, which she ignored. Matt showed her how to fold the torn shirt into a makeshift sling for his arm.

"Better?" she asked when they'd finished.

He let out a careful breath and rolled his shoulder. "Yeah."

"We need to get you to the ER."

"Nah, I'm good now."

"And you say *I* don't listen." She slid her arm around him to pull him upright, muttering to herself. "No one ever listens to me. Not that I can blame them. I believed in Riley and look how that turned out."

Matt slid a hand to the nape of her neck and tilted her face up, his own solemn. "I'm listening to you," he said. "I'll always listen. I might not agree, but I swear to you, I'll always listen. I didn't mean to hurt you, Amy."

Just like that, her throat clogged. Her eyes burned. "Matt—"

"I never wanted you to give up on Riley," he went on quietly. "The kid made a mistake, that doesn't mean she *is* a mistake." He stroked her hair out of her face. "She's making restitution. She's finding out how to make things right when she screws up. That's because of you, Amy. You set her up to succeed. Don't you see? The *best* thing that could ever have happened to her is having you in her corner." He paused, eyes warm as they roamed over her features. "Now more than ever, don't give up on her."

She stared into his eyes and shook her head, incredibly aware of the heat of his body under her hands. "I won't. I... can't."

"Good," he said. "Because I can't give up either. Not on her. Not on you. And not on us."

Her heart stopped, and he smiled, which kick-started her heart again, painfully. Then he rose to his feet, slipping his good arm around her shoulders, leaning on her as he caught his breath. He turned toward the rocks.

"Matt—"

But he was already climbing back up.

"Matt—"

"I'm fine."

Great, he was fine. But she was so *not* fine. She was worried sick. She stayed right behind him, though what she was going to do if he fell, she had no idea. At least she had a really great view, since he was stripped to just his pants and boots.

"We could see better if you shined the light out in front of us instead of at my ass," he said mildly.

Crap. She redirected the light and ignored his soft laugh.

Finally they made it back to her campsite.

They sat on the log in front of her fire, Matt holding his arm tight to his chest.

"You're not okay," she accused.

"Might have torn something," he admitted.

"How are we going to get you back?"

"I'll be fine by morning."

"It *is* morning. And you have to be back!"

"Amy." Using his good arm, he pulled her in against him. "It's just a job."

She couldn't believe it, couldn't believe what he'd done for her. She burrowed through her backpack and came up with the Dr. Pepper she'd packed. At the time, it'd felt a little pathetic, carrying one of Matt's sodas simply to be reminded of him. But she was so glad she'd done it. She opened it and handed it over to him.

He looked as if she'd handed him the moon. She waited until he'd downed it. "Matt," she said quietly, "you love your job."

"I do. But I loved my last job, too, and I put that job ahead of everything else, including my own instincts and my marriage. I'm not doing that ever again."

"Ever is a long time."

"*Ever*," he repeated firmly. "And something else I'm not doing ever again..."

"What?

"Taking off my shirt unless you take off yours." He knocked her backward off the log and followed her down.

"Careful of your shoulder!" she squeaked, flat on her back, held to the ground by two-hundred-and-twenty pounds of sexy forest ranger.

"It's not my shoulder you should be worried about," he said, then covered her mouth with his. She cupped the curve of his jaw, feeling his stubble scrape against the pads of her fingers. His lips moved against hers, and though she meant to stop this craziness before he got hurt any further, she found herself kissing him back hungrily, not able to get enough of him.

How could she have forgotten how she felt when he kissed her like this? She was panting for air when he rolled to his back. "Are you okay?" she managed.

"No. Come here."

She moved over him. His fingers were surprisingly dexterous given that he had limited motion and had to be hurting like hell. Dexterous and gentle and tender as he got her out of her clothes in record time. He urged her up, then up some more, until she was sitting on his chest. "Matt, what—"

"More," he said, pulling at her until her knees were on either side of his ears. "There," he said with deep satisfaction.

There was nothing gentle or tender about him now, not when he nipped her inner thigh, or spread her legs even farther and buried his face between them. With one stroke of his tongue, he had her in a heated frenzy, crying out as she climaxed. Before she'd stopped shuddering, he'd guided her down onto his body and shoved his pants down enough to push inside her as his mouth found hers again.

She could taste herself on his tongue. She was trying to be careful with his shoulder but her nails dug into his back. He swallowed her cries as he thrust up into her, powerful and primal. She couldn't think, all she could do was feel, and what she felt so overwhelmed her that she felt her eyes fill.

His eyes were dark and heated as he looked up at her. "Again," he said. "Let go for me again."

That was all it took to send her flying. He was right with her, shuddering in her arms, his good hand gripping her hip as he pulled her down and tucked his face into the crook of her neck. She could feel the heat of his breath against her skin as he struggled to control his breathing.

She couldn't have controlled hers even if she'd tried. He was still buried deep inside her, and she held him close, savoring the feel of their bodies joined together.

Finally she lifted her head and looked into his clear, gorgeous light brown eyes, and that's when she knew.

He was it for her.

No matter what happened, no matter what he said now, that fact remained.

"I've made some pretty spectacular mistakes in my life," he said quietly. "The latest was when I let you think I'd given up on us."

She tried to climb off him but he held her tight, pulling her down to him, pressing his lips to her temple. "Stay. Stay with me."

"I understood why you might have given up," she said. "I'd lied to you."

"Yeah." He nodded. "Which just proves that I'm not the only one who can make a spectacular mistake." He smiled at her. "That's good to know."

She couldn't smile back. Her heart was in her throat. She'd learned a lot about herself lately, mostly that it was hard to ask for forgiveness, and harder still to give it. To let go and trust. But worth it. Oh, God, so worth it. "I'm so sorry," she whispered.

"I know," he said. "And I'm sorry, too. So damn sorry that I hurt you. But I swear to you, Amy, if you give me another chance, I'll never hurt you again. Not for anything. You can trust me." His gaze held hers prisoner, and it was too much.

Way too much. She felt too open and...naked. She dropped her head to his chest. "I do trust you," she whispered. "I just don't know what I'm doing."

He stroked his good hand down her back. "You'll figure it out. I have faith in you."

Lifting her head, she stared at him, then laughed. "You're not going to be the hero and offer to solve all my problems?"

"I'm not here to solve your problems. I'm here to support you in your own decisions. I'm not going to walk away, Amy. Not now, not when the going gets tough, not ever. I'm right here at your back."

"For how long?"

"For as long as you'll have me. I love you, Amy."

Staggered, she stared at him. "But you don't do love."

"I never said that. I said love hasn't worked out for me. But all it takes is the right one. You're the right one."

No one had ever said such a thing to her before, and it made her heart swell hard against her ribcage. "I love you, Matt. So much."

He smiled like she'd just given him the best gift he'd ever had. She settled against his good side, and they stared up at the star-laden sky. "I knew I'd find something on this journey," she said. "I wasn't sure what, but I knew it'd be something special."

They pulled into the North District office at nine a.m., one full hour late, and Matt knew that hour was going to cost him, in a big way.

He didn't regret being late. Couldn't. He'd meant what he'd said to Amy, that he was no longer putting his job ahead of his life. That had been habit, a self-preservation technique.

And it was chicken shit.

He'd learned something about himself here in Lucky Harbor.

The town trusted him. His friends trusted him. Amy trusted him. And he could trust himself and let happiness in.

Amy was his happiness.

The ranger station parking lot wasn't usually a hotbed of activity, but this morning the entire lot was jam-packed with cars.

"What's going on?" Amy asked.

Matt was staring at the lot. "I have no idea."

They got out looking like a ragtag team from *The Amazing Race*. Matt was still shirtless, the sling in place. Amy's clothes were torn from her breathless, in-the-dark climb down to where Matt had fallen. She was disheveled and glowing.

Not from the climb.

Just looking at her warmed Matt from the inside out.

"Mallory's car is here," Amy said, pointing it out. "And Grace's. And isn't that Josh's car? And Ty's truck?

And Sawyer's cop car? What—Why is everyone here? Do you think they're all here supporting you?"

Yeah, that's exactly what he thought.

Proving it, the station door opened, and people filed out, his coworkers, and then Jan, Lucille, Lucille's entire posse . . . half the town.

"What the hell?" Matt said.

Sawyer reached him first. "Got Riley's assailant in custody. The idiot showed up at the diner last night with a knife, threatening everyone in sight if they didn't produce Riley, and Jan beaned him with a frying pan. She's pressing charges, and Riley will do the same." Sawyer looked at Amy. "Jan told Riley that they were even now. The slate was cleared, and Riley could rent out that little hole-in-the-wall studio apartment above the diner if she wanted."

Ty and Josh reached them. Josh's attention narrowed in on Matt's makeshift splint. "Ah, hell," he said, sliding the torn shirt aside, examining the shoulder until Matt hissed in a breath. "You did it again, didn't you?"

Lucille pushed her way between the two big men, barely coming up past their elbows. "Well?" she demanded of Matt. "I came out here and missed my morning talk shows. The least you can do is give me an exclusive quote on the situation."

Matt shook his head. "I don't know the situation."

Lucille went brows up, looking as if she'd just swallowed the canary. "So if I told you that we all came here to see your sexy tush fired, you'd believe me?"

Matt slid a look to Josh and Ty, both of whom were wearing dark sunglasses and matching solemn expressions, giving nothing away. Some help.

Lucille smiled and patted him on the chest like he was a sad puppy. "Aw, you're too cute to tease. We all came this morning to plead your case. Ty and Josh here told your boss that you couldn't be here because you were busy saving a woman who'd gone into the forest alone." She turned to Amy. "Did you need saving again, honey?"

"Actually," Matt said, holding her tight to his good side. "She saved *me*."

"Sweet," Lucille said. "I saved you, too, don't forget." She elbowed Ty. "See, Facebook isn't *completely* evil." She beamed with pride. "Oh, and you're cleared of any inquiries or blights on your record," she said to Matt casually. "Those Facebook pics were pretty damning." She turned to Amy. "I was thinking an exclusive show."

"Show?"

"Your art. You came to Lucky Harbor to follow your grandma's decades-old adventure, hoping for the same life-changing experiences, right? Do you have any idea what a great story that makes to go with the art? It's fantastic. I can't even make that stuff up. You're going to sell like hotcakes. We're going to make buckets of money."

"How did you know all that?" Amy asked. "About my grandma and everything?"

"Honey, I know all. The question is, did you get your life-changing experience?"

Amy looked at Matt and smiled. "I did."

Matt's entire heart turned over in his chest. "Damn," he said, pulling her in. "Damn, I love you."

"Watch the arm!" Josh warned.

"He's not watching that arm," Ty said as Matt kissed Amy again.

"Christ," Josh said.

Matt ignored them all and kept kissing Amy. A surge of emotion rocked him to his core when she responded with everything she had, and the kiss got even a little more heated. He was vaguely aware of everyone cheering and hooting and hollering, but he didn't give a shit. He had everything he ever wanted, at last.

Raising his head, he looked down at the woman whose smile made it seem as if she were lit up from within. She was filthy, exhausted, probably half starved, and a complete mess. But she took his breath and owned his heart, and he'd never seen anything more beautiful. "Be mine, Amy."

"I already am."

The Chocoholics' Brownies-to-Die-For

Ingredients

4 large eggs
1 cup of sugar
1 cup of brown sugar
1 cup of butter (2 sticks)
1 1/2 cups of sifted cocoa powder
2 tsp of vanilla
1/2 cup of sifted flour
1/2 tsp of salt

Use the mixer to beat the eggs on medium speed until they turn light yellow. Add both sugars and salt. Mix well. Then gradually add the rest of the ingredients: vanilla, butter, cocoa powder, and flour. Keep mixing until it is all combined but the batter is still lumpy.

Pour into an 8″ x 8″ greased, nonstick pan and place it in the oven at 300 degrees. After 45 minutes, use a toothpick to check the brownies. Check every five minutes for a total cooking time of up to 60 minutes. When the toothpick comes out clean, remove brownies and let them cool before you cut them.

Voila! Your chocolate fix.

ER doc Josh Scott has his
future all mapped out.
But Grace has a different plan...

Please turn this page
for a preview.

Forever and a Day

Chapter 1

♥

Chocolate makes the world go around.

Tired, edgy, and more than a little scared that she was never going to get her life on the happy track, Grace Brooks dropped into the back booth of the diner and sagged against the red vinyl seat. "I could really use a drink."

Mallory, in wrinkled scrubs, just coming off an all-night shift at the ER, snorted as she crawled into the booth as well. "It's eight in the morning."

"Hey, it's happy hour somewhere." This from their third musketeer, Amy, who was wearing a black tee, a black denim skirt with lots of zippers and kick-ass boots, the tough girl ensemble softened by the bright pink Eat Me apron she was forced to wear while waitressing. "Pick your poison."

"Actually," Grace said with a yawn. "I was thinking hot chocolate."

"Or that," Amy said. "Be right back."

Good as her word, she reappeared with a tray of

steaming hot chocolate and big, fluffy chocolate pancakes. "Chocoholics unite."

Four months ago Grace had come west from New York for a Seattle banking job, until she'd discovered that putting out for the boss was part of the deal. Leaving the offer on the table, she'd gotten into her car and driven as far as the tank of gas could take her, ending up in the little Washington State beach town of Lucky Harbor. That same night she'd gotten stuck in this very diner during a freak snowstorm with two strangers.

Mallory and Amy.

With no electricity and a downed tree blocking their escape, the three of them had spent a few scary hours soothing their nerves by eating their way through a very large chocolate cake. After that, meeting over chocolate cake became habit—until they'd accidentally destroyed the inside of the diner in a certain candle incident that wasn't to be discussed. Jan, the owner of Eat Me, had refused to let them meet over cake anymore, so the Chocoholics had switched to brownies for a while. Grace was thinking of making a motion for chocolate cupcakes as the next dessert. It was important to have the right food for those meetings, as dissecting their lives—specifically their lack of love lives—was hard work. Except these days Amy and Mallory actually *had* love lives.

Grace did not.

Amy disappeared and came back with butter and syrup. She untied and tossed aside her apron and sat, pushing the syrup to Grace.

"I love you," Grace said with great feeling as she took her first bite of delicious goodness.

Not one to waste her break, Amy toasted her with a pancake-loaded fork dripping syrup and kept eating.

Not Mallory, who was still carefully spreading butter on her pancakes, her diamond engagement ring catching the light with every movement. "You going to tell us what's wrong, Grace?"

Grace stilled for a beat, surprised that Mallory had been able to read her. "I didn't say anything was wrong."

"You're mainlining a stack of six pancakes like your life depends on it."

This was a true statement. But nothing was wrong exactly. Except...everything.

All her life she'd worked her ass off, running on the hamster wheel, heading toward her elusive future. Being adopted at birth by a rocket scientist and a well-respected research biologist had set the standards, and she knew her role. Achieve, and achieve high. "It's nothing really. Except I've applied at every bank, every investment firm, every accounting firm between Seattle and San Francisco."

"No nibbles?" Mallory asked sympathetically, reaching for the syrup, her ring flashing again.

Amy shielded her eyes. "Jeez, Mallory, stop waving that thing around, you're going to blind us. Couldn't Ty have found one smaller than a third world country? Or less sparkly?"

Mallory beamed at the rock on her finger but otherwise ignored Amy's comment, unwilling to be deterred. "Back to the nibbles," she said to Grace.

"Nothing too noteworthy," Grace said. "Just a couple of possible interviews for next week, one in Seattle, one in Portland." Neither job was exactly what she wanted, but they'd both be a steady—and solid—paycheck.

Grace had grown up back east, from toddlerhood through getting her CPA. Drowning beneath the debt load of her education—her parents had been of the "build character and pave your own road" variety—she'd followed that job offer to Seattle, wanting a good, solid position in the firm. Just not one that she could find in the Kama Sutra.

Now late spring had turned to late summer, and she was still in Lucky Harbor, living off the temp jobs she'd picked up. She was down to her last couple hundred bucks, and her parents thought she was still in Seattle counting other people's money for a living. The pleaser in her was withering daily.

Her parents believed in hard work and rising above the norm's potential. Since they were both esteemed in their respective fields, it was safe to say that they'd accomplished their goals there.

Grace was still working on doing the same. She'd strived hard for each of her twenty-eight years to live up to the standards of being a Brooks, but there was no doubt she felt the pressure. In her heart she belonged, but in her brain—the part of her who knew that she was only a Brooks on *paper*—she'd never really pulled it off.

"I don't want you to leave Lucky Harbor," Mallory said. "But one of these interviews will work out for you, I know it."

Grace didn't necessarily want to leave either. She'd found the small, quirky town to be more welcoming than anywhere else she'd ever been, but staying wasn't really an option. She was never going to build her big career here.

"So with two interviews lined up, what's the problem?" Amy asked.

What *wasn't* the problem? "Well, let's see." She stabbed a few more pancakes from the tray and dropped them on her plate. "I'm still fibbing to my parents so they won't worry." She hated that, so very much. She'd done it to make them happy, but that wasn't making her feel any better. "I'm whittling away at my meager savings. I'm in limbo...pick one."

"Yeah, none of those things are the problem," Amy said.

"No?"

"No. The problem is that you're not getting any."

Grace sagged at the pathetic truthfulness of this statement, a situation made all the worse by the fact that both Amy and Mallory *were* getting some.

Lots.

"Remember the storm?" Mallory asked. "When we almost died right in this very place?"

"Right," Amy said dryly. "From overdosing on chocolate cake, maybe."

Mallory ignored this and pointed her fork at Grace. "We made a pinky promise. I said I'd learn to be a little bad for a change. And Amy here was going to live her life instead of letting it live her. And you, Miss Grace, you were going to find more than a new job, remember? You were going to stop chasing your own tail and go after some happy and some fun. It's time, babe."

"I am having fun here." At least, more than she'd ever let herself have before. "And what it's time for, is work." With a longing look at the last stack of pancakes, Grace stood up and brushed the crumbs off her sundress.

"What's today's job?" Amy asked.

When Grace had first realized she needed to get a

temporary job or stop eating, she'd purposely gone for something new. Something that didn't require stuffy pencil skirts or closed-toe heels. Something that didn't require sitting in front of a computer for fifteen hours a day. Because if she had to be off track and a little lost, then she *was* going to have fun while she was at it, dammit. "I'm delivering birthday flowers to Mrs. Burland for her eightieth birthday," she said. "Then modeling at Lucille's art gallery for a drawing class."

"Modeling for an art class?" Mallory asked. "Don't art classes use nude models?"

"That's not today." Nope, nude was *tomorrow's* class, and Grace was really hoping something happened before then, like maybe she'd win the lottery. Or get beamed to another planet. "I'm a hand model today."

Amy looked her over. "If I had your body, I'd totally model nude."

Grace shook her head, dropped the last of her pocket money onto the table, and left to make the floral deliveries. At the bank, she'd always had to get up before the crack of dawn, ride a train for two hours to get to work, put in fifteen hours, then get home in time just to crawl exhausted into bed.

Things were majorly different here.

For one thing, she saw daylight.

So maybe she could no longer afford Starbucks. At least she wasn't still having the recurring nightmare where she suffocated under a sea of pennies that she'd been trying to count one by one.

Two hours later, Grace was just finishing the flower deliveries when her cell phone buzzed. Out of habit, she looked at the screen with her eyes squinted. Because everyone knew *that* made it easier to hear bad news. But there wasn't any more bad news to be had, she reminded herself. She'd already pretty much hit rock bottom. Even so, she took a big step back from the large tree she stood near, not wanting to tempt fate to prove her wrong by striking her with a lightning bolt.

She didn't recognize the incoming number, so she played mental roulette and answered. "Grace Brooks," she said in her most professional tone, as if she were still sitting on top of her world. Hey, she might have had to give up designer clothes, but she hadn't lost her pride. Not yet anyway.

There was a brief pause. "I'm calling about your flyer," the man said. "I need a dog walker. Someone who's on time, responsible, and not a flake." The man, whoever he was, had a hell of a voice; low and a little raspy, but she was stuck on his words.

Her flyer? "A dog walker," she repeated. Huh.

"I'd need you to start today."

"Today...as in *today*?" she asked.

"Yes."

Okay, clearly he'd misdialed. And just as clearly, there was someone else in Lucky Harbor trying to drum up work for herself.

Grace considered herself a good person. She sponsored a child in Africa, she dropped her spare change into the charity jars at the supermarket, and she gave her restaurant leftovers to the homeless. Or at least she used to, back in the days when she could afford a restaurant. In any case, someone had put up flyers looking to get work, and that someone deserved this phone call.

But dog walking...She could totally do dog walking.

Offering a silent apology for stealing the job, she said, "Sure, I can start today."

There was a brief pause. "Your flyer lists your qualifications, but not how long you've been doing this."

That was too bad because she'd sure like to know that herself. She'd never actually had a dog. Turns out, rocket scientists and renowned biologists don't have a lot of time in their lives for consequentials such as dogs.

Or kids...

In fact, come to think of it, Grace had never had so much as a goldfish, but really, how hard could it be? Put the thing on a leash and walk, right? "I'm a little new at the dog walking thing," she admitted.

"A little new?" he asked. "Or a lot new?"

"A lot."

Another brief pause, as if he was considering hanging up, and Grace rushed to fill the silence. "But I'm very diligent!" she said quickly. "I never leave a job unfinished. And I'm completely reliable."

"The dog is actually a puppy," he said. "And new to our household. Not yet fully trained."

"No problem," she said, and crossed her fingers, hoping that was true. She loved puppies. Or at least she loved the *idea* of puppies.

"I left for work early this morning and won't be home until late tonight. I'd need you to walk the dog by lunch time."

Yeah, he really had a hell of a voice. Low and authoritative, it made her want to snap to attention and salute him, but it was also...sexy. Wondering if the rest of him matched his voice, she made arrangements to go to his house in a few hours and walk the puppy, where there'd be someone waiting to let her inside. Her payment of forty bucks cash would be left on the dining room table.

Forty bucks cash for walking a puppy...

Score.

Grace didn't ask why the person opening the door for her couldn't walk the puppy. She didn't want to talk her new employer out of hiring her because hello, *forty bucks*. She could eat all week off that, if she was careful.

At the appropriate time, she pulled up to the address she'd been given and sucked in a big breath. She hadn't caught the man's name, but he lived in a very expensive area, on the northernmost part of the town, where the rocky beach stretched for endless miles like a gorgeous postcard for the Pacific Northwest. The dark green bluffs and rock stacks were piled like gifts from heaven for as far as the eye could see. Well, as far as *her* eye could see, which wasn't all that far since she needed glasses.

She was waiting on a great job with benefits to come along first.

The house sat across the street from the beach, all sprawling stone and glass. Beautiful, though she found it odd that it was all one level, when the surrounding homes were two and three stories high. Even more curious, next to the front steps was a ramp. A wheelchair ramp. Grace knocked on the door, then caught sight of the Post-it note stuck on the glass panel.

Dear Dog Sitter,

I've left door unlocked for you, please let yourself in. Oh, and if you could throw away this note and

*not let my brother know I left his house unlocked,
that'd be great, thanks. Also, don't steal anything.*

Anna

Grace stood there chewing her bottom lip in indecision. She hadn't given this enough thought. Hell, let's be honest. She'd given it *no* thought at all past "Easy Job." But she was thinking now, and she was thinking that walking into a perfect stranger's home seemed problematic, if not downright dangerous. What if a curious neighbor saw her and called the cops? She looked herself over. Enjoying her current freedom from business wear, she was in a sundress with her cute Payless-special ankle boots and lace socks. Not looking like much of a banking specialist, and hopefully not looking like a breaking-and-entering expert either...

But what if this was a setup? What if a bad guy lived here, one who lured hungry, slightly desperate, act-now-think-later women inside to do heinous things to them?

Okay, so maybe she'd been watching too many late-night marathon runs of *Criminal Minds*, but it could totally happen.

Then, from inside the depths of the house came a happy, high-pitched bark. And then another, which seemed to say: "*hurry up, lady, I have to pee!*"

Ah, hell. In for a penny... Grace opened the front door and peered inside.

The living room was as stunning as the outside of the house. Wide open spaces, done in dark, masculine wood and neutral colors. The furniture was oversized and sparse on the beautiful, scarred, hardwood floors. An entire wall of windows faced the Indian summer sky and Pacific Ocean.

As Grace stepped inside, the barking increased in volume, intermingled now with hopeful whining. She followed the sounds to a huge, state-of-the-art kitchen that made her wish she knew how to cook beyond the basic boxed mac and cheese and grilled cheese sandwiches. Just beyond the kitchen was a laundry room, the doorway blocked by a toddler gate.

On the other side of the gate was a baby pig.

A baby pig who barked.

Okay, not a pig at all, but one of those dogs whose faces always looked all smashed in. The tiny body was mostly tan, with a black face, crazy bugged-out eyes, and a tongue that lolled out the side of its mouth. It looked like an animated cartoon as it twirled in excited circles, dancing for her, trying to impress and charm its way out of lockup.

"Hi," she said to him. *Her?* Hard to tell since its parts were so low as to scrape the ground along with its belly.

The thing snorted and huffed in joyous delirium, then hopped up and down like a Mexican jumping bean.

"Oh, there's no need for all that," Grace said, and opened the gate.

Mistake number one.

The dog/pig/alien streaked past her with astounding speed and promptly raced out of the kitchen, and out of sight.

"Hey," she called. "Slow down."

But it didn't, and wow, those stumpy legs could really churn. It snorted with sheer delight as it made its mad getaway, and Grace was forced to rethink the pig theory. Also, the sex mystery was solved.

From behind, she'd caught a glimpse of dangly bits.

It—*he*—ran circles around the couch, barking with merry enthusiasm. She gave chase, wondering how it was that she had multiple advanced degrees and yet she hadn't thought to ask the name of the damn dog. "Hey," she said. "Hey, you. We're going outside to walk."

The puppy dashed past her like lightning.

Dammit. Breathless, she changed direction and followed him back into the kitchen, where he was chasing some imaginary threat around the gorgeous dark wood kitchen table that indeed had two twenty dollar bills lying on the smooth surface.

She was beginning to see why the job paid so much.

She retraced her steps to the laundry room and found a leash and collar hanging on the doorknob above the gate. Perfect. The collar was a manly blue and the tag said TANK.

Grace laughed out loud, then searched out "Tank." Turned out, Tank had worn off the excess energy and was up against the front door, panting.

"Good boy," Grace cooed, and came at him with his collar. "What a good boy."

He smiled at her.

Aw. *See?* She told herself. *Compared to account analysis and posing nude, this job was going to be a piece of cake.* She was still mentally patting herself on the back for accepting this job when right there on the foyer floor, Tank squatted, hunched, and—

"No!" she cried. "Oh, no, not inside!" She fumbled with the front door, which scared Tank into stopping mid-poo. He ran a few feet away from the front door and hunched again. He was quicker this time. Grace was still standing there, mouth open in shock and horror, little Tank took a dainty step away from his *second* masterpiece, pawed his short back legs on the wood like a matador, and then, with his oversized head held up high, trotted right out the front door like royalty.

Grace staggered after him, eyes watering from the unholy smell. "Tank! Tank, wait!"

Tank didn't wait. Apparently feeling ten pounds lighter, he raced across the front yard and street. He hit the beach, his little legs pumping with the speed of a gazelle as he practically flew across the sand, heading straight for the water.

"Oh, God," she cried. "No, Tank, *no!*"

But Tank dove into the first wave and vanished.

Grace dropped the purse still dangling off her shoulder to the sand. "*Tank!*"

A wave hit her at hip level, knocking her back. She stepped out again, frantically searching for a bobbing head.

Nothing. The little guy had completely vanished, having committed suicide right before her eyes.

The next wave hit her at chest height. Again she staggered back, gasping at the shock of the water as she searched frantically for a little black head. Because she was concentrating, wave number three washed right over the top of her. When she came up sputtering, she shook her head and then dove beneath the surface to search there.

Nothing.

Finally, she was forced to crawl out of the water and admit defeat. She pulled her phone from her purse and swore because it was off. Probably because she kept dropping it.

Or tossing it to the rocky beach to look for drowning puppies.

She powered the phone on, gnawed on her lower lip, then called the man who'd trusted her to "be on time, responsible, and not a flake." Heart pounding, throat tight, she waited until he picked up.

"Dr. Scott," came the low, deep male voice.

Dr. Scott. *Dr. Scott?*

"Hello?" he said, his voice that same calm as before, but there was an underlying impatience now. "Anyone there?"

Oh, God. This was bad. Very bad. Because she knew him.

Well, okay, not really. She'd seen him at the diner a few times; he was good friends with Mallory's and Amy's boyfriends. Dr. Joshua Scott, II, was thirty-four—which she knew because Mallory had given him thirty-four chocolate cupcakes on his birthday last month, a joke because he was a health nut. He was a big guy, built for football more than the ER, but he'd chosen the latter. Even in his wrinkled scrubs after a long day at work, with a stethoscope hanging around his neck, his dark hair tousled and his darker eyes lined with exhaustion, he was drop-dead sexy. The few times that their gazes had locked, the air had snapped, crackled, and popped with a tension she hadn't felt with a man in far too long.

And she'd just killed his puppy.

"Um, hi," she said. "This is Grace Brooks. Your... dog walker." She choked down a horrified sob and forced herself to continue, to give him the rest. "I might have just lost your puppy."

There was a single beat of stunned silence.

"I'm so sorry," she whispered.

More silence.

She dropped to her wobbly knees in the sand and shoved her wet hair out of her face with shaking fingers. "Dr. Scott? Did you hear me?"

"Yes."

She waited for the rest of his response, desperately gripping the phone.

"You *might* have lost Tank."

"Yes," she said softly, hating herself.

"If that's true, I owe you a big, fat kiss."

Grace pulled her phone from her ear and stared at it, then brought it back. "No," she said, shaking her head as if he could see her. "I don't think you understand, I *lost* Tank. In the water."

He muttered something that she'd have sworn sounded like "I should be so lucky," but that couldn't have been right.

"I'm two minutes away," he said. "I got a break in the ER and was coming home to make sure you showed."

"Well, of course I showed—"

But he'd disconnected. "Why wouldn't I show?" With a huff, she put her phone back in her purse and got up. Two minutes. She had two minutes to find Tank.

THE DISH

Where authors give you the inside scoop!

♥ ♥ ♥ ♥ ♥ ♥ ♥ ♥ ♥ ♥ ♥ ♥ ♥ ♥

From the desk of Cynthia Garner

Dear Reader,

You've now met several characters from my Warriors of the Rift series, and in SECRET OF THE WOLF you get to know Dante MacMillan and Victoria Joseph. Dante's a man with a lot of people depending on him, from his colleagues to his sister, who's just getting over chemotherapy treatments and an unexpected divorce—as well as three lovely four-legged friends named Big Ben, Studmuffin, and Sugardaddy.

Some of the real events that happened in the Phoenix area while I was writing this book included a huge dust storm called a haboob. The first one that blew through the area shut down Sky Harbor Airport. The monster was around 5,000 feet high when it slammed into Phoenix, but radar indicated it had reached heights of 10,000 feet prior to hitting the city. It was caused by the winds that come with our monsoon season, but instead of a rain storm the Phoenix area got a dust storm.

I think I'd rather have monsters in the form of werewolves and vampires, thank you very much. A 10,000-foot-high wall of dust is too apocalyptic for me. (Come to think of it, I may actually prefer a zombie apocalypse over a haboob. The one we had was very reminiscent of that one scene in *The Mummy*. Of course, if Brendan Fraser came along for the ride...)

While Dante and Tori didn't have to put up with monster dust storms, they did have to work with other monsters while they focused on a special project during their off-duty hours that brought them close in more ways than one.

As with *Kiss of the Vampire*, I have extras up on my website: a character interview with Tori, some pictures of Scottsdale where the story takes place, and a character tree showing the Council of Preternaturals and their hierarchy.

Look for the next installment, *Heart of the Demon*, coming soon! Finn Evnissyen may not be all he seems to be.

Happy Reading!

Cynthia Garner

cynthiagarnerbooks@gmail.com
http://cynthiagarnerbooks.com

♥ ♥ ♥ ♥ ♥ ♥ ♥ ♥ ♥ ♥ ♥ ♥ ♥ ♥ ♥

From the desk of Jill Shalvis

Dear Reader,

A few years ago, my family went camping. We brought our boat, and on the first day there, we launched it on the lake for the duration of our stay. My husband gave me my choice of driving the truck and trailer to the campsite or driving the boat across the lake to the dock. It was windy, and I'm a boat wuss, so I picked the truck. Halfway around the lake, I got the trailer stuck on a weird hairpin turn and had to be rescued by a forest ranger. He was big and tough and armed and overworked, and undoubtedly underpaid as well, but the man helped me out of a jam so my husband wouldn't kill me. Ever since then, I've wanted to write a forest ranger into one of my books as a hero.

Enter Matt Bowers. Big and tough and armed and overworked and underpaid. Like my real-life hero, he also stopped and helped a damsel in distress. Of course, Matt gets a lot more in the bargain than my poor beleaguered forest ranger ever got. Matt Bowers gets waitress Amy Michaels, beautiful, tough, jaded...and in desperate need of rescuing. She just doesn't know it yet.

Hope you enjoy watching these two warily circle each other on their path to true love. Like me, neither of them takes the easy way. I mean, what's the fun in that?

Our family had a great summer at that lake, and it's a great summer for me this year too with not one, but three Lucky Harbor novels. So if you enjoy AT LAST, don't miss sexy Special Ops soldier Ty Garrison in *Lucky in Love* and handsome doctor Josh Scott in *Forever and a Day*, coming in August.

Happy Reading—all summer long!

Jill Shalvis

http://www.jillshalvis.com

http://www.facebook.com/jillshalvis

♥ ♥ ♥ ♥ ♥ ♥ ♥ ♥ ♥ ♥ ♥ ♥ ♥ ♥ ♥ ♥

From the desk of Molly Cannon

Dear Reader,

There used to be a bar way out in the country where my husband and I would go with a bunch of our friends to dance on Saturday nights. We'd drive for miles and miles down these dark, unlit roads, and then in the distance we'd see the glow against the night sky from the pole lights in the parking lot. We'd pull in, the gravel crunching under our tires, and the place would be packed. After we found a place to park, we'd scramble out of our cars and head inside. The sound of country music and the smell of beer would hit us like a wave when we walked in the door. And the building—it was gigantic, a big, barn-like place—but we'd find a table and settle in for a night of two-stepping, drinking beer, and hanging out with our friends.

As I danced, I couldn't help but do a little people watching. The women would all be dressed to the nines in their dancing outfits, trying to catch someone's eye. The men would be on the prowl but doing their best to play it cool. I'd keep my eye on the blonde woman in the yellow dress: She'd come with one guy, but she danced with another one all night long. Or the tall, stern-looking cowboy at the bar who never took his eyes off the short, dark-haired girl in the pink shirt for a single second. She huddled up with a group of girlfriends, so I wondered if he'd ever work up the courage to ask her for a dance. There might be a couple arguing in one corner, and a couple kissing in another. It was always quite a show: love, lust, broken hearts, maybe some cheating, and a lot of hanky-panky—all played out to the quick-quick, slow-slow beat of a country song. That dance hall is gone now, and the countryside has been swallowed up by neighborhoods and paved roads with streetlights, but I haven't forgotten the nights I spent there.

So it's no accident that the first scene of my book AIN'T MISBEHAVING takes place in a parking lot. Not just any parking lot, but the parking lot outside of Lu Lu's, the local watering hole in Everson, Texas. When Marla Jean Bandy decides it's time to quit spending nights home alone after her divorce, when she decides it's time to bust out and have some fun, Lu Lu's is just the kind of place I thought she needed. Decked out in a tight red dress and her best cowboy boots, she's ready to get back out there and have a good time...until Jake Jacobsen, a childhood crush, shows up and tries to run interference. Marla Jean is about to find out that a parking lot on a Saturday night can be full of delicious possibilities.

I hope you enjoy AIN'T MISBEHAVING and have fun getting to know Marla Jean, Jake, and all the meddlesome, well-meaning folks in Everson, Texas.

Happy Reading!

Molly Cannon

www.mollycannon.com
Facebook.com
Twitter @cannonmolly

Find out more about Forever Romance!

Visit us at
www.hachettebookgroup.com/publishing_forever.aspx

Find us on Facebook
http://www.facebook.com/ForeverRomance

Follow us on Twitter
http://twitter.com/ForeverRomance

NEW AND UPCOMING TITLES

Each month we feature our new titles
and reader favorites.

CONTESTS AND GIVEAWAYS

We give away galleys, autographed copies,
and all kinds of exclusive items.

AUTHOR INFO

You'll find bios, articles, and links to personal websites
for all your favorite authors—and so much more.

GET SOCIAL

Connect with your favorite authors, editors, and
other Forever fans, and share what's important to you.

THE BUZZ

Sign up for our monthly romance newsletter,
and be the first to read all about it.